THE JOURNEY OF

The Jade Ring

BOOK ONE

D1554692

THE JOURNEY OF

The Jade Ring

BOOK ONE

Linda Brown Carlson

Shui-sa
Tree Press
Rancho Mirage, California

The Journey of The Jade Ring, Book One

Copyright © 2022 Linda Brown Carlson

All rights reserved. No part of this publication may be reproduced, distributed, or transmitted in any form or by any electronic or mechanical means, without the prior written permission of the author, except in the case of brief quotations embodied in critical reviews and certain other non-commercial uses permitted by copyright law.

This is a work of fiction. All incidents and dialogue, and all characters except some historical figures, are products of the author's imagination and are not to be construed as real. Where historical figures appear, the situations, incidents, and dialogues concerning those persons are entirely fictional and are not intended to depict actual events or to change the entirely fictional nature of the work. In all other respects, any resemblance to actual persons, living or dead, events, or locales is entirely coincidental.

ISBN 979-8-9857966-0-5 (paperback)

Library of Congress Control Number: 2022906839

Published by

Shui-sa
Tree Press

Rancho Mirage, California
https://lindabrowncarlson.com/

1st edition

Editor: Lynn Jones Green

Cover/interior design and layout:
Mark E. Anderson, www.aquazebra.com

AquaZebra™
Web, Book & Print Design

Printed in the United States of America

Dedication

To my husband, Wayne

Epigraph

Love is composed of a single soul
inhabiting two bodies
—Aristotle

Acknowledgments

Although writing a novel is a solitary activity, making the book a reality takes many helping hands. Foremost, I want to thank my husband and soul mate, Wayne, for, without his love, understanding, support, and encouragement, The Journey of the Jade Ring would never have become a reality.

As a proud member of the Palm Springs Writers Guild, I have connected with published and debut authors through the guild and found pure enjoyment in participating in critique groups sponsored by the guild. I am indebted to Daniel Cook, Carol Mann, Larry Lauritzen, B. Channing Hillway, Pat Erickson, Candace Fagan, Nancy Ako, Judy Thompson, Kathy Bjork, and Ariella Moon. Their generosity of time and inspiration spurred me on to complete my debut novel. Thank you. I am grateful for your friendship.

Additional thanks to editor Lynn Jones Green, publisher Shui-sa Tree Press, cover/interior designer Mark E. Anderson at AquaZebra Web, Book & Print Design and photographer Kathy Rappaport for the author photo.

— Linda B. Carlson
Spring of 2022

Prologue

A heavy mist hangs in the air surrounding a man, obscuring all recognizable landmarks and sounds.

The fog swallows his question: "Where am I?"

Unable to make sense of this place, he realizes he cannot remember much of his past identity. When a thunderous voice calls to him from a brilliant light, the man raises his hands to shield his eyes.

"I am your Spirit Guide," the voice announces. "I am here to help you transition through your *inter-life*. Please follow the path."

The man walks through the vapor, which obscures the unfamiliar pathway. It is fresh, the earth damp and verdant as it leads into a forest of *shui-sa* trees standing majestic and proud. Now the slanted rays of the sun filter through the canopy of the ancient redwoods, and a gentle breeze creates fluttering shadows on the ground. Engulfed by their immense size and their deep red bark, he finds the forest to be somehow familiar. He has the overwhelming sensation of coming home.

Two thick roots spread equal distance apart, where the massive central tree trunk meets the earth, creating a space just right for sitting. He leans against the trunk, sensing the oneness of the noble tree, breathing in its essence, trying to comprehend its mystery of eternal truth, wisdom, and knowledge.

The voice speaks again, jolting him from his thoughts. "These magnificent guardians symbolize the world's center, where heaven and earth touch, where all times and places converge. You remain with your memory intact for a while after death. Before rebirth, you change, losing the recall of your past life in preparation to assume the shape of your next experience. You must prepare yourself to become flesh and blood again—soon—as a boy in China. You will do outstanding works."

"I do not remember my previous life," the man said, gazing at his feet. "I am not sure I want to go back. It is so pleasant here among these magical trees."

"It is not a matter of choice," the voice answers. "In time, everyone here will lose their façade and find they are children again in a new place. In time, your soul merges with the light. However, it remains aware and continues to learn. Consult any of the Master Spirits here in the trees for guidance."

Silence engulfs him. As he sits, a stunning girl—dressed in a yellow silk dress, with dark eyes as bright as the moon and hair the color of midnight—appears to float through the woods toward him. At first, she stops, stares, and then, after waving, she walks his way.

"These last few days, I have not felt like myself," she says, stroking her hair. "I have less and less memory of my past or who I am. I have meandered, hoping to find someone in the forest to help me." She gestures to the open space beside him. "Do you mind if I sit with you for a time? I dislike being alone."

The man's cheeks flush with pleasure. "I would appreciate your company. I thought I might be all alone, too." He stares skyward, his eyes puzzled. "Even my name is a mystery. My Spirit Guide told me I am going to China soon."

"Do you remember your past or who you were?" she asks, taking a seat beside him to share the noble tree's trunk.

"No, my memory is faint." The man gazes into the canopy of leaves and branches. "However, these trees are familiar, almost as if they are a part of me." Looking back at her, he asks, "Do you know your name or where you will go?"

"My Spirit Guide did not tell me, and alas, I too do not know my name." Her eyes sparkle. "For fun, I will be Claudia, and I will call you Louis." She giggled.

"Claudia," he says as he reaches out to take her slender hand. "Your jade ring is familiar. I have the most peculiar sensation I somehow know you. Could we know each other from another time?"

"I do not know," she says. With these words, she leans forward and kisses Louis, a kiss so sweet he knows how he wants to fill the empty pages of his existence.

Louis and Claudia spent their last days in the forest together, walking among the millennia-aged trees. The music of the wind soars through their branches, enhancing the quiet tranquility of their magical universe. Sometimes they sit by the luminous water of a brook. Other times, they listen to insects' quaver and delight in the prattle of the birds' calls and responses with their mates. The fireflies decorate the trees with the radiance of stardust at night, and a sliver of the silver moon hangs over an arched footbridge crossing a stream. They fall deeper and deeper in love.

In a lush emerald meadow of soft grass, Louis leans on one elbow and confesses, "The images fade faster now." He tries to focus on the features of Claudia's face. "I can see shadows of my next existence. My spirit feels pulled to a distant place.

A woman waits for me there. I hear her voice saying, 'Come.'"
Louis bolts upright. "It is time for me to leave you and the
forest to be reborn."

"I hear no one." Claudia grabs his hand to pull him back. "I
do not want you to go. You cannot go away now. What will I do
without you?" Her eyes teared. "What if we never meet again?"

"Do not be afraid. We will find each other in life, time after
time. I do not know how, but I am certain we will be lovers
again, as we have been here among the ancient trees.

Claudia forces her ring into his hand. "Louis, take my ring
with you. Remember, I love you."

Louis kisses her with profound tenderness. In that moment,
he vanishes from the forest.

Chapter 1

Ancient China: Zhou Dynasty
Spring and Autumn Period of 500 BC

Gōngshu Bān knelt alone by his mother's shallow grave. He threw his unwashed body over the fresh mound of dirt and sobbed. "Why did you leave me?" he begged. "I have no one. What do I do? Someone took our hut. I am scared."

The battle cries of feudal warriors on horseback and archers on foot thundered past him. They failed to distract him from his grief. His eyes stung from the dust storm kicked up by their horses. The boy stood, gazing at the delicate ring—her ring on his thumb, the only thing of beauty left in his world. Its dark green background, the color of lotus leaves suspended in a pond, reflected white clouds chasing each other in a never-ending circle. He rolled it around and tried not to cry.

Tears mixed with the dirt on his face, leaving streaks of mud down his cheeks. *This ring is all I have left,* he thought. The memory of her washed skin—after she cleaned the earth from her feet and hands from toiling in the fields—remained vivid. The sun had caused her face to wrinkle and to become the color of a golden-brown raisin.

Gōngshu Bān remembered her answer when he asked, "Why do you work? Other mothers stay in their huts."

His mother cradled him in her arms and wept. "Our life has not always been like this. Although your father descended from a noble family, you must remember, the warring nobles of Lu killed him and all of our relatives. They took our land. You and I escaped to the safety of this village when you were two years old. I have to work in the fields to take care of you."

"No one cares about me now," he whispered to the ground, thinking she could still hear him. "All I have is my shirt and your ring."

He held the ring in the palm of his hand, trance-like, wishing she could tell him what to do next.

Suddenly, the ring glowed and warmed. He heard his mother's voice calling to him: "I have returned to the forest of ancient shui-sa trees in the world's center, where heaven and earth touch. I await my next life. Always do good deeds, my son. The ring will guide you," the quiet voice said.

"Mother, is it you?" he asked, searching for the source of the words. "Come back," he pleaded. "What do you mean? Come back!" He strained to hear her words, but heard only the sounds of a distant battle carried by the breeze.

He tarried with his bare arms wrapped around his knees, unwilling to abandon her, praying to hear her speak again.

Long afternoon shadows signaled the coming of evening. Gōngshū Bān rubbed his chest, trying to dislodge the deep-seated ache he felt and ease the hunger pangs rumbling in his empty stomach. *Who will feed me? Who wants a boy of seven?* These questions and fears swirled in his mind. He walked with tentative steps away from her grave, his thoughts unfocused, toward the safety of his village walls, gripping the ring in his hand.

The boy took no notice of the weary travelers on the other side of the road, their bundles hanging from carrying poles. Ox carts—loaded with millet, prodded along with men carrying long sticks—eventually passed. As he walked, a couple of lads twice his age, caught his attention as they jostled each other.

When the boys called his name, he recognized them as the ruffians who harassed the younger boys when no adults were in sight.

They jeered at him. "What are you doing out here by yourself? Where's your 'mommy'?" they taunted.

Gōngshū Bān ignored them, continuing to increase his pace.

The taller tyrant blocked his way. The second boy grabbed his shirt. "Where are you going?" he repeated.

"Leave me alone," replied Gōngshū Bān.

"What's in your hand?" the bully asked, noticing Gōngshū Bān's fingers curled into a fist. "Let me see it," he said, trying to pry Gōngshū Bān's hand open.

They scuffled, and the taller one knocked Gōngshū Bān onto the ground. The other boy joined the fray, overpowering the seven-year-old. Punching and kicking, they pried his fingers loose.

"Ah-ha! A ring! Where did you get this, you dirt eater? Did you steal it?"

Gōngshū Bān lunged at the assailant. "Give it back! It's my mother's!"

The fracas attracted the attention of several pilgrims traveling on the road. One man came to Gōngshū Bān's aid. "What is this about?" the man asked.

"They took my mother's ring," he said through clenched teeth.

"Where is your mother?" asked another man.

"She lies in the earth," Gōngshū Bān said, tears filling his eyes.

The first man addressed the assailants: "Give the ring back to this child and be on your way before we dispense our justice to you two thieves."

"Here," the tall one said, tossing the ring at Gōngshū Bān's feet. He motioned to his friend. "Come on, let's leave this baby."

"Thank you." The child bowed to the travelers, lifted the ring from the dirt, cleaned it, and slid it on his thumb. "I have nothing more."

The men departed, leaving Gōngshū Bān to continue toward his village, mulling over his mother's passing and her strange words. He wiped the perspiration from his forehead, realizing he'd been lucky to escape the attempted robbery. Now he needed to stop his gnawing stomach.

His focus blurred by hunger, he didn't see a powerful black horse carrying a feudal warrior, a man clad in a bronze helmet, which was adorned with a dragon mask, and lamellar leather armor. He never realized the man was headed straight toward him, hooves pounding, churning up a dust cloud.

At the last instant, another traveler appeared and snatched the boy out of the horse's path. The rider kept going, never looking back, never intending to give way to a small boy.

"Why are you here alone?" his rescuer asked, his tone gentle. "It is not safe for one so young to be so far away from a village. One of the traveling soldiers might snatch you and carry you away to be their slave. How old are you?"

Gōngshū Bān lifted his tear-stained face. The stranger's face appeared to glow from within, yet did not frighten him.

"Seven. My mother—I just left her grave. Some boys . . ."

He raised his eyebrows, offering a questioning gaze. "Do you pass Sin Yang?"

"Yes," the man said. "I am on an assignment to Mingquin, a little past Sin Yang. I will be glad to go with you if you wish. Afterward, then I will continue on my trek."

Gōngshu Bān grasped the stranger's hand with a firm grip, not wanting the man to change his mind. "Thank you. I would like your help."

"What are you going to do?" the stranger inquired. "Are there relations you can stay with, or is there anyone in the village to help you? Did your mother leave you any food or money?"

"I don't know." Gōngshu Bān shrugged his thin shoulders. His voice trembled. "Mother said all our relatives have left this life. Somebody took our hut." The boy hesitated. "Maybe I can work in the fields." He kicked the dirt. "I am scared they will say I am too little."

"Perhaps you might ask an elder. I am sure a wise man would guide you."

"I know some of our old men. They would often let me sit with them when mother worked." Accepting the thought, he replied, "I will ask them."

When they approached the guarded gate in the fortified walls of Sin Yang, the man paused and turned to the child. "I must leave you here. I wish you luck."

The boy bowed to the stranger. "Thank you, kind one."

With a wave of his hand, the traveler disappeared as he had appeared.

Alone, Gōngshu Bān ambled toward the center of the village, kicking the dust with his bare feet, passing a row of stick hovels he had once called home. The rattling of the pots and aromas of the evening meals made his empty stomach rumble.

He paused beside a tiny vegetable patch behind the shack where he once lived. Scanning the area to ensure no one had noticed him, he crouched to pull a yam out of the ground. As he stood, an old woman came out.

"Thief! Thief!" she yelled, alerting all her neighbors.

The frightened boy dropped his prize and ran. A few women gave chase, but they were not fast enough to catch him. He darted in and out through the yards and between buildings to escape the shouting women.

As he reached the central square, huffing and puffing, he stopped in mid-stride. He saw several familiar men standing by the well, waiting for him. He made a hasty bow in respect.

Lao Wen Gui, the highest-ranking elder, stepped forward with gray, thick chin whiskers, accompanying his bushy eyebrows and bulbous nose. Floppy ears stuck out from under his tan cap. A dark-brown, belted robe engulfed his bony frame.

"Why are you running?" the leader asked.

"I left mother's grave," the child answered, hanging his head, hoping to not have to explain all that happened.

Two women who had chased him arrived. "This boy tried to steal one of my yams," the taller lady wheezed, out of breath.

"Is this true?" the elder asked.

"I am hungry. Mother is gone. This woman took our hut and our vegetable patch. The yam belonged to us. I have no money."

"Stealing is a severe offense. If you were an adult, we would cut off the hand you used."

Gōngshu Bān's eyes grew wide, grabbing his hand at the thought of losing it.

"I will take charge of this offender," the elder assured the women. "You will not see this boy again."

What will he do with me? Will he sell me as a slave? Gōngshu Bān's thoughts reeled.

The women departed, muttering how children had no respect for the rules.

Lao Wen Gui motioned the elders to sit on benches under a nearby willow tree, with the youngster sitting at their feet.

"You must be desperate to steal food. When did you last eat?"

"Two days ago," he said.

The elder's frail fingers touched the boy's shoulder. "We are sorry your mother left this life. We feared this might happen. She worked too hard, from sunup to sundown."

Gōngshu Bān focused on the elder, not sure what to expect. He flexed his hand, still thinking about its fate, curious about the elder's assurance the women would not see him again.

The man continued. "We are fond of you and realize you are now alone. While what you did is wrong, hunger drives men to take drastic measures. You spent many hours with us listening and learning while your mother toiled in the fields. I believe evil does not dwell in your heart. But if you stay here, you will fall prey to a path of crime. We have arranged for you to live and study with Master Sima, a scholar and inventor. We told him how you created tiny birds from leaves that can glide through the air. He takes students into his home, like you, who are—smart, eager to learn, and hard workers."

Am I smart? The boy dropped his gaze. *Trying to steal a yam was dumb.*

"When Master Sima learned of your situation, he agreed to take you as his student and teach you to read, to write calligraphy, to play a Qin, to study the stars in the heavens, and to understand valuable life lessons after your mother left this world."

Glancing from one elder to the other, not understanding the meaning of some of the man's words, Gōngshu Bān fidgeted where he sat on the ground.

"We sent word to him about your mother's passing. The master replied he is ready to meet you right away."

The child's chest tightened. He thought he might be sick, but focused his complete attention on Lao Wen Gui, trying to calm the butterflies in his still empty stomach.

"Master Sima lives in a sizable town high on Mount Lu, far removed from the war and turmoil here."

The boy's eyes darted from one elder to another.

"The master descends from an influential lord," the old man continued. "His wealthy family made it possible for him to study with Master Kong, a wise man."

Gōngshu Bān jammed his hands into his armpits, his mind racing. *Who is he? Will he have food?* His bottom lip trembled. "How far away is it?" he asked, scanning the group of old men. "I have always lived here."

"It will take a day and a half to reach the top of the mountain," the elder said. "We will begin our journey tomorrow. Tonight, you will stay with my family."

Gōngshu Bān's shoulders relaxed, and he blew out a long breath. "Oh, thank you. I have no other place to sleep." He opened his hand, staring at his mother's ring. "This is all I have to pay you for your kindness," the boy said, his voice a whisper.

The elder's eyes gleamed. "I do not require payment. It is my good deed for you. I will keep the ring for you while we make our way up the mountain. It appears your shirt is pocketless."

"Thank you. I have no safe place to keep it. Two boys already tried to take it from me on the road, but some travelers stopped them."

He handed the ring to the elder, who examined it and raised his gaze. "This ring is a true treasure, child," the man said. "It is *yu,* the divine gem, the stone of the heart, the most precious jewel in the entire land. It is indestructible, and many people say it can give immortality to its owner by the August Personage of Jade, the ruler of heaven."

"What is 'immortality'?" the boy asked.

"It is a strange concept to understand. It means never having to leave this world," the elder explained.

"But it is my mother's, and she is not here."

"Yes, but now it is yours, and she lives on in your memory. Your ring holds magical powers."

"Magic?" Gōngshu Bān's hands slapped his cheeks.

"I will keep it safe and return it to you when we arrive at Master Sima's home. Your mother left you a cherished gift."

The boy furrowed his brow. *I have no one to take care of me and no other choice.* Finally, he answered, "You have always been kind to me. I know nothing of the mountain or Master Sima, but I must trust you, Wise Elder."

"The sun is setting. It is time to go home," Lao Wen Gui said.

"Safe travels, Gōngshu Bān," the other elders called. "Do your best."

The child bowed to the elders before walking with the older man to his humble home of mud-brick walls, stick roof, and dirt floor. Lao Wen Gui bent near to the ground to enter the low doorway. Gōngshu Bān followed him. When his eyes adjusted to the dim light, he recognized some of the elder's immediate family waiting in the single modest room.

The elder motioned to a washbasin and a towel on a crude table. "You will want to wash your face and hands before you eat."

Gōngshu Bān bobbed his head in agreement before splashing the water in the basin like a bird in a puddle.

The smoky aroma of their nighttime meal permeated the compact space. Gōngshu Bān knelt at the table beside the elder, eager to eat. He grabbed his bowl, lifting it to his mouth, but stopped when Lao Wen Gui stood, holding his vessel of rice toward the heavens. "We invite you, ancestors, to share our food."

The boy's eyes grew wide. "What does that mean?" he murmured.

"This is part of our custom to pay tribute to our departed family members," the elder explained. "They need food and drink in their afterlife, just as we do. We honor and take care of them after they leave this life, so they will greet us when we arrive. Our ancestors are vital to us."

Did someone wait for mother? Or is she alone? Tears spilled from his eyes. Gōngshu Bān offered a part of his rice to his mother, wherever she might be, and hoped someone greeted her.

After they finished their meal, Gōngshu Bān lay atop a straw mat on the floor. He remembered a song his mother sang to him at night about a little lost duck who found his way home. *I am like that duck,* he thought. *Maybe tomorrow I too will find a new home.*

鲁班

The morning sun's warm glow streamed through the single open window of Lao Wen Gui's house, awakening the household members and Gōngshu Bān.

A modest fire took the spring chill off the room, its wood smoke escaping through the small hole in the roof.

Two little children played chase around the central table, their squeals annoying the grandparents until their mother brought bowls of rice and dried fish to the table for everyone to eat.

"We are fortunate to have dry weather," the older man said when they finished eating. "We have a long journey ahead."

He handed a pair of straw sandals to the boy. "You will need these. Part of our path is rugged once we leave the major road."

Gōngshu Bān examined the crude footwear, the sole woven from reeds, cords threaded through a central twist in the back, then to a loop on each side by the toes, forming a triangle. The elder had to tie the strings to hold them on. The boy took a few steps.

"How do you walk in these?" the child asked. "I always go barefoot."

"They may feel strange at first, but you will become accustomed to them. We must be on our way." The elder slung a pouch cross body and carried a coat blanket.

Their journey to Mount Lu began in the second month of the spring, in the fifth year of Jī Gai's rule. Gōngshu Bān gazed at the morning sky. Today it somehow appeared bluer than usual. He took a deep breath, enjoying the peach blossom-perfumed air.

When they passed through the outer wall gate to the central road, Gōngshu Bān peered over his shoulder. Fear overwhelmed him as the entrance closed with a thud. He grabbed the wise elder's arm.

"Are you going to tell Master Sima about the yam I stole from the garden? I am sorry; I did not know what else to do."

"I see you are regretful," the elder replied. "We all make mistakes. When we learn from them, we are stronger. You will gain many life experiences from Master Sima."

"Will the master like me?"

"If you are obedient, study hard and remember your lessons well," the old man said. "He will recognize you are a gifted child and treat you as a son."

A son? Why would a stranger want me? However, the old man's answer comforted him. The farther they walked, the more his initial fear melted into an eagerness to reach his new home and meet his teacher.

They passed the rice and millet fields on the Yangtze River bank where his late mother had toiled each day.

Stooped field hands, dressed in moss green tunics over mud-colored shirts, had their trousers rolled up to their knees. They sang work songs to pass the time. Most were barefoot; others wore crude shoes like Gōngshu Bān's sandals. A sloped, broad-brimmed straw hat protected them from the sun.

One worker with a round basket on his back carried his millet to an empty cart.

Gōngshu Bān laughed, pointing. "Over there, the basket makes the man look like a turtle."

"Yes, it does." Lao Wen Gui chuckled. "I never thought of that. Master Sima will value your wonderful imagination."

Leaving the river, a smooth stone road curved into a spacious dirt path as they climbed the mountain. Lao Wen Gui pointed out the rugged ridges of the Seven-Pointed Peaks stretching out before them, now veiled in a thin mist. The closer knolls were dark sapphire, while each subsequent ridge faded into lighter shades of blue in the distance.

"Those spires rise to support the roof of heaven," the elder explained as he raised his gaze toward the hills. "Mount Lu is that oval-shaped mountain. Can you see the mountains resembling five old men standing side-by-side?"

"Yes, there they are!" Gōngshu Bān squealed.

"Beside them, you will find the twin gate-towers of Stone Gate. It is next to Poyang Lake. Tomorrow, we will travel the mountain's western side with a ravine and a crystal-clear waterfall."

Gōngshu Bān focused on the imposing cliffs looming above them. His shoulders slumped, grumbling. "How will we make it to the top?" he asked.

"They say the longest journey begins with the first step," the elder offered.

魯班

The path narrowed the farther they climbed. When Lao Wen Gui stumbled, he used his red shui-sa walking stick to steady himself as he trod each stage along the way. The child followed in his footsteps; two solitary travelers winding their way higher and higher.

At the next sharp bend in the trail, Gōngshu Bān stopped, put his hands on his knees, and gasped for air. "I want to go back. It is hard to walk. These sandals hurt my feet."

"Going back is not possible. You have no one to care for

you." Lao Wen Gui furrowed his brow, narrowing his eyes. "You would end up as someone's slave, lose your hand or, worse, be killed," he said, his voice firm. "Master Sima is your only chance to avoid trouble. We must continue, and you must keep walking."

"Who made this path? It is so steep and narrow. If we go up so high, will we reach heaven?"

"They say Pangu, the creator of the world, made it." The elder lifted his gaze. "These extraordinary rock formations are a sign of his supernatural power. Take a deep breath of the fresh air.

Gōngshu Bān filled his lungs with the cool air. "There are no village odors. No pigs."

"All of this is Pangu's mountain paradise. At sunset, we will view this valley from one of those peaks. Then, you will recognize the vast scale of his universe and understand his supremacy."

The child huffed and took a few hesitant steps.

"Perhaps this is the best time to rest and eat. We can sit on this log," the man said, pointing to a fallen tree beside the path covered on one side with soft green moss. The elder reached into his shoulder bag and handed a bundle and a gourd of water to his traveling companion before taking his food from the sack.

"We have sweet rice cakes for tonight and tomorrow morning."

"Thank you," Gōngshu Bān said with a half-smile. "I am hungry."

After eating, they continued their journey. As night engulfed them, the eerie forest sounds made the hairs on the back of the child's neck prickle. "What made that noise?" he whispered.

"Most likely, a mouse searching for someplace to spend the night, just as we are." The elder put his arm around the boy's shoulders to reassure him. "We will take shelter at the base of this majestic pine tree." He wrapped the boy in his coat blanket.

The old man fell asleep, weary from the day's strenuous climb, but the child lay awake in the dark surroundings, jumping at the slightest sounds. He wondered how the elder could sleep and what creature might pounce upon them during the night.

鲁班

"Awake," Lao Wen Gui said, shaking the boy.

Gōngshu Bān woke with a start. "Where am I?" he asked through half-opened eyes. The soft dawn light revealed a heavy dew making the gloomy woodlands appear scary and smell musty.

"We must continue." the elder said.

The boy closed his eyes. "I am too tired and sleepy."

"You can sleep tonight. Master Sima expects us mid-day."

The child struggled to his feet, surveying the surrounding trees, bushes, and brambles. "At least nothing ate us."

"Maybe they thought I might be too old, and you were too skinny to be a proper meal," the elder joked.

"I am hungry enough to eat anything."

"We will wait to enjoy our rice cakes when we reach the mountain's peak."

"These sandals make my feet hurt," the boy said, stumbling over a bare root growing on the trail.

The pathway had several switch-backs as they gained altitude. When Gōngshu Bān slipped on the wet path, a sharp rock cut a jagged gash in his knee. Panicked when blood trickled toward his ankle, he cried. "Help me! Am I going to join my mother?"

"You are fortunate." The elder tended the boy's wound. "It is not as awful as you think, and no, you will not leave this world. Your leg might be sore for a day or two." He tore a strip of cloth from the hem of his long shirt and bandaged the cut before helping the boy to his feet. "We need to continue," he said, his voice firm.

Gōngshū Bān hobbled for a while, slowing their progress. He wondered if they would ever reach Master Sima's home. *Why did mother leave me? I want to go back.*

The weather changed several times along their journey. At first, the fog made it hard to distinguish the mountains' formations. Soon, streams of light pierced the thick mist. Without warning, the sun announced the day. Like magic, the vapor disappeared in time for the travelers to take in the lake's view, which reflected the inverted peaks of Mount Lu. Birds fluttered through the pinion pines. Sounds of the woodland animals beckoned them to continue their journey.

At the summit, they ate their rice cakes. Gōngshū Bān gazed at the cloud-covered valley where he had once lived. "It is so quiet. Is this heaven? Are we the only people on the earth now? It is so different. So far . . . far away."

He rubbed his arms, hugged himself, and looked around, expecting to find the Ruler of Heaven. *I am scared.*

The day progressed. They passed the waterfall the elder had promised, where the crystal-clear water gushed over the rim with a roar cascading into the pool below. Gōngshū Bān stared at the unfamiliar sight, covering his ears. "Beautiful! I wish mother could see this. Where does the water come from?"

"The spring rains travel through the mountain's valleys into this stream, before the water flows into the Yangtze River and out to sea."

By late morning, Gōngshu Bān recognized buildings with strange rooftops in the distance. Walking closer, he wrinkled his nose. *Pew! Stinking pigs.* "Does Master Sima live here? Where are their huts with sticks on top?"

"These houses differ from ours. An outside wall surrounds them. Pounded dirt bricks make the houses' walls, and they have tile roofs instead of thatch. This roof helps to keep out the rain. They face south to keep the north wind at bay and arrange them in groups of buildings called 'bays,' separated by courtyards and gardens."

"What is a courtyard?"

"It is an area of ground inside the walls of the house. Often, it is a kitchen with stone benches, flowers, and places where people grow vegetables," he said. "You will find one when we arrive."

鲁班

They arrived at Master Sima's three-bay house and stood at the southeast wooden door carved with peach blossoms and a pair of swimming fish. They waited for a servant to greet them.

Gōngshu Bān wiped his sweaty palms on his dingy gray shirt and swallowed hard to calm his nerves. When the squeaky door opened, they entered through a passageway leading to the first courtyard used for cooking. Pots hung over an open fire, tended by a cook. Servants hustled to arrange the food on trays for their lunch.

"Something smells good," he said. "I am hungry from walking all day." He rubbed his stomach. "I hope we will eat soon."

"Remember, we will honor our ancestors before the meal, as we did last night."

"Yes, I remember. I wish Mother was here."

From the second courtyard, Gōngshu Bān discovered ornate columns painted black. He hid behind Lao Wen Gui's robe, trembling. *Is this a ruler's palace? I should not be here.* He followed the elder into the inner hall, where Master Sima waited, the sweet fragrance of incense perfuming the area.

The room stretched the entire width of the house. Latticed windows lined each side of the outer walls, allowing the sunlight to stream through the west side, casting intricate shadows and streaks of light across a massive rosewood dining table. Stacked orange and indigo silk pillows flanked thick sitting mats. Master Sima's ancestral altar occupied a place of importance on another wall.

Master Sima wore a droopy mustache, and a trimmed beard. A blue-ribbon tied in a bow held his hair, streaked with white, pulled back in the typical educated fashion. He clutched a brown coat blanket wrapped around his simple, floor-length white robe.

His kind eyes and quiet manner helped ease Gōngshu Bān's fears, but the child stood as still as a stone.

Lao Wen Gui and Master Sima bowed to each other. The elder nudged the boy to bow.

"Welcome to my home," Master Sima said with outstretched arms. "I am pleased you are here. I trust your journey did not tire you."

Gōngshu Bān did not answer. He only moved his head from

side to side.

"I have things to make you feel at home," the master said. "First, a new name."

Gōngshū Bān clutched his hands around his shoulders. *What is wrong with my name?*

"We will call you 'Lu Bān' because you now live here on Mount Lu."

A servant, dressed in a citrine tunic, entered the room carrying a stack of garments, handing them to Master Sima. Lu Bān's eyes widened when Master Sima held them out toward him. "Next, fresh clothes."

The man in the tunic reached for the boy's tattered, scratchy long shirt to remove it.

Lu Bān grabbed the fabric, bending to evade the servant, not wanting Master Sima to view his scrawny, naked body. The elder signaled his assurance with a tip of his head.

With reluctance, he let the man tug the garment over his head. A new floor-length cream-colored linen gown settled against his skin, followed by a shorter gray coat. A belt with a cast-bronze belt hook, in the shape of a bird's head, fastened the garment. Lu Bān's fingers traced the buckle's outline. *I must be dreaming.*

Master Sima glanced at his old friend and acknowledged his approval. "Child, now you resemble a genuine scholar. I imagine you are both hungry."

Lu Bān's eyes brightened. "Yes, I am."

"Come, it is time to eat," said Master Sima as he led his guests to a short table where they sat cross-legged on a thick mat. Lu Bān had never seen so much food. Ginger or anise-flavored cooked rice cakes rested on a black lacquered tray.

A servant served them Black Dragon tea in small, white ceramic cups and steaming soup in porcelain bowls painted orange and blue.

The noodle soup with hefty bites of chicken surprised Lu Bān. "Mother never put meat in our soup. Just broth and foxtail noodles. The soup is good!" He finished the golden liquid in his bowl with a slurp, patting his stomach. "Can I have more?"

In a short while, Master Sima grinned, as Lu Bān finish his second bowl. "Now, with your belly full, I will show you where you will sleep."

They all walked to the rear of the house, where two compact rooms were in each corner.

"Lu Bān, you are my only student. Your room will be the one on the east side, so you might enjoy the morning sun. I have discovered that better ideas find me at daybreak. I hope you will too." Master Sima slid the opaque screen open. It made a *swoosh* sound against the floor.

Lu Bān bowed and walked to a thick straw mat on a raised platform. He inhaled and sighed. "Oh, fresh hay."

He ran his hand around the smooth edge of a bronze washbasin on a black lacquered corner cabinet before picking up two simple wooden candlesticks on another table to examine them. A carved chest and basket rested against an outer wall under the window opening.

"A room of my own?" Lu Bān said, facing his Master Sima. "How can this be?" He collapsed on his knees at the master's feet. "How can I thank you, Kind One?"

"Study hard. Do your best. My teacher, Master Kong, took no money from his students. However, he expected us to pass our knowledge on to others to make our world a better place.

I will expect you to do the same," Master Sima said. He put his hands under the boy's arms to help him to his feet and led his new student to the center room in the back of the house.

"Here is where you will begin your lessons. You and I will spend most of your time here. It would be my parents' room if they still lived. Now I use it for my workshop because it gives me more space. Would you like to go inside?"

Lu Bān entered the workspace, heart-pounding, tingling from head to toe. He imagined the things that might happen. The child caught his breath when he saw animal models on a table in front of the center-wall window.

"What are these pictures? Everything is new to me." He ran to a pile of narrow pieces of split planks stacked along a wall, picked up a piece, and slid his fingertips over the smoothness of one side and the roughness of the back. His eyes brightened. "What are these?"

"Those are slips of bamboo used for recording thoughts."

"And these strange things?"

"They are the four treasures of the study." Master Sima walked to the table to point out the treasures arranged on the center table. "They are a brush, ink, inkstone, and silk for calligraphy, a way of writing. You will learn how to use these," he said, a gleam in his eyes projecting an inner light. "Though it will take time," he added.

Lu Bān, missing one of his front teeth, smiled back at Master Sima and bowed to the wise old man who had arranged this for him.

"Thank you, Old and Respected One. You are kind to this shameful boy. I know my mother is pleased."

"Ah, yes, your mother." The elder reached into his coat and

produced the jade ring. "I believe this is yours," he said, and handed it to Lu Bān.

He took the ring from the elder. The cool stone made his skin tingle. He thought he heard his mother's voice in the distance.

Lao Wen Gui bowed to Master Sima, who returned the bow. "I must be on my way back to our village." Turning to the boy, he said, "Achieve your best, Lu Bān. May your ancestors protect you." The elder waved and walked out the door.

The boy swallowed hard when the door closed with a soft click. He rubbed the back of his neck and grimaced. *Come back. I am scared.* The ring vibrated. *Mother? It is magic. She would tell me to do my best.* Putting the ring in his coat pocket, he drew in a deep breath and raised his face to Master Sima. "When do we start, Master?" he said with a broad grin. "I am ready."

"We will begin when the morning sun shines through your window." Master Sima motioned toward his attendant. "For now, Chen Bo will help you put your clothes away before our evening meal."

Lu Bān followed Chen Bo back to his room.

The servant gestured to a wooden chest. "In here, you will find additional long robes, three pairs of trousers, and a coat blanket for when the weather is cold. Master Sima will expect you for dinner when the sun drops below the bottom branch, there." He pointed to a ginkgo tree outside. "A thick cover for your mat is in the basket under the window. I will call you in case you fall asleep. Master Sima expects you to be punctual."

"Thank you," Lu Bān said, waiting for the sliding opaque screen door to close. Removing the ring from his pocket, he held it to his chest. "You would not believe it, Mother. A room of my own, new clothes, and all the wonderful food I can eat," he said, kissing the ring. "Now, I need a safe place to hide you. You might get lost."

Searching the room, he found a loose brick in the wall, perfect for protecting his treasure. He slid the ring into the space and edged the brick back into position. Hearing a noise outside the window, he stared into the growing gloom, but didn't see anyone or anything.

Lu Bān fell asleep. When he woke with a start, the sun had slipped below the horizon. Panicked, he cried, "Where is Chen Bo? I am late."

Lu Bān, out of breath, arrived in the dining room to find Master Sima sitting cross-legged on his mat. His kind smile was missing.

Master Sima's lips tightened. "You are tardy."

"Chen Bo said he would wake me if I fell asleep. He didn't. I am sorry, Master."

"It is not Chen Bo's duty to awaken you. You must rely on yourself. Punctuality is of utmost importance. Do you understand?"

Lu Bān bobbed his head. "Yes. I will not let it happen again."

"We will start afresh in the morning," Master Sima said. "Tonight, we will enjoy our meal."

Master Sima rang a small ceramic bell. Chen Bo brought bowls of fragrant lemongrass soup with dumplings to the dining room, serving Master Sima first. Chen Bo ignored Lu Bān's glare and returned to the kitchen for rice cakes.

Why did you trick me? Lu Bān wondered.

鲁班

The following day, after breakfast, Lu Bān seated himself at his table in the workshop.

"My table is *Zhang Mu,* or camphor wood, painted with colorful patterns of lotus seeds." Master Sima slid his hand over its worn surface. "I have spent many hours at this table over the years. It belonged to my father, and his father before him."

Lu Bān noticed the gray in the master's hair. *It must be old.*

The sun streamed through the windows, illuminating the top of Lu Bān's table. He examined the wood grain surface. "These squiggles look like feathers. I like birds."

"Yes, they do," Master Sima agreed. "Lao Win Gui told me about your fascination with birds. We call the material *Ji Chi Mu,* sometimes called Phoenix tail or chicken-wing wood. I hoped you might enjoy it."

"What are these?" Lu Bān questioned, running his fingers over the smooth blue bumps inlaid around the table's edges.

"The stones are turquoise. Although turquoise does not possess the sparkle of transparent stone, we prize it for its ancient heritage and unique blue-green color. The gods say it increases your mental, physical, and spiritual abilities."

"'Turquoise' . . . I like the word." Lu Bān hesitated, thinking about the precious stones. "Lao Wen Gui said my mother's ring is jade, the divine gem given by the Jade Ruler of Heaven. What did he mean?" he asked.

"Jade has many qualities. It has magical powers to protect and bring good luck. It is the concentrated essences of love, the protector of generations, living and departed, the stone of the heart and the jewel of heaven," Master Sima said. "There are many stories of the Jade Emperor who started his life as the crown prince of a heavenly kingdom. At birth, he emitted a wondrous green light filling the heavens. As a kind, intelligent, and wise child, he devoted himself to doing good for everyone. He rose to the status of emperor when his father left this life."

Lu Bān knitted his brows, focusing his attention on Master Sima's every word.

"In the beginning," the master continued, "the world was a terrible, monstrous place with no gods to protect the humans. An evil entity wanted to rule both heaven and earth. He went to a cave where he passed three thousand trials, each lasting three million years. After he accomplished each test, he emerged unbeatable, making all life miserable."

"Is the earth that old?"

"Many years older," Master Sima assured him. "A deity who sought to do good deeds came to earth—disguised as a man—to challenge this tyrant to a fight. The man won the battle, ridding the land of this wicked god forever. The humans cheered and praised this man's noble actions, declaring him the Jade Emperor, the Supreme Sovereign. He rules with benevolence."

"How do you know these things?"

"I learned many important subjects when I studied with my teacher, Master Kong."

Master Sima continued. "Injustice, war, and evil ran rampant in our world. He established a moral code of conduct for us to follow based on the individual principles of mutual respect, virtuous behavior, and family ties. I want you to study these ideas."

"We still have war," Lu Bān said. "Warriors killed my relatives."

"War is not bad when fought for righteousness, defending against mistreatment, or righting a wrong. We should stand against war if it is an abuse of power to conquer other people," Master Sima counseled.

"Why are some men good, and others are not?"

"By nature, all men are alike. However, by practice, they become farther apart," Master Sima said. "The more a man meditates upon respectable thoughts, the better will be his world and the world at large." The wrinkles around Master Sima's eyes accentuated his kind smile. "We will talk more about this subject in the future."

"I will think on it, Master."

"Let us begin with a calligraphy lesson. Are you ready?"

"Yes, Master."

Master Sima knelt beside his student's table. He picked up a handful of foot-long flat sticks. "We will use these thin bamboo slips to practice writing. First, hold the calligraphy brush with care and roll it in ink, like this, to form a delicate tip."

Lu Bān positioned the brush between his thumb and fore-finger, adjusting it several times before turning the barrel to get the brush's feel. He squished his eyebrows to concentrate, dipped the end hairs in the black ink, and rolled the brush.

"Yes, you have made a grand start." Master Sima scruti-nized his new student's attempt and demonstrated the next step.

"Now, use caution to apply the ink to the slip in controlled, graceful symbols. These symbols convey ideas. This figure means 'eternal.' It will help you practice the eight different calligraphy strokes."

The boy's eyes sparkled as he viewed the ink spread out in perfect proportions on the smooth bamboo, based on the brushstroke's proper pressure and speed.

"Try your symbol beneath mine."

Lu Bān followed the master's directions, completing the symbol as close to the one his teacher drew as he could. He searched his teacher's face, expecting high praise, crestfallen when Master Sima said, "Although your figure is a wonderful beginning, it will take several months of practice to make it perfect."

Lu Bān's shoulders slumped. "Months? That long?"

"I understand your disappointment," Master Sima said. "When I began my instruction with Master Kong, my execution fell short, too. He told me, 'A man who moves a mountain begins by carrying away small stones.' You moved the first rock on your journey. You must learn patience."

Lu Bān retreated to his room when he finished his lessons. The screen made a swishing noise when he closed it. He removed his mother's ring from its secret place, held it close to his heart, lifted his eyes, and told her about his day.

"Today is the best day ever, although I failed to make the symbol like Master Sima's. He said it would take a long time. I promise to work hard. You will be proud." He kissed the ring. "I must hurry to dinner. I cannot be late again," he said before placing the ring in its secret niche. He did not notice Chen Bo outside the window, watching his every move.

Chapter 2

Several months later, Lu Bān knelt at his table, concentrating on writing, drawing, and completing his mathematics lessons during a summer storm. The lightning threw a white-hot flash of light around the room as a rumble shook the walls.

"Our mountain location put us closer to heaven," Master Sima chuckled. "We must be inside an irritated cloud,"

"Mother told me an angry god produces thunder with a drum and mallet to punish people guilty of secret crimes, while his wife makes lightning."

"You have an exceptional memory. The god's name is Leigong, and his wife is Dianmu. You need not worry unless you have committed a secret crime."

"No, Master Sima, I keep no secrets and only hope my mother is proud."

"Someone must have a concealed a crime to cause this intense tempest. Even the birds are silent."

"I love birds. I sketched one I saw in the courtyard to show you. How is it they fly?" Lu Bān searched for his chalkboard. "It is missing!" His hand flew to his storage chest. "What happened to my drawing? Someone took it," he gasped. "Why would anyone want my sketch?"

"No one uses this room except the two of us. Are you sure you left it here?"

"Yes, Master. I had it here yesterday morning before lunch."

"Do not worry. We will find it. Perhaps you took it to your room?"

Master Sima opened the cabinet to remove a set of pictures, illustrating how the bones and muscles enabled birds to fly. "Until you find your drawing, you can study these and create sketches of your own."

The storm's lightning and thunder accompanied Lu Bān back to his room to search for his chalkboard. When he arrived, many things were not where he'd left them earlier. He sped to where he kept his mother's ring, jerking out the brick to stare at the vacant space. His stomach roiled.

"It is not here!" he shrieked, running back to their workshop. "It disappeared! Mother's ring is missing," he wheezed, out of breath, collapsing on his mat. Tears poured down his distraught face. "Who did this? Why?" Lu Bān balled his fist, giving it a vigorous shake. "When I find them, I . . ."

Master Sima stood before him, arms crossed. "Now is a perfect time to learn a lesson about controlling your emotions. I can understand your fury. Master Kong taught me when anger rises, you must weigh the consequences."

Lu Bān's cheeks burned. His arms relaxed, hanging by his side. "Although I still want to hit them, I guess I might get a bigger punch back."

"Wait here. I will return," his teacher said.

鲁班

Master Sima called his servants together in the kitchen courtyard, questioning them about the ring. Each denied any knowledge of its disappearance as they stood in the sweltering July weather after the storm passed.

"You heard Leigong's thunder. One of you owns the truth. One of you is guilty of a secret crime. You will suffer torments in your next life if you took the ring and then lied. You may even return as a pig." He studied their faces, hoping to detect nervousness. "I will be lenient if you confess by morning."

Master Sima returned to the workshop, stooping beside Lu Bān, who remained in a daze. "I believe we will learn who took it tomorrow. The thought of suffering in a future life is a powerful motivator."

魯班

The cook entered the kitchen courtyard at daybreak. Her shriek pierced the early morning quiet upon finding Chen Bo lying on the ground. A pool of blood had oozed from his chest. A bloody dagger with a yellow dragon-carved hilt lay next to the body.

Master Sima hurried to determine what had happened. Lu Bān arrived as Master Sima picked up two bamboo slips beside the corpse and read the words:

My actions shame my ancestors. Your new student now holds your attention. Seeing him hide his ring, I believed I could sell it, become rich, and move away. He took it out, talked to it, and hid it again. I thought it might indeed hold magic. I am a fool. I beg your forgiveness. The ring is in my pocket.

An uncomfortable silence settled over the courtyard. Lu Bān searched his teacher's face, asking, "Am I the cause?"

Master Sima put his palm on Lu Bān's shoulder. "You did nothing wrong, child. Jealousy and greed are the terrible monsters who took his life." He examined Chen Bo's pocket, retrieved the ring, handing it to Lu Bān. "He did not damage it. I imagine you will find he also returned your chalk drawing."

Lu Bān took the ring back to his room. He held it to his breast before slipping it on his thumb. The ring emitted a slight sound and warmed. "It fits. The magic made my thumb grow." Lu Bān stared at the ring on his hand. "You are safe now, Mother."

魯班

Five years passed. On one of Master Sima and Lu Bān's regular walks through the narrow town streets, men hustled to and from shops, carrying trays of fragrant pies, baskets of fruits and vegetables, avoiding the carts rumbling over the stones. Lu Bān laughed at two barking dogs chasing a stray cat into a side street.

Master Sima stopped to rest under a majestic shui-sa tree, grateful for the shade from the relentless afternoon sun. The tree's fragrance filled their nostrils.

The master said, "Lu Bān, since your arrival, you have worked each day with diligence. You have learned to read, to draw buildings, to understand the night sky secrets, and to write elegant calligraphy. Of all the students who have studied here, you are my best scholar. It is time to turn our studies to life and the philosophy of doing good deeds for others," Master Sima explained. "Helping to improve the lives of your fellow man is paramount. Do you remember the lesson of our ruler?"

"Yes," Lu Bān said. "He keeps the Mandate of Heaven as long as he protects his people more than he cares for himself. If the ruler becomes selfish, the gods will appoint a new one."

"Correct," Master Sima replied with a nod. "As you grow toward manhood, you must understand this is an ethical code, a guide to personal behavior. Your mother's ring is a perfect reminder. Jade is a symbol of moral integrity and purity."

Lu Bān rolled the ring around on his thumb, hoping to absorb those qualities.

"These traits are of prime importance, as is helping to enhance the lives of your fellow man," Master Sima said. "We call good deeds 'replacement of blessings' or 'rewards for goodness.' You will find either rewards or troubles in your next life based on the way you live now. The more virtuous actions you perform, the better your life will be."

Lu Bān reflected on when he lived with his mother. "Did I do something wrong in my past life to cause mother to depart this life?"

"No, you are not responsible. We all leave this life at our appointed time."

"I understand, Master." Lu Bān bowed. "I will remember to pursue good deeds."

They resumed their walk. The majestic white cranes preened their black-tipped feathers at the lake's edge. Their high-pitched *karrooo* calls filled the midmorning air. They stopped when an army of youthful men caught their attention, grunting with buckets of water hanging from their carry-poles to irrigate a nearby field.

Still preoccupied with his teacher's words, Lu Bān wrinkled

his forehead. "Is there some way we may help those boys?" Without thinking, he fingered the jade ring. *There must be a better way to move water from the lake to the fields.* Closing his eyes, he fell, trance-like, through a deep mist. He had a crystal-clear picture of the workers. The ring warmed, growing hotter and hotter still, as if transferring the solution to his mind.

Lu Bān's eyes snapped open, reaching for a stick to draw a diagram of lines and square boxes in the dirt.

Master Sima considered his sketch. A relaxed smile crossed his face. "Your suggestion is excellent. Let us work to make your idea a reality."

They tried several ways to shape the channels and fashion the gates over the next year. At each failure, Master Sima reminded his pupil, "Our greatest glory is not in never falling, but in rising every time to try again."

"It appears I often fall," Lu Bān said, wiping sweat from his brow. "Getting up is the challenge to think of another way to solve our problems."

Student and teacher worked together until they invented a novel way to irrigate the land, using troughs fitted with wooden gates to release the water when needed. It took another year for Master Sima to convince Lu Shi Huan, the landowner, their plan would work and to fund the project.

Their efforts increased food production for their neighbors and helped feed the town's needy. They also enabled Lu Shi Huan to prosper beyond his fondest dreams, setting him on a course of prominence in the village.

鲁班

Lu Shi Huan, the son of a mid-level official in the palace of Duke Ding of Lu, assumed his father's government position and his lands after his father left the earth.

A year later, in late summer, Duke Ding passed, leaving the throne to his son, Duke Ai. An ambitious man, Lu Huan sought to garner favor with the new duke at every opportunity, passing sensitive information about the duke's enemies, potential strife among the landowners, and rumors of palace intrigue, always under cover of darkness in a secluded alcove of the fortress.

The duke rewarded Lu Shi Huan's efforts, elevating him to the level of an earl and then to a lord, serving at the duke's pleasure with four other lords.

Lord Huan's status came with obligations. The duke used his pledged servant to secure an alliance with a rival, Duke Jing of the Qi State, by arranging the marriage of one of the duke's relatives to Lord Huan.

Realizing his lordship, wealth, and position hung in the balance, Lord Huan consented to the union, one fraught with strife from its inception. Their union produced a daughter, but no son, presenting Lord Huan with an inevitable dilemma. *Who will take care of us when we are old?*

According to custom, when his daughter reached her fifteenth year, she would marry and live with the new husband's family, leaving Lord and Lady Huan with no one to care for them as they age. He needed to find a worthy man without parents to solve his problem when his daughter came of age in a few years.

After Master Sima approached Lu Shi Huan with Lu Bān's irrigation system, he realized this innovation would give him the advantage over the other growers by increasing his crops, thus adding to his wealth. He also recognized Lu Bān's potential as a talented inventor.

Never wanting to miss the opportunity to garner the duke's favor, Lord Huan shared his thoughts with the duke, hoping to impress the royal with his knowledge about the system before anyone else.

The duke, always interested in taking advantage of his neighboring dukes, encouraged Lord Huan to follow Lu Bān and report promising inventions.

Lord Huan set about to discover more about the irrigation's creator. He learned Lu Bān, an orphan, had become Master Sima's student several years ago.

An orphan, he mused. *If he married our daughter, they would live with us. Duke Ai would have to approve. Is Lu Bān my answer?*

魯班

No longer a skinny child, Lu Bān grew into a muscular, well-built, tall, eighteen-year-old with coal-black hair and the soft hairs of a mustache and chin whiskers. He continued to study mathematics, the stars and architecture—creating new designs never discovered. One drawing occurred when Lu Bān struggled to produce a draft for a Dragon Temple for Jiangxi City.

Stuck for inspiration, he stretched out on a pile of indigo, yellow, and green silk cushions, held the jade ring between his fingers, and closed his eyes to summon its help. Mist surrounded him like a cozy blanket, drawing him into the depths of a warm sea. In his vision, he visited the Dragon King of the Eastern Ocean to ask if he could borrow his magnificent Underwater Crystal Palace as a template. The king, flattered by Lu Bān's high praise, agreed to lend him the palace for three days and had it flown over by a team of dragons.

As Lu Bān worked on his version, he realized the crystal palace was too intricate. He failed to produce a workable drawing during his three-day allotment.

When the dragons returned to collect the palace, they clustered around the building and lifted. They snarled, heaved, and strained, to no avail. It would not budge because Lu Bān had nailed it to the ground.

The Dragon King became furious. He dispatched an army of dragons, crabs, and sea monsters to retrieve the structure. Because none of the creatures knew how to remove the nails, the palace remained in place.

As the sun rose on the fourth day, the sea creatures scuttled back to the water. However, the dragons kept straining to lift the building until they collapsed from heat exhaustion. Their dark-crimson-dried-out bodies curled around the palace, each presenting an impressive spectacle.

Lu Bān awoke from his dream, erased his sketches, and drew plans for a new variety of Dragon Temples.

When Master Sima arrived at the workshop to check on Lu Bān's progress, he found the young man hunched over his worktable, his azure robe's hem puddled on the floor, sketching with unmatched urgency. Master Sima examined the new designs. "These pictures take my breath away. I've seen nothing like them."

Lu Bān took a slow lungful of air to savor the moment. "I want to be the land's greatest craftsman."

"You are well on your way with these illustrations. When you finish the Dragon Temples in Jiangxi, we will enjoy a tidy sum of money. Soon, everyone across the country may search for your skills. Remember the will to win, the desire to succeed, the urge to reach your full potential. These are the keys to unlock the door to your success."

Chapter 3

On a glittering spring morning, when the fragrance of cherry blossoms perfumed the breeze, the teacher and pupil walked to a clearing outside of town.

Filled with high spirits and excitement, Lu Bān carried his creation, attached to one end of a hank of silk string wound around a rectangle of bamboo sticks. The day had arrived to test its ability.

The raucous crow called from a tree when they passed the park carrying an unfamiliar object. It caught a few of the townspeople's attention.

"What do you have?" one man shouted.

"Something I call a *bamboo sparrow*," Lu Bān said.

"What does it do?" screeched another.

Master Sima teased. "Follow us. It will amaze you."

Arriving at the field, a sizable crowd had gathered. An imposing figure of a government official observed them from a distance.

Lu Bān thought back to a day three years ago when he'd entered their workshop. He'd watched the old master kneeling at his worktable, sketching a familiar object inspired by a sparrow hawk spiraling in the sky.

"I wonder if you could make a wooden bird fly?" Master Sima wondered aloud.

Lu Bān focused on the drawing, pondering the shape, size, and proportions. *Would it work? Could it fly?*

"This would be a wonderful project to try," Lu Bān said at last. "I will use your sketch as my model."

Lu Bān began his quest to carve a suitable piece of bamboo.

Today, after years of more work, they would discover if his creation could soar. The breeze increased. Master Sima ran as fast as he could, clutching the sparrow. Lu Bān released the silk line with superb skill until the wind lifted the sparrow toward the sky.

"Look to the heavens!" one spectator yelled. "It floats!" Others in the circle clapped and cheered. All at once, disaster struck. The crowd uttered a collective gasp as the sparrow flipped over and crashed to the ground, breaking into a thousand tiny pieces.

The crowd's cheers turned to boos. "I am going home," one man shouted. "There is nothing more to learn."

Lu Bān's heart sank. He knelt beside his sparrow and scooped up the splintered bits of bamboo.

A man in the front row asked in a low voice, "Will you try again?"

"Three years of effort reduced to a pile of rubble." Lu Bān groaned, standing. "I have failed."

魯班

Following Duke Ai's orders to keep Lu Bān under surveillance, Lord Huan stood some distance from the spectators, observing the activity in the park.

Lu Bān's idea is ingenious. If he can make it fly, it will be a perfect way to send messages to the warriors on a battlefield or spy on the enemy.

Although he witnessed the bird soar and then crash, Lord Huan realized the bird's potential and a solution to his dilemma. He formulated a plan.

Lu Bān has no family and is a student of Master Sima, the scholar. If I persuade Duke Ai to sanction my daughter's marriage to Lu Bān, therefore becoming my son-in-law, I will know about his creations before anyone else. Thus, the duke will have the advantage over his enemies and keep me in his good graces. My next task is to gain the inventor's confidence and convince him to marry my daughter.

A warmth spread through Lord Huan's body as his plan took shape in his mind.

My daughter will not leave, and I will control Lu Bān's genius. My hope lies with his bird.

魯班

"I am sure it will fly." Master Sima patted Lu Bān's shoulder when they reached the workshop after the disastrous failure. "You understand what does not work. Learn from this defeat and refine your idea."

Lu Bān's chin trembled, breathing out a deep, weighted moan. He buried his head in his hands. "Perhaps I am not as talented as I thought. The task is too difficult."

Master Sima's reassuring smile made the corners of his eyes crinkle. "Master Kong would tell you, 'Believe in yourself, and the rest will fall into place.' You can do it. If you want to be the best builder and inventor ever, you must try hard things."

Lu Bān remained quiet for a time, fingering his mother's jade ring on his little finger to avoid his mentor's gaze. He closed his eyes, drawing another deep breath. A sense of tranquility enveloped him, just as he'd always experienced when his mother wrapped her arms around him to calm his fears.

Lu Bān ignored his self-doubt. He raised his eyes to stare into Master Sima's. "I will do my best. With your drawings, vision, and confidence, I will begin before I lose my nerve."

He selected a piece of bamboo and worked on a design inspired by his bird sketches from childhood.

Over the next year, Lu Bān split bamboo rounds into thin strips, polished them, curved them by heating and sweating them over a fire, forming them into the shape of a magpie, his favorite bird. In a few weeks, he would test his improved bird.

魯班

On the eighth day of the eighth month in the Lunar New Year, Lu Bān knelt before Master Sima's ancestral altar. He held the jade ring to his heart, closing his eyes.

"Mother, I give all honor to you. I wish for your blessing today for a successful flight." A sharp tingle shot through Lu Bān's body as the ring warmed. "Thank you, Mother. I know you are with me."

The ring continued to heat. A familiar scent of a verdant shui-sa tree forest filled his nostrils, followed by a fleeting flash—a faint image, a figure dressed in yellow—for a momentary glance before vanishing.

Jolted by the vision's disappearance, he opened his eyes, still kneeling at the altar. The ring lost its green shimmer and cooled to its natural state as Lu Bān strained to resurrect the mental picture.

Master Sima's voice beckoned him. "Come, it is time to test your bird."

Together, Master Sima and his pupil made their way to the clearing on the outskirts of town. An enterprising vendor moved his cart to the field and hawked rice cakes and juice as the crowds gathered again. This time, twice the number of people came after word spread of the previous year's wooden sparrow experiment.

"Good luck, Lu Bān!" one man yelled.

A broad grin flooded Lu Bān's face, causing his eyes to resemble slits, mirroring his enjoyment of the communal experience.

"I will wager two spade coins your bird falls from the sky like before," a man in a blue robe taunted. Opposing murmurs passed through the crowd, with several offers to accept the bet.

"I will take your gamble!" a man dressed in orange hollered. "I believe it will fly!" More applause followed.

Lu Bān searched the clouds, eager to find signs of movement. After a brief time, he noticed a faint breeze. The rustling sound of leaves in the trees increased. Bit by bit, the wind grew stronger until it blew with a constant strength.

Again, Master Sima ran with the magpie. Lu Bān released coils of the silk string, and the bamboo bird jostled until it floated with ease above the exuberant cheers of the crowd.

The orange-robed man pumped his arms in victory, hurrying to collect his wager. "You owe me two spade coins," he said to the blue-robed man. "I will take them now."

The loser raised his hands, closed his eyes in defeat, pressed his lips together, taking his time before paying the money to his rival.

"The bird is a success," Master Sima said, patting Lu Bān's back. "You did it."

The crowd's nonstop congratulations bolstered Lu Bān's spirits. His shoulders relaxed. Rather than continuing to hold the line, he tethered it to a stake in the center of the field. Like magic, the magpie stayed in the air.

A day passed. The bird still soared as spectators filtered in and out of the park to check on its progress. By the second and third day, the crowd had grown enough to encircle the clearing.

As the wind softened, the magpie drifted to the ground. Astonishment settled over the audience. Well-wishers gathered around to applaud Lu Bān's success.

Lu Bān squared his shoulders, beaming. He clutched his creation before him. "As the bird soared high above us, it reminded me of an actual bird hovering in place." He held the bird aloft, and in a loud, confident voice, raised over the people's extended cheers, "In honor of the bird, I will call this a *kite*."

A dignitary emerged from the crowd's edge, walking with purpose toward Lu Bān. He appeared to be a high-ranking official based on his elegant attire and an elaborate guan headdress covering his hair-knot. The town's folk parted to make way for the officeholder.

On his imposing, rotund figure, he wore an emerald *Yi*, an open, cross-collar robe. Intricate braid decorated its full, voluminous sleeves and a long body garment of patterned, green silk under the *Yi*. A contrasting print *bixi*, or skirt, over his trousers, reached to his knees. A *Pei* ornament of jade and gold hung from his sash on an elaborate red cord. It swung from side to side as he walked.

"You are a talented inventor," the man said. "I have followed your progress."

Lu Bān bowed. His scalp prickled. Without thinking, he clutched the kite to his chest. *Why would you watch me?*

The man acknowledged Lu Bān's hair pulled up into a bun and his pointed hat. "I see you have observed the *guan li* capping ceremony. How many years are you over twenty?"

Lu Bān bowed again to the man to show his respect. "I am almost twenty-one."

"I understand you are without a family," the man snapped, his tone sharp.

Lu Bān's shoulders drooped. Obligated, he recounted how he'd become an orphan, and how Master Sima had befriended him as a small child.

"And you never married."

"No, sir, I lack parents or money to negotiate a proper proposal." Lu Bān said, his voice soft. "I fear I will never marry."

The man flashed his perfect teeth and extended his arms. "I have the solution. I have no son, but I have a daughter. She likes to draw, sketch, and invent things. I believe you would be a splendid match for her. She possesses the skills a woman needs to provide for her husband. You are without a father. I am without a son." He touched Lu Bān's arm. "I have settled it. I will take you to be my *son*," he said, his voice projecting authority and self-confidence.

Before Lu Bān could respond, the man spun and walked away. He glanced over his shoulder. "I will speak to Master Sima about a marriage arrangement."

Lu Bān took a step back. His mouth gaped. He stood speechless. *Marriage? Become a son?* Parents arrange their children's marriages. How could he marry? He had no gifts for her parents, or ancestral tablets, or a house of his own. Why would such an important man consider him fit as a son-in-law? *What if she is ugly?* His eyes brightened. *Why not? Marriage, after all, is the father's idea.*

It had been a splendid day for Lu Bān. The successful flight of his kite, and now he had a man telling him he would marry his daughter.

Could it be the magic?

魯班

Master Sima and Lu Bān relaxed together in their courtyard. A gray Chinese nightingale, with its orange beak and bright yellow throat, began its mating song as the last rays of full sun filtered through the tea tree behind their bench.

Over tea, Master Sima started his assessment of the day. "Lu Bān, I am full of pride. You improved upon my idea of a flying bird, and you made the dream a reality."

"I owe it all to you, Master," Lu Bān said. "The kite's success is beyond belief. Thank you for your confidence and encouragement."

"Now you have an uncommon opportunity. The official who spoke to you today is Lord Huan. He enjoys influence and position with our ruler, Duke Ai." Master Sima sipped his tea and continued. "Before he became a prominent lord in the State of Lu, I knew him as Lu Shi Huan. Our paths crossed several years ago, after you and I perfected the irrigation system for his fields. I met him when I convinced him to pay for the project and our work. After many more meetings, he agreed to our terms."

A slow recognition filled Lu Bān's face. "That is what he meant when he said he had been keeping track of me."

"Your idea made him affluent, and he parlays his wealth into having his way when he desires something. It now appears he wants you." Master Sima sighed. "Lu Bān, my parents arranged my marriage to a wonderful woman. Although we were strangers when we married, we grew to love and respect each other. To our great sorrow, we had no children, but we were joyful. Fond memories of her still linger."

"I am . . . sorry," Lu Bān stammered. "You never spoke of a wife."

"Tradition dictates sons mourn when their elders leave, and one is not to cry or grieve in public for anyone who comes from an inferior rank, including parents mourning for their children. We bury them in silence and do not speak of them again. Following this line of reasoning, a husband should not mourn for a spouse because she is lower in stature in this *dyad*."

"This is not right." Lu Bān shot back. "If you loved your wife, how could you not show your grief?"

"I followed the accepted code of behavior. I washed my wife's body, dressed her in white, placed her in a wooden coffin, and buried her on the hill overlooking the lake she cherished." Master Sima touched his chest. "I will forever carry my love for her here in my heart."

A lengthy silence passed before Lu Bān inquired, "How did she leave this life?"

Master Sima dabbed at moist eyes. "Recollections of those days still cause me sorrow. I can still smell the smoke and remember the flames. I lost my beloved wife to a fire many years ago."

"You never remarried?"

"No, as a philosopher and scholar, I do not need a wife now. My parents departed this life. I produced no son. Now, servants take care of me. Many students like you have kept me company over the years."

Lu Bān folded his hands, bent forward to rest his forearms on his knees, staring at the ground.

"How can I leave you? If you had not taken me in, I would not be here now. Orphaned children had no value in our village. I had no hopes of marriage. Now a preeminent official tells me I will marry his daughter, abandon you, and live with them. It is an unanticipated idea."

"Lord Huan's arrangement is an opportunity for you to marry a wealthy girl and live with an affluent family," the master replied. "While it is unwise to refuse his offer, I can understand your dilemma." Master Sima extended his hand to touch Lu Bān's shoulder. "I love you as a son, but I desire the best for you. With the resounding success of your kite and your talents, you will be in demand throughout the country. It is only a matter of time before you receive other opportunities, and you will eventually leave."

Master Sima took a heavy breath, then he continued: "I should not make this decision for you. You must decide if you wish to marry. If not, you must live with the consequences. Lord Huan possesses the wealth and power to make your life miserable."

"I never considered marriage before. Lacking status, why would he pick me?" Lu Bān paused. "Would you talk with Lord Huan to evaluate his daughter? You know I value your counsel."

After a lengthy silence, Master Sima agreed. "I will meet

with him on your behalf. We should have a better understanding of her qualities and Lord Huan's intentions tomorrow."

魯班

According to tradition, a groom's family starts a marriage proposal, and a matchmaker handles the details of contacting the girl's parents. However, Lord Huan decided to broker the marital agreement and made the unusual offer to come to Master Sima's home at the appointed time for their first meeting.

The two men bowed before taking a seat on a thick mat at a squatty table flanked by black columns in the house's second bay. Lord Huan's eyes sparkled as he painted a picture of his daughter.

"Although she is a girl, her schooling continued past age nine with the finest teachers," Lord Huan said.

"Teachers?" Master Sima's eyebrows shot up so far, they almost reached his hairline. "How is that possible?"

Lord Huan gave a toothy grin. "I used my position and authority to place her with private tutors. My daughter enjoys writing poems and is the master of The Four Arts. She plays the *Qin* and lute with skill and excels in both calligraphy and painting."

Master Sima tipped his head to one side. "She can play Go?"

"My daughter is proficient at the game of encirclement chess. Her ability to conquer her opponent's territory and surround vacant points with her stones is impressive. Why, she can defeat me on occasions." Lord Huan puffed out his chest. "She possesses a refined talent for sketching and painting flowers, and she has the gift to create the fine art of needlework." He leaned toward Master Sima. "You recognize this skill is a symbol of a diligent woman, and the *standard* of an obedient wife."

Lord Huan narrowed his eyes as he continued. "You realize I can command Lu Bān to marry my daughter. However, I would rather it is your agreeable decision."

Lord Huan appeared to care about his daughter. Master Sima listened and wondered, *Why else would he offer this unusual proposal, considering his social status? Does this man have other motives for the marriage?* The master stroked his chin whiskers. *Her qualities reflect a well-bred girl—but what about her independent thinking? This trait concerns me the most.*

Master Sima stood to escort Lord Huan to the door. "I will contemplate the situation and discuss it further with Lu Bān."

A satisfied smile filled Lord Huan's face. "My case is convincing. I expect you to persuade Lu Bān to accept my offer," he said, giving Master Sima a bow of respect.

Master Sima mirrored the bow.

Over evening tea, Master Sima recounted his dialogue with Lord Huan. "His daughter appears to be an extraordinary girl. He has become a man with much power and influence. Rejecting his wishes could lead to hard consequences for you. He expects me to meet him again tomorrow."

"Lord Huan's social status is far above my standing," Lu Bān replied. "I keep wondering why he would want me. What should I do?"

"It will be your decision and yours alone. Whatever you decide, or wherever you go, go with your heart. But keep your head about you."

鲁班

Sleep eluded Lu Bān, thrashing, uneasy about the whole notion of marriage. He arose, put on a red silk ceremonial robe. Moving to light the candles on his table, their smoke rising in swirls, he retrieved his mother's jade ring from the secret wall niche. *Could the ring help me understand what to do?* He held it in his left hand and closed his eyes. He tried to summon his mother's spirit to guide him.

The stone appeared cool at first. It warmed, becoming hotter, almost too hot to hold. His mother's vision appeared. Although her lips moved, he could not understand her words. Her eyes crinkled at the corners. A placid expression filled her face, as if giving her blessing.

The figure disappeared as he reached his hand to touch her. In an instant, the ring lost its fire and returned to its cold, green, natural-stone state. Lu Bān kissed the ring, replacing it in its safe place. At peace, he fell asleep. He dreamed of a forest of shui-sa trees and a girl dressed in yellow.

魯班

The following day, Lu Bān told his master about the events of the night over breakfast. "I believe my mother approves."

"Perhaps," sighed Master Sima. "Let us wait until I speak with Lord Huan this afternoon."

Master Sima sat and listened again while Lord Huan paced, explaining his plan. "Because I am without a son to carry on my ancestral lines, this marriage would be an excellent solution for both my family and Lu Bān."

The whole marriage notion seemed out of the realm of usual. Lord Huan appeared to liken the situation to a farmer purchasing livestock for his farm. Master Sima realized Lord Huan's daughter was not a typical bride-to-be.

"I will admit," Lord Huan said, "she has not always been an obedient young child. But she has matured and is now submissive and respectful. My daughter possesses many exceptional traits. She is smarter than most boys are and deserves a husband with whom she can blossom and live life to her fullest measure." He stopped to face Master Sima and held his hands out, palms up. "Can you not understand? I see much potential in Lu Bān?"

"I recognize you care for your daughter," Master Sima said. "I love Lu Bān as much as if he were my son. He has been with me for most of his life, and I want what is best for him."

Master Sima walked to the latticed covered window with slow steps, peering into the garden filled with fragrant spring flowers of yellow and crimson for a few moments. He remained motionless as a yellow butterfly landed on his hand, then flew away, reminding him of his wife. Turning to face Lord Huan, he bowed. The raspy chatter of a magpie seemed to voice his approval. It made him smile.

"I will give my consent for Lu Bān to marry your daughter and agree to act on Lu Bān's behalf if their astrological charts are compatible."

Lord Huan relaxed his posture.

"Bring your daughter's *Zi Wei Dou Shu*, or "Four Pillars"— birth year, month, date, and time—to me tomorrow," Master Sima instructed. "Because Lu Bān has no ancestral altar, I will hold the document on mine"—he gestured to his right— "for the customary three days. I will engage a *fortune teller* to compare their charts and *solve the doubts*."

"Excellent. I will bring the certificate as you wish," Lord Huan said.

魯班

Lord Huan walked home with determined steps, head held high, his arms swinging by his side, delighted to have the answer he wanted. He inhaled a deep, satisfying breath. *It was easier to convince the old fool of my plan than I thought—Master Sima, master of what? Ha! I am the master, for my skills have persuaded him. 'What I wanted,' he thinks. Duke Ai will be pleased. Now, I need a reward*, he thought, feeling aroused. *I will pay a visit to my* little flower *after I tell the duke of my success.*

魯班

Arriving home, Lord Huan went straight to his official work-room and chose a slip to compose his terse message to Duke Ai. It read: *I won. Our plan proceeds.* He tucked the writing slip into the official correspondence pouch and called for his trusted assistant to deliver it to the palace.

The courier arrived, acknowledged the instructions, and departed. On his way, he passed Lady Huan, dressed in a knee-length black robe wrapped in the front, trimmed in orange, with billowing sleeves, covering her full figure over her long full skirt, on her way to see her husband.

A crooked, sly smile crossed her worn face, seeing the bag in the courier's hand. They exchanged knowing glances before continuing in opposite directions.

"Did you revisit Master Sima today?" Lady Huan asked, hands on her hips. "You need to drop this foolish idea to trick this peasant into marrying our daughter."

"Lu Bān has extraordinary abilities for solving problems and building things." Lord Huan narrowed his eyes. "One day, his name will be on everyone's lips as a great artisan. They might erect a statue in his honor."

"Your plan is a poor bet." Her voice raised. "Your foolish ambitions will destroy our life. What if he produces nothing valuable for the duke? We will be stuck with this worm; you will lose your position with the duke *and* our family's standing. The Tián general is a better match. I know his father—"

"Yes," he pinched his mouth with a sour expression, "I am aware of your *connection* to the general. Lovers, weren't you? As if anyone could love you."

"You understand nothing of love except your love for power at the cost of this family," Lady Huan snapped. "And don't think I am unaware of your little *mistress* in the outer city," she said, jabbing her long finger in the air, "whatever her name is. You are not as ingenious as you think."

"All men have a woman who can fulfill their needs. You lack this capacity."

"Think beyond your crotch. A match with the general's son would strengthen your position with Qi State. It will be to your advantage to have an ally if the rumors of war are true, and you find yourself on the losing side. You admitted before, they are stronger than our state."

"Save your breath to cool your porridge. I have made my decision. I am taking our daughter's Zi Wei Dou Shu to Master Sima for the fortune teller to compare their charts tomorrow, whether you like it or not."

Lady Huan spun in a huff; her black skirt whirled. Her parting words were, "The consequences will be yours."

Lord Huan placed his elbow on the table, resting his jaw on his palm. *I made a deal with the devil when I agreed to marry the Qi ruler's daughter to strengthen the alliance with Duke Ai. True. I received an exalted position in the government, but at the cost of constant bickering. Why did she have to be such a quarrelsome, conniving woman? Our lives are more miserable by the day.*

He reached for the flame stick to light one of his favorite incense cones after one of their frequent arguments. Curls of smoke ascended from the censer, spreading the deep aroma of styrax with its sweet, balsamic, faint, somewhat spicy and animalic amber-like undertones throughout the room. The fragrance always stoked his desire for his mistress, Huo Jing. Her arms would provide the comfort he sought.

魯班

Lady Huan passed into the garden where the courier waited. He handed her the slip he carried from Lord Huan. Her face clouded when she read the words. Handing it back, she also slipped him a few metal coins for his trouble. After the messenger left, Lady Huan formulated a plan to thwart this marriage.

魯班

Lord Huan delivered the birth document to Master Sima the following day. He beamed and bowed. "I will return in three days. I trust the charts are compatible."

On the third day, Lord Huan paid another visit. Jasmine tea perfumed the room. Master Sima greeted Lord Huan with a bow. "Please join me on the mat. Would you care for tea?"

"Yes, I would enjoy a cup," Lord Huan said.

"Here is the divination comparing the position of the five major planets, the sun and moon, in your daughter's diagram with Lu Bān's." Master Sima unrolled the chart. "See?" He pointed to the intersecting lines. "The fortune-teller says the heavenly signs are in alignment, the yin and yang balance." Master Sima paused for several breaths. "I will support Lu Bān's marriage to your daughter. However, the ultimate decision remains his."

Lord Huan's broad grin exposed his perfect teeth. "I am sure Lu Bān is the right man for my daughter. You will understand. They will be happy and give us many sons. I *suggest* you *urge* Lu Bān to accept my offer," he said, emphasizing his suggestion and veiled command.

魯班

Lu Bān waited for Lord Huan to leave before he joined his mentor in the inner hall. He wore his mother's jade ring on his little finger.

"Lord Huan insists you are the right match for his daughter," Master Sima said.

"I would like to marry and enjoy the blessing of children." Lu Bān fingered the vibrating ring. "I believe this to be my one chance. What happens now?"

"Because Lord Huan negotiated the proposal with me, we

need not follow the usual steps." Master Sima held up his fingers. "First, families need not meet face-to-face. Second, we have evaluated each other's appearance, education, and character. Your social position does not appear to concern Lord Huan."

"I keep wondering why he would choose me. I have no lineage, even though my mother said my father came from a noble family."

"We can proceed to the actual betrothal if you are positive marriage is something you desire," the master instructed.

Lu Bān took a slow, deep breath. He again rolled the ring around on his finger. "I am ready."

"To set a date for the marriage, you need to present a *juyi*, or 'engagement token,' to Lord Huan for his daughter."

Lu Bān tilted his head. "I have the perfect gift," he said with a broad grin.

魯班

Two days later, Lu Bān and Master Sima met with Lord Huan for the last time.

Lu Bān bowed. "I give honor to Master Sima," he said. "He accepted me when I had nowhere to go, after my mother left this world. He took me in and treated me as his son, guiding and teaching me with unmatched compassion."

He continued, "Through him, I learned to hold faithfulness and sincerity as my first principles, to treasure knowledge and to practice kindness toward my fellow man. I celebrate our ancestors' importance, although I knew none of my family. I arrived here with the clothes I wore that day and one other item—my mother's precious jade ring." Lu Bān stared at the object he held in his hand. "It has comforted me knowing it belonged to her. Today, it is still my one true, valuable possession."

Lu Bān glanced at Master Sima before shifting his gaze back to Lord Huan. "After much consideration, and with Master Sima's approval, I will accept your marriage proposal." He held out his mother's ring. "Please give this *juyi* engagement token to your daughter as my sign that I wish to marry her."

"I am pleased with this gesture," Lord Huan said, holding the delicate ring. "Thank you. It is a thoughtful gift." Lord Huan bowed to Master Sima. Lu Bān returned the bow. "May your mother rejoice. I will take this to my daughter, who waits in eager anticipation for my return."

魯班

Lord Huan's daughter waited in the inner hall of their spacious five-bay house for her father's return. She paced in silence, stopped to peer out a small window covered with a bamboo string screen, unfolded and refolded the cuffs of her robe, and walked back and forth again. *I wish he would hurry. The suspense is unbearable.*

"You will wear a hole in the floor if you keep walking," her mother said. "Sit down. Your father is making a terrible mistake arranging your marriage to this peasant. You would be happier with the general's son. He is handsome and has a future."

The dutiful daughter's eyes flashed. *Since when do you care if I am unhappy? Staying in this house with or without a husband is torture.*

The bride-to-be began her preparations for this day last

year when she reached the marriageable age of fifteen. After observing the *Ji Li* hairpin ritual, she coiled her long hair, the color of midnight, into a topknot held in place with decorative pins. Her parents also determined her *style* name, which she and Lu Bān would learn when the proposal became final.

When Lord Huan arrived, he gazed at his daughter through adoring eyes; he saw a beautiful bargaining chip. A gold and pearl ornament hung from the pin in the center of the required top knot in her hair. Matching dangle earrings swayed from her delicate ears. She wore a pale-yellow silk robe, held in place with a broad, bright gold sash, wrapped around her like sunshine. She stood on wooden platform shoes, painted white.

Lord Huan took his daughter's hand.

Trembling, she met her father's gaze, caught between excitement and fear. She knew whatever the decision; she had to obey him or risk severe punishment.

"You are the most charming girl in the world," her father said, bending down to kiss her forehead. "Any man would be fortunate to have you for a wife."

"Humph," Lady Huan snorted, thrusting her long nose in the air. "*This man* is not worthy of our family's position. How could you carry out this terrible proposal? Our daughter should marry someone who would add to our status, not some loathsome nobody. General Yan's son is a better choice."

"Silence, wife!" Lord Huan exploded. "I have heard enough of your protests. You forget, *I* decide!"

Lady Huan folded her arms across her chest and turned away in silent disapproval.

The daughter rolled her shoulders forward, wanting to disappear from her parents' argument, now sure she would suffer her mother's wrath, like always, after the quarrel. *I am like a space in a game of Go with a black stone and a white stone warring to capture the same space.*

"*This man* is perfect for us. He is a talented inventor, and through his work, he will bring honor to our household." Lord Huan glared at his wife, speaking through clenched teeth. "*He* will be *our* son and live with *our* family, so Lu Bān and *our* daughter can take care of us as we age."

Lord Huan drew in a slow, steady breath to calm his anger. "I have made the arrangements." He held the jade ring in his palm for his daughter to glimpse. "Lu Bān offered this *juyi* as his pledge to marry you."

The daughter glanced from her mother to her father, weighing her dilemma. *I cannot refuse my father's authority. But accepting the token will add to Mother's fury.*

She took the ring, hesitated, and slipped it on her finger. A tingle shot through her body as she saw a spark of light emanate from the jade ring. The ring warmed. She blinked, and for an instant, a vision and the scent of a shui-sa tree forest flashed before her. She sensed an immediate connection.

"This *is* the man. I am sure he is the one for me." She held out her hand, wearing the ring. Happiness and peace flooded her face. Her billowy sleeves, trimmed in red and black cuffs, filled with air as she twirled around and danced. She hugged her father and moved to show the ring to her mother.

Lady Huan huffed and left the room with no acknowledgment. *Mother will never forgive me, I fear.*

Lord Huan noticed his daughter's watery gaze. "Pay no attention to your mother's reaction. She envies your talents, for she possesses none."

The daughter fidgeted with her sleeve, mulling over her father's words. *Jealous? Why? I do not understand. She is a grand woman of status in our town.*

"I can now reveal your style name to you and Lu Bān." Lord Huan refocused on the marriage proposal. "He will call you *Yun*, which means 'cloud.'"

Yun felt a warm glow fill her, letting the name settle in her mind. "I like it. It is an exquisite name to begin my new life," she said. *I wish I could start it in another house, away from my mother.*

"By your acceptance of the jade ring, I now pledge you and Lu Bān to each other."

Did I ever have a choice? she thought. *Although, I am confident he is the right one.*

At that moment, a pair of magpies exchanged their quiet, musical warbling outside. Yun relaxed. *Even the birds approve of this match.*

Lord Huan again kissed her forehead. "Based on the chart Master Sima gave me, I have consulted the fortune teller to choose a marriage date to bring the most luck to you as a couple. She determined your luckiest day will be six weeks from today."

Yun positioned her fingers in a prayer-like pose. *Please, let him be handsome and kind, not old and ugly.*

魯班

Lady Huan overheard her husband's conversation with Yun. *I have six weeks to find a way to rid us of this peon. Yun will thank me in the long run. Perhaps I could arrange for someone to take him away to the barbarian lands beyond the Zhou Kingdom's boundaries.* She rubbed her chin, working on her plan.

Ah, yes, he will be here for the traditional parent's dinner alone, without Master Sima, the night before the wedding. The men could intercept him on his way home. By the time someone misses him, it will be too late. I am sure the courier I have paid to give me information will find some way to do the deed. I will make it worth his time and trouble. Everyone will think the worm ran away, afraid to go through with the marriage.

Until then, I need to proceed with planning the wedding. I have much to arrange: the musicians, guests, and family members to invite; wedding clothing; and expensive food to order. This ruse will cost a fortune, but it is my husband's fault for not listening to me. He will thank me when he realizes his folly.

魯班

The official reply from Lord Huan arrived by messenger, addressed to Master Sima. Lu Chi, the servant, received the slip and took it to his master in the private garden protected by a solid wooden gate, where Lu Bān and his mentor waited for the marriage proposal's last word.

A heavy scent of lemon blossoms hung in the evening air as Lu Chi delivered the message, leaving the men alone.

"This is a formality," Master Sima began. "Lord Huan already decided you should marry his daughter."

Lu Bān's stomach flip-flopped. "My utmost concern is living with his family. Why would he choose me when he could pick from many others, equal to his status?"

"Yes, I have wondered the same thing. It is most unusual

to consider a girl's wishes above all else."

"If Lord Huan indeed loves his daughter, why would he not take into consideration her happiness?" the young man asked. "You taught me, without feelings of respect, nothing distinguishes men from beasts. I believe reverence should extend to everyone—not just men."

"Yes, I agree." Master Sima read the note. "The most appropriate date to bring you luck is six weeks away. There are many things for you to learn and decisions to make to prepare for your marriage. Lord Huan will expect you to be aware of the protocol accorded to his social standing."

Lu Bān exhaled, relieved. "It will give me time to study my duties. Would you be my guide, as you have been my teacher these many years?"

Master Sima touched Lu Bān's shoulder. "You are like my son," he answered. An unfocused gaze filled his face. "I remember my apprehension and excitement as I prepared for marriage. First, you will need to learn two different tea-pouring ceremonies, the honoring of ancestors, and the choice of a "good luck man," someone who fathered many offspring, to help you select and deliver a new bed to your room in Lord Huan's house."

Lu Bān raised his eyebrows. "Does someone come to mind?"

"One of my longtime friends, Lin Wan, would qualify. He has fourteen children. Ten of those are sons. I am certain he will consent to assist you."

"Ten sons? He will bring me good fortune. I remember meeting him with you at the lake."

魯班

Following customs, Lin Wan agreed to be Lu Bān's good luck man. They took several neighborhood children along to Lord Huan's five-bay house to deliver the fresh bed the day before the wedding. They placed it in a room on the east side of the house reserved for the newlyweds.

Lin Wan opened a cloth bag and poured its contents over the bed. "We scatter red dates, oranges, lotus seeds, peanuts, and pomegranates to represent abundance and fertility, to make sure your future offspring are well-fed." He invited the children onto the bed as an omen of fertility.

Through a glassy-eyed stare, Lu Bān beheld the boys' and girls' giggle and play. Fatherhood. Would he be a dutiful father? Master Sima seemed like a father. He decided to follow his example.

魯班

Dressed in a black robe trimmed in white, Lu Bān prepared to walk to Lord Huan's home to dine with Yun's parents. *Tomorrow, my life changes forever. One moment, I imagine the wonderful things in store. The next instant, I want to run away. I hope this is the right decision.*

So accustomed to fingering the jade ring in times of need, he reached to touch it, and for a brief moment, he forgot he had given it to Lord Huan. A fleeting vision of his mother passed through his mind in a forest among millennial-aged trees. She paused, smiled, and waved. "This woman will bring you great joy, my son."

魯班

Lu Bān stood at Lord Huan's door for a few extra heartbeats to calm his nerves and review the protocol he learned from Master Sima for tonight's tea ritual, and, summoning courage, he knocked on the door.

Lu Bān followed a servant into the inner hall, where Lord and Lady Huan waited. The room reflected Lord Huan's wealth, status, and position. An imperial tree rambled across the surface on one of the wall screens—birds representing the four seasons, perched on white-blossomed branches. Sandalwood incense perfumed the room.

The opposite wall screen depicted two graceful, four-foot-tall, black and white cranes among a backdrop of elegant bamboo plants. A Qin musician played soothing background melodies.

Lu Bān offered a bow of respect.

"Greetings," Lord Huan said, gesturing for Lu Bān to sit to his right.

Lady Huan, wearing several jewels on her fingers, took her place opposite her husband. The men sat cross-legged on a thick mat at a low, carved rosewood table, while a servant positioned porcelain cups, painted with bluebirds, and a small bronze cauldron beside Lu Bān.

Lu Bān replayed in his mind the instructions for pouring tea. He reached for the teapot, and as a sign of respect, he bowed and poured tea for Lord Huan, handing the teacup to him with both hands. Lord Huan accepted the offering with two hands, responding with a tip of his head.

Lady Huan refused to take her cup and flashed an icy stare before turning to face the wall. *This marriage was a huge mistake. I could not allow my husband's plan to succeed and jeopardize our status. The courier insisted I pay him in advance, but everything is now set for this scum to disappear tonight.*

A sudden, frigid chill struck Lu Bān's core. *Tonight is not the wonderful beginning I hoped. Living here may prove disastrous.*

Lord Huan's scowl softened. "Lu Bān, I welcome you to my home and my family. I recognize your talents and pray you will be content with my daughter. You will add many sons to my family."

Lu Bān's palms sweated. "Thank you, Lord Huan. I hope to father many sons and enjoy a long life with Yun." His mind raced. *What happens if I do not produce a son or any other children?*

Lord Huan handed Lu Bān a package wrapped in red silk. "Please accept this pair of lacquered chopsticks and two wine goblets. They are symbolic, for you are receiving the joy of my family, in the person of my daughter."

Lu Bān accepted his gift and bowed. "I vow to give honor to your ancestors. I pledge to be a dutiful husband and to be your grateful, respectful son." *My life continues to change by the moment. Will tonight ever end? I pray this marriage is not a colossal mistake, and tomorrow is different.* He smiled at Lady Huan, hoping she could not detect his apprehension. *I fear this woman can make my life miserable.*

魯班

The evening complete, Lu Bān bowed, bidding Lord Huan farewell, before stepping out into the warm, humid night, his path lit by a faint, waxing crescent moon. Reviewing the events of the evening, he questioned his decision to marry into a family with one hostile parent. *I pledged my mother's jade ring and my word I would marry Lord Huan's daughter. There is no turning back, but I hope Yun will not have her mother's demeanor. My mother's vision said I would be happy. I must trust her and the ring. I will find out tomorrow.*

He was walking beside a long row of east-facing rock walls toward Master Sima's home. Two men suddenly appeared from the shadows toward the end of the wall and pounced on him from behind, each grabbing one of his arms.

"Let me go!" he shouted. "I have no money, only chopsticks and wine goblets." He grunted and pulled against the men, struggling to free himself.

"We do not want your money, only you," the taller man said, increasing his grip to subdue Lu Bān. "Come with us, and we will not hurt you."

"Help!" he shouted. "Let me go! Someone, help me!" His voice echoed along the empty street.

An older man rounding the corner hurried toward the struggling men holding a red shui-sa walking stick. "Let him go!" he shouted, poking the pole in the shorter man's eye, who yelped in pain, turned Lu Bān loose, and fell to the ground. The rescuer kicked the man's groin, rendering him immobile, gasping for breath.

Lu Bān used his free hand to ram his palm at the tall man's nose. Blood sprang from the assailant's nostrils along with a scream of agony, breaking the silence. The man lost his grip, freeing Lu Bān's other hand to punch his attacker's throat as hard as he could, causing him to collapse to Lu Bān's feet.

Lu Bān put his hands on his knees, panting to catch his breath.

"Are you alright, Lu Bān?" the familiar voice said. "We

need to hurry away from these two before they recover."

"Master Sima . . . what are you doing here?"

"I thought you might like company on your walk home after your dinner," he answered. "It appears I made an excellent decision."

Lu Bān retrieved the package from Lord Huan, dusting it off. "Who are these rogues? What did they want with me?"

"I recognize both of them. They come from the outer city. People hire them on occasions to persuade citizens to release their purses or agree to certain demands. We will report them to the authorities tomorrow. They are notorious malefactors, in and out of jail often." Master Sima squinted at Lu Bān in the dim light. "Are you hurt?"

"Nothing grave," he answered, brushing a sore spot on his cheek and another on his arm. "I am glad to see you." He chuckled. "You wield a mean walking stick."

"We had better rest. You have a busy day tomorrow. I would not want you to be late for your wedding."

Chapter 4

Weeks passed. Spring gave way to summer. According to wedding customs, Yun retreated from her ordinary routine to prepare for her imminent departure from her unmarried, carefree life. For two days before the wedding, she lived in seclusion in a separate part of the house with two of her closest friends, Dandan and Lan.

The night before the wedding, they sang songs from their childhood. The song "I Am a Little Bird" reminded them of their lighthearted life. They flapped their "wings" and sang:

I am a little bird, soaring and chirping, free and happy

I have no sadness

I have no worries

I only love to laugh

Continuing to laugh, still pretending to fly like birds, Lan sang "When We Were Together," and the girls joined in:

When we were together, together, together

When we were together, we were so happy.

Smiling, you looked at me.

Laughing, I look back at you.

When we were together, we were so happy.

Lan reached for Yun's hand. "We will always be friends. Do not worry."

"I will miss you," Dandan said, tears staining her cheeks. "We can never tell secrets and laugh as we have all these years.

Now you will belong to Lu Bān."

"Although I must obey him, I am sure my mother will believe I should still mind her." Yun's shoulders slumped. "I have no escape. Remember, I will still live here."

"What about the wedding night? Are you afraid?" Lan wondered.

"I am," Yun confessed. "Mother offered few details, other than I should study the 'dowry paintings' she packed in my marriage chest after the wedding. I am nervous."

"Can we have a quick look?" Lan said, scooting to the edge of her mat. "Do they tell you what to do?"

"I am not sure," Yun said with a blank stare. "I know I am not supposed to open the box. They moved it to our wedding room yesterday."

"Could we sneak in to take a peek?" asked Dandan.

"No! My mother would beat me if she caught us."

"My oldest sister told me it hurt," Dandan said, "but it only lasted a moment. She said I needed to wait until I married to understand."

"I prefer not to consider that part," Yun said, changing the subject. "I wonder if he will be handsome."

Dandan wrinkled her nose to tease Yun. "His face might resemble a dog."

They stopped giggling as Lady Huan entered the room, the scent of sandalwood following her. An uncomfortable hush fell over the girls. They remained silent as Yun took her place on her mat.

"Although I would wish a better marriage for you, The Respected One Above decreed it, and I must follow his wishes, just as you must accept your husband's desires. I share no joy in performing the ritual of combing your hair. But it is my duty to repeat the words, even though I do not share their sentiment," she said, her tone flat. Without further comment, Lady Huan knelt behind Yun. Her fleshy fingers gathered her daughter's long hair with her left hand, holding a tortoise-shell comb with her right.

Yun held stone-still as the teeth grazed her scalp, gliding through her hair, and listened to her *lingtáng*. "This first time through your hair means from beginning to end. May you be together all your lives. The second time is for closeness and harmony in your marriage for a hundred years until a ripe old age." She paused. "The third time is a wish for many grandchildren. And the fourth offers hope for wealth and a long marriage until your hair, and your eyebrows, are white."

Lady Huan leaned close to her daughter, determined not to show any emotion. She stroked Yun's hair one last time. Rising, she departed without another word, leaving Yun alone with her girlfriends.

魯班

A secret smile crossed Lady Huan's face. *If everything goes as planned, there will not be a wedding tomorrow.* An owl's hoot called after her as she passed through the garden to the primary house. She froze, clutching the neck of her robe. *A bad omen?*

魯班

Yun reflected on her mother's words as she ran her slender fingers through her hair. "I trust we will enjoy the harmony my parents lack. I pray he is gentle and kind." Yun focused on her two friends. "I hope he will experience affection for me. What will I do if I do not please him?"

"He will devote himself to you. Do not worry." The girls hugged one last time before they blew out the candles and fell asleep.

Yun rolled the jade ring around her finger when it vibrated with intensity. A sense of calm settled over her when she closed her eyes. A vision of a man walking hand-in-hand with a girl dressed in yellow in a verdant forest of shui-sa trees startled her. They stopped to rest in a lush green meadow lying on the soft grass. They talked, and the girl gave the man a jade ring she wore just before he kissed her and vanished.

Yun's eyes snapped open, her heart pounding. Examining her ring, she realized, *This was the same ring. He is the right man!* she told herself. *Tomorrow is our wedding day. Tomorrow, I will be a married woman, and I will be his wife.*

鲁班

Lady Huan wondered, *Where is the courier? He should be here by now with my joyous news. I spent a sleepless night waiting for his report.* She observed her reflection on the polished disk, practicing her shocked expression for when she and her husband would hear the dreadful report of Lu Bān's disappearance. *I need extra face cosmetics today to cover the circles under my eyes.*

Dressed in a red and gold brocade robe and skirt, she paced the inner hall, listening for any signs of the messenger. *Time is getting short, only three clock candles before Yun appears for our tea ceremony.* She called a servant for bitter tea to calm her nerves.

The warm sensation of the beverage gave her courage. *Waiting is torture.* A raucous call of a crow sent a terrified shiver down her spine. *An ill omen? What if the plan failed, and they got caught?* Her mind raced. *My actions might have cost all of us our lives.*

魯班

At dawn, a servant awakened Yun and her friends. Dandan and Lan returned to their homes to prepare for the wedding later in the day.

Yun knelt in the soft glow of Dragon-and-Phoenix candles to meditate. A half-hour passed before she stepped into an oval wooden tub of warm, fragrant water infused with pomelo, a variety of grapefruit, to cleanse her of evil influences and serve as a cosmetic to soften her skin.

Outside, bird songs entertained her as she scooped up the citrus-scented water, letting it trickle over her slender body. The jade ring on her finger vibrated, sending concentric rings radiating on the water's surface, expanding to the wooden edges. An obscure image of a man appeared, walking through a forest. A sense of peace and happiness washed over her as she rested, trancelike, in her bath.

Yun's "good-luck woman," Huizhong, a trusted friend of the family whose parents, husband, and children were still living, interrupted her solitude. "It is time for you to retire from your soak and get dressed," she said, offering Yun a towel. Huizhong picked up a tray filled with jars. "First, I will apply your makeup and help you put on new, white-silk underclothes."

Yun remained motionless in the light of the Dragon-and-Phoenix candles as Huizhong performed the meticulous *Shang Tou* hairdressing ritual. She gazed into the bronze, polished disk, while Huizhong brushed her hair with care and grand ceremony, tying her hair in a bun, the style of a married woman.

"May you always obey your husband, may God bless you with many children, and may you enjoy many joyous days with your new husband," Huizhong said, putting the last touches on Yun's hairstyle. "Now, your father's marriage gift," she said, opening a red silk-covered box.

Yun took out the gold dangle earrings. "My grandmother wore these on her wedding day, according to my father. She left this life before my birth. My father saved them for me." Yun put them on and admired her reflection.

A servant brought Yun a bowl of *tangyaun* with pink and white rice balls. Yun tasted the sweet broth as Huizhong said, "This soup represents a complete and loving marriage. May it be so for you and Lu Bān."

Yun finished and bowed to Huizhong. "You are a faithful friend of our family. I am most grateful. Thank you for your help. I am still nervous, though."

"Every bride is anxious on her wedding day. We expect it," Huizhong said. "Come now. It is time to emerge from your retreat."

Yun howled with laughter as Huizhong carried the blushing bride to the next room on Huizhong's back so Yun's feet did not touch the ground. She remembered the times when, as a child, she had wrapped her arms around her father's neck, riding on his back.

She stepped into a pair of tiny red shoes, placed in the center of a sieve to strain out evil. Yun slipped into her crimson silk wedding skirt and jacket, embroidered with elaborate gold and silver figures, and she attached a small mirror to reflect wicked spirits away until she arrived inside the bridal chamber.

"Red is a dominant, joyous color. They say it will bring good luck and drive away evil spirits on your wedding day," Huizhong said. "You are stunning. Now for the finishing touch." Huizhong placed the bridal Phoenix Crown on Yun's head. A ruby "curtain" of tassels and sparkling beads hung from the headpiece to cover her face.

Yun's heart beat faster at the possibility of seeing her husband for the first time. She wrinkled her nose. "I hope he is not ugly," she murmured, fidgeting with her skirt. "I will not be able to tell one way or the other through all these beads."

"Your mother and father are waiting for you," Huizhong said, straightening the heavy headdress.

鲁班

"Are you ill?" Lord Huan asked when Lady Huan emerged from her dressing area, her face pale and her posture stooped.

"I did not sleep well," she said with a shrug.

"I suspect it is not from your excitement to have our new *son* join our family," her husband said, a tone of sarcasm in his voice.

"I am sure it is all the pressure to make the arrangements for the musicians, food, decorations, and the guests. We want everything to be perfect for the wedding." She swallowed hard. "I will be glad when today is over. Nothing will be the same ever again."

"Do your duty." Lord Huan's tone was firm. "It is time for the tea ceremony."

魯班

Yun joined her father and mother, her wedding preparations complete, bowing first to them and then to the ancestral tablets. She knelt before her parents and offered sweet bites of dried plums and pistachios before she served tea. Yun filled the porcelain cups half-full of white tea made from the camellia tea bush's immature buds. The tea splashing into the cups was the only sound in the room. She handed a cup to her father, on her right, who smiled at his daughter. Then she gave one to her mother, who did not lift her gaze to make eye contact. Yun bowed again.

"I apologize to you, my father and mother, for any wrongdoing, and I hope you will pardon my transgressions." *Will mother ever forgive me?* She folded the ceremonial tea napkin into a triangle to keep away any evil *Qi* energy.

"You are an obedient daughter," Lord Huan said after he finished his tea. "Lu Bān is a lucky man."

With the tea ceremony concluded, they waited in total silence for Lu Bān's arrival and his procession from Master Sima's house.

Chapter 5

The encounter with the would-be robber had left Lu Bān somewhat dazed and shaken by the time they reached the house's safety. Master Sima called Lu Chi to bring tea to calm Lu Bān's mind.

With the tea served, the servant withdrew from the two men, leaving them alone in the cozy garden, with the crickets sharing the local gossip.

"Master," Lu Bān inhaled a conspicuous breath, "the scoundrels who grabbed me said they did not want money, just me, and if I went with them without a fight, they would not harm me." He examined his reflection in the polished bronze disk. "I escaped with this scrape on my cheek and a bruise on my arm. Luck smiled upon me tonight. If you had not come along when you did—what do you think they wanted?"

"Your wedding is tomorrow," Master Sima began. "Perhaps someone wants to prevent you from marrying Yun. Would there be a jealous man who hoped to marry her? With you out of the way, he could make his case."

"Or Lady Huan, who does not want me as a son-in-law. She preferred some general's son. I am sure she hates me."

"Enough to have two men take you by force?" Master Sima asked. "That is a serious action. If true, Lord Huan would be in much trouble, for even if he had nothing to do with the crime, any member of his household would also suffer whatever punishment the duke dispensed. The *Lianzuo System* encourages family members to police their households out of fear of retribution for the other person's transgressions."

"The way she behaved at dinner tonight, I believe she could be cold-hearted enough to plan my capture. She knew I would be alone, walking home in the dark. I doubt I will ever know the truth. I intend to tell Lord Huan about the attempted abduction, but not my suspicions. It would be a terrible way to begin my marriage, living in the same house."

"It is time to prepare for the wedding if you plan to proceed," Master Sima reminded Lu Bān.

"I gave my mother's ring and my word," he said with a faraway gaze.

魯班

Lu Bān dressed in a long, scarlet silk gown, full sleeves trimmed in a braid with an eternal knot design, and matching shoes. He placed a crimson silk sash in an X across his chest with a silk ball attached to his shoulder. Then he knelt before Master Sima's ancestral altar. His mentor performed the *Jia Guan*, the "capping" ritual.

"To prepare for your marriage and, as a symbol of entering adulthood, I place this hat, decorated with fragrant cypress leaves, on your head," Master Sima said, wearing a red and gold brocade robe over scarlet pants. "May your ancestors be with you. May you have a long, joyful life with Yun."

Lu Bān stood and bowed to the ancestral tablets representing Heaven and Earth. *I wish Mother could be here.* He bowed to the altar and Master Sima.

魯班

As part of the ceremony, Master Sima removed the silk ball from Lu Bān's shoulder and placed it on top of the bridal sedan chair covered in silk and fresh flowers.

In an instant, the din of firecrackers emitting an odor of sulfur, deafening gongs, and beating drums marked the start of the procession from Master Sima's home. All participants wore variations of red and gold costumes, creating a sea of scarlet rippling along the street.

Lu Bān led the parade, accompanied by a small child from the town, as an omen of future sons. The child's hand reminded him of when a stranger took his tiny hand and saved him from certain slaughter, and how his life had changed.

Master Sima, friends, relatives, and well-wishers carried lanterns and banners and followed the bridal sedan chair supported by four hired men. Musicians with cymbals, drums, and gongs provided the music for a red dancing "lion," played by two dancers in yellow, red, and white brilliant outfits. They jumped, growled, and pranced about like the lion they portrayed.

Other revelers appeared in various cherry or lemon-colored feather dragon masks, along with a giant orange, fluffy dragon with exaggerated white and black swirls painted where the eyes would be. The procession created quite a spectacle. Lu Bān's caravan joined Yun's waiting relatives outside her father's house, greeting the parade with a cheer, followed by more firecrackers.

Lady Huan fainted, her red clothing resembling a pool of

blood surrounding her body.

魯班

Yun hid behind their carved wooden door to glimpse her future husband through the open fretwork as Lu Bān led the parade to Lord Huan's house. The jade ring on her finger sprang to life with a warm glow and tingle. The vibrations transferred to her right hand when she touched it. *This is a good luck omen,* she realized.

"He is much taller than I expected and appears muscular," she said in hushed tones to Huizhong. "His coal-black hair, eyebrows, mustache, and chin whiskers make him appear older, yet his *eyes.* They sparkle and seem kind. I see a familiar twinkle."

When Lu Bān approached the entry, Yun jumped back to prevent him from glimpsing her.

Dandan and Lan, Yun's best friends, blocked his entrance. They played the door game, a fun gesture to delay Yun's exit. Lu Bān held up two red envelopes as part of the ritual.

"I have *Li Shi*, token money for you if you will let me in," he said.

They teased him, peppering him with questions. "Do you feel affection for Yun? Are you sure you want to marry her?"

"Yes, of course," he said, trying in vain to squeeze through the opening.

Yun appeared beyond the entrance, her face obscured by the beads on the Phoenix crown. She stood in the doorway. Her relatives showered her with rice and red and green beans to attract the attention of *Jīnjī*, the good-luck golden chicken.

Lu Bān liked what he saw, although her face remained

covered. He exhaled. *At least she is not fat.* His face lit within, and he bowed.

The participants of the wedding threw rice into the bridal sedan chair. Huizhong once again carried Yun from the house on her back to the chair.

Lu Bān, joined by Lord Huan, stood back while the men carried Yun around the house's perimeter to symbolize her family's departure and becoming Lu Bān's wife. Firecrackers continued to scare away any remaining evil spirits, causing the children to put their fingers in their ears to muffle the noise.

Lord Huan noticed the cut on Lu Bān's cheek. "What happened? You haven't been to the marriage bed yet." He gave Lu Bān a sly smile.

"Two men tried to abduct me last night on the way home from your house after dinner. If it had not been for Master Sima's thinking that I could use some company on the way back, I would not be here."

"Who were they?" Lord Huan jerked his head, his eyebrows raised. "Did you recognize them? Did they rob you?"

"No, the taller man told me they did not want money, although I did not have any. He said they just wanted me. They promised if I went without resistance, they would not hurt me. I did not tarry long enough to find out." Lu Bān scrutinized Lord Huan's reaction to his next question. "Why do you think someone would want me out of the way the night before my wedding?"

Lord Huan did not answer right away. He appeared to be running scenarios through his mind, worried he might have a good idea. Instead, he offered, "Perhaps someone who wanted to marry Yun. With you out of the way, his parents might seek a marriage proposal."

"Master Sima wondered the same thing. I guess I will never have the answer. From now on, I will be more careful walking in the dark."

The chair stopped at the house's front door, refocusing their attention on Yun, who stepped onto a red mat to ensure her foot did not touch the bare earth. She stepped over an iron basin with lit charcoal, another symbol to keep evil spirits away and attract prosperity to the couple before she entered the doorway.

Lu Bān followed his bride, and then the rest of the guests entered the house.

No one had noticed Lady Huan's absence with all the noise, cheers, and excitement. A servant helped a very pale, shaken Lady Huan to her feet. She straightened her robe and hair and pinched her cheeks to restore their color in time for the next wedding phase.

In contrast to the elaborate preparations, the simple wedding ceremony followed. Yun and Lu Bān walked to the family altar before the sun passed its highest point in the sky to begin their new life together.

Lu Bān felt the crowd's stares boring into him, like the entire weight of their future lay on his shoulders.

"We pay homage to our Earth, our Ruler, to our family ancestors, and *Tsao-Chün*, the kitchen god," they said in unison, bowing each time as they identified the four entities. Bowing to Master Sima, they said, "We offer this fragrant tea, with two lotus seeds in the cup, as a gesture of our respect."

Master Sima took the cup, drank the tea, and handed a single wine goblet to Lu Bān. The couple bowed to Master Sima and each other. Their fingers touched. The jade ring vibrated, sending a quivering sensation through their hands, heat spreading to their toes as they sipped from the chalice, their smiles confirming their shared exhilaration. They ate sugar molded in the shape of a rooster to end the marriage ceremony.

Lu Bān starred at Yun for a moment. *At last, I can raise the red beads on the bridal Phoenix Crown and view Yun's face.* Lifting the beads, completely transfixed, Lu Bān's breath caught. "You are exquisite," he said.

Yun's glowing, oval face, her new-moon-shaped eyebrows, and her sweet dimples in her cheeks entranced him. Her eyes shaped like peach blossoms in the spring, long and upcurved at the corners. Under her lashes, a pair of misty black pupils gazed back at him. Her mouth resembled a cherry, small, rosy, and somewhat arched.

Lu Bān thought, *I cannot wait to savor it. She is a feminine splendor, and she belongs to me. Fortune blesses me today.*

魯班

Lord Huan spared no expense to provide an elaborate wedding feast to show his wealth and power. Crimson flowers and lucky bamboo decorated the house's inner hall where the wedding banquet took place. Red "happiness" banners adorned each side of the doorway.

The soft glow of hundreds of candles bathed the room. A group of paid musicians played quiet music; the tinkling sounds of a *Guzheng*, a zither-like instrument, blended with the lower trembles of the *Pipa, Qins*, and lutes.

Lord and Lady Huan led the procession into the hall.

"Where have you been?" Lord Huan asked through clenched

teeth. "You missed the outside rituals."

Lady Huan remained silent, wondering what might happen next. Would the authorities appear at any moment?

Everyone entered, their order based on age and importance in the family. Lord Huan's two brothers and their wives followed the bride's parents, then Master Sima. Lu Bān and Yun entered next. Huizhong, the family friend, and Lin Wan, Lu Bān's "good luck man," preceded Yun's cousin, Weici. Yun's friends, Dandan and Lan, and the rest of the guests took their places last, kneeling at the tables.

Lu Bān searched the room. A sense of relief, wonder, and nervousness washed over him like an ocean wave.

Yun's nervous smile reflected her thoughts of dread, not fully understanding her role as a wife. She tried to push any uneasy feelings out of her mind. The jade ring on her finger warmed, signaling reassurance.

The newlyweds knelt together at the honorary table, facing the guests.

Vases—overflowing with orchids, the symbol of love, and pink peonies, representing spring and renewed life—sat in the center of the table, bedecked with orange blossoms for fertility and lotus flowers celebrating creation and a lasting relationship.

Lord Huan stood, holding a goblet, and a hush fell across the room. "May our ancestors rejoice as we welcome our new son into our family and Master Sima, our new relative," he said. He took a sip of wine and held a bowl of rice high above his head as an offering to their lineages. "We invite you to join our feast."

Clutching her wine goblet with a tight grip to stop her hand from shaking, Lady Huan consumed its contents in a few gulps.

Their host continued. "Each course we serve today holds a particular meaning for the newlyweds. First, let us wish Lu Bān and Yun wealth with this dish of redfish," Lord Huan said as plates of fragrant ginger fish arrived. "Please enjoy yourselves."

"I will one day be rich from designing buildings and inventing things," Lu Bān boasted to Yun. "You will see."

Yun's face glowed. "I am eager to view your drawings. My father told me of your talent. I like to draw too," she told her groom.

Before Lu Bān could comment, Yun's father rose again from his mat when servants entered with enormous platters, steam rising from the presentation. "Roast suckling pig served whole, symbolizes my daughter's purity and virginity," he said, causing Yun to blush, lowering her gaze.

Lu Bān reached for her hand beneath the table and gave it a brief, reassuring squeeze.

The father continued: "We wish a peaceful future for our couple, as symbolized by the pigeon course."

Lu Bān broke off one of the pink orchards and presented it to Yun, a smile spreading across his entire face.

Yun blushed, matching the flower's color, and mirrored his smile.

More food appeared for the wedding guests. Lord Huan said, "The chicken, cooked in red oil, symbolizes our desire for the couple to enjoy a prosperous life."

"Chicken in red oil is one of my favorites," Lu Bān said, trying to make polite conversation.

"I believe we will be wealthy," Yun said. "My father said our charts show we will have a successful marriage."

"Um-hum," Lu Bān voiced his agreement with a mouthful

of succulent chicken.

"Now, for the last course," announced Lord Huan. "Dragon shrimp and chicken indicate the Dragon and the Phoenix are in harmony. Our family's Yin and Yang elements balance." He held his goblet up once again to toast the newlyweds.

Lu Bān and Yun raised their glasses, too. "Our good fortune begins tonight," he said. Their goblets touched, making a light *clink*.

Lady Huan regained her composure in time for Dandan, Lan, and Yun's cousin, Weici, to perform the time-honored wedding dance.

The musicians played a familiar tune as the three girls walked single file to the middle of the room. They each held a scarlet silk handkerchief in their hand and extended their other hand to the center, creating a three-pointed star. They danced in a circle until the music stopped, then bowed to Lord and Lady Huan, the elder relatives, Master Sima, Lu Bān, and Yun.

鲁班

A flash of orange caught Lord Huan's eye at the garden gate. Excusing himself, he went to check out the strange sight.

Curious, Lady Huan followed a safe distance behind, concealing herself behind a screen to listen. She drew in her breath when she recognized the voice.

The fluffy orange dragon from the parade stood in the shadows. "Come closer," a quiet, familiar voice said.

Lord Huan hesitated, tilting his head before he approached his visitor.

"I thought I would come to see this genius of yours, now

that he is part of your household, for better or worse." Duke Ai said. "You realize if he fails, your entire family is in jeopardy."

"Yes, my lord, he is an honorable man. I am sure he will do his best. You have my word."

"Yes—your word," he smirked. "I expect to have some invention to help me regain control of the army from Ji Kanazi, the chief minister who holds the purse strings of our state. I just learned when Prince Yangsheng, the son of Duke Jing of Qi, lived in exile within our borders, he married Ji Kanazi's sister. After Duke Jing's passing recently, the prince is now Duke Dao of Qi. We have enough bad blood with Qi without relatives involved. They continue to gain in strength."

"I am familiar with Ji Kanazi's tight fist on the money," Lord Huan replied. "He has increased the field tax, not only based on the parcel's size but also the quality of the soil. Might you be able to persuade him to tax my fields on size only?"

"I will see what I can do . . . depending on the helpfulness of your new son."

"Thank you, my lord."

"What does your wife think of this recent addition? Many at the palace knew she favored a general's son from Qi."

"She is a woman; who cares what she thinks?" Lord Huan raised his voice louder than he intended. "She understands her place in my house, and she does as I say, or she puts herself at risk of,"—he drew back his hand, making a swipe at the air—"severe punishment. She remains a business proposition between you and me, nothing more."

Lady Huan suppressed a laugh. *What a pompous ass he is, groveling before the duke. He is the duke's running dog, chasing a non-existent bone. Ha.* Realizing the conversation was ending, she slipped back to her place at the table.

Duke Ai appeared startled, glancing toward the house. "Did you hear a slight titter?"

"Perhaps crickets. They are active at this time of year." Lord Huan guessed. "I had better go inside. I have wedding guests to thank."

魯班

With the banquet finished, Yun's parents escorted the nervous newlyweds to the bridal chamber. Lord Huan walked with Lu Bān; Lady Huan and Yun followed several paces behind them.

"Have you ever been with a woman?" the lord asked. "Did Master Sima teach you how to please her? I do not believe Lady Huan did her duty to prepare Yun. For that, I apologize."

Not expecting such a personal question, Lu Bān stammered, "Um . . . Uh, I have not known a woman." His face flushed crimson. "I have . . . engaged in self-indulgence on a few occasions. However, I do not want to waste my rain. Master Sima tells me a man has a fixed amount. If you use it to pleasure yourself, you will not have enough to produce children. He said when I am married, my wife will provide replenishment. I suppose we will learn together." He took a deep breath, blushing again. "I am eager to practice."

"Obey all of your husband's desires," Lady Huan said in a hushed tone, leaning close as they walked, "even though you may find some things less desirable. It is what wives must do."

A blank stare crossed Yun's face. Her entire body tensed. "What do you mean?" Her eyes grew wide, tears welling. "Will he hurt me?"

Her mother did not answer.

She hates Lu Bān. Yun stifled a tear. *Why does she punish me?* The jade ring's pulsating calmed Yun's fears. *This is my destiny.*

魯班

The couple stood by the bed. The dragon candles gave the room a vibrant glow to drive away evil spirits. They continued their wedding rituals by drinking honey and sweet wine from two goblets linked by a red thread. Yun and Lu Bān took a few sips, exchanged cups, and they consumed the rest. Yun's parents withdrew, leaving the couple alone.

Their eyes locked. Lu Bān said, "You are more wondrous than my fondest dreams. I pledge to be a respectful husband." He took her hand and pulled her to him. His untried urge in his groin pressed against her. He placed his lips on hers. To his surprise, Yun brushed his lips with her tongue. His hands slipped down, tracing the curves of her delicate body.

He felt her quiver. He kissed her again. With passion, she responded with unbridled restraint. Although they were both novices, nature's plan guided them. He removed her wedding clothes. They fell to the floor in a pool of red silk. In an instant, she stood naked; his gaze transfixed. He studied her delicate limbs and fingers, her luminous porcelain skin radiant against her hair, the color of midnight. He released the decorative pin holding her hair, allowing it to pour down over her shoulders.

Yun experienced feelings deep within, unexpected yet wondrous. Lu Bān's touch made her skin tingle. Moisture formed between her legs. Her heart pounded with such force; she was sure it would leap out of her chest. She moaned as he drew her close to kiss her.

With the care one would use with a delicate vase, Lu Bān picked her up and placed her on the fresh bed, their bed. He removed his robe. Yun saw her husband's manhood for the first time. Blushing, she lowered her eyes. *Here I am, on the brink of womanhood. Why has my mother not prepared me for this moment, for what is about to happen? Did she want me to fail?*

With delicate tenderness, Lu Bān took his wife in his arms. He caressed her soft flesh while continuing to kiss her all over her body. He rolled a nipple between his fingers before covering her stiff nipple with his mouth. With tenderness, he prepared to enter her for the first time. He pushed until resistance stopped him.

Yun trembled. Her heart raced, in part from fear, but also from anticipation.

"Does it hurt?"

"Yes, but I am to obey your desires," Yun said.

With a second push, he pierced her maidenhead. Her fingers clutched his back as she caught her breath. The initial pain dissolved into pleasure she could not believe.

She responded to his rhythmic strokes with thrusts of her own. He kissed her with more craving than she imagined. She answered with kisses of her own. Passion's fire filled them both as they found their rhythm.

Yun felt waves of contractions deep within her. Lu Bān stiffened, and with a cry of ecstasy, he filled her with his seed. Tears of joy trickled down her cheeks. Lu Bān collapsed, exhausted, on top of her.

Lu Bān kissed his wife again and rolled off beside her. He stroked her face and wiped the tears from her cheeks. "I love you," he murmured. "I never believed this dream could be a reality. My life is now complete."

Yun, overcome with love, cooed, "My heart and soul are yours forever, my husband." She placed her head on his shoulder, snuggling beside him. *My fears were for nothing.*

They fell into a deep, relaxed sleep, content with each other. They awakened several times throughout the night to repeat their lovemaking.

Chapter 6

"This is a perfect day," Lu Bān said. "The weather is warm. You are my wife, and the birds sing our 'new life song' for us. How did I get so lucky?"

The newlyweds relaxed in the kitchen courtyard on a stone bench, eating bowls of rice. Yun poured tea for her husband. An evergreen tea-tree provided shade and produced leaves for their beverage.

"It is a flawless day," agreed Yun. "Our good luck started with the success of your kite. It caught my father's attention and brought you into my life. I am content, my husband," Yun said, picking up the teapot to fill Lu Bān's half-empty cup. "More tea?"

"Yes," he said, inhaling a deep breath of fresh morning air. "I do not want to go to work."

"Why not pass the day here with me? We can walk to the park and enjoy the cranes," Yun suggested. "Master Sima could not expect you today, does he?"

"I have an idea. If I organized a workshop here, the trip to Master Sima's house would be unnecessary. This way, I can be near you while I work. I could ask your father for permission to use the empty room next to ours. If he agrees, I will bring my tools and drawings back with me after we visit Master Sima tomorrow to pay our respects."

Yun wrapped her arms around her husband's shoulders. "It would be wonderful to be together each day. Perhaps I could even draw my table designs there." She hesitated. "If it pleases you, my husband," her eyes sparkled, "I am eager to show you something I have worked on as a surprise wedding present for the past year without my parent's knowledge. My mother would disapprove of me spending time on such a strange object. She believes the best use of a needle is to make needlework designs on cloth."

"What else would you do with a needle?" he asked, his eyebrows arching, his arms crossed over his chest.

"Wait here for a moment, and I will show you."

Lu Bān waited as Yun disappeared into the bedroom she had once occupied. She came back with a long, slender package tied up with twine. She removed the cloth from the parcel. "I call it my 'portable roof' on a stick. It is more for keeping the sun off than the rain." She held it over her head and showed how it worked. "I made it from five-year-old, hollow mulberry sticks. They are strong, yet flexible enough not to crack. To make the top circle, I used twenty-eight of them as rigid spokes, fitted around the upper part of this long, round, wooden shaft. There is a handle on the other end."

Lu Bān inspected the object.

"They support the silk covering," she continued. "Underneath, there is another set of shorter sticks. I attached one end of each stick with a thread to a hollow wooden ring that slides up-and-down on the central shaft. It makes a zigzag design where they attach to the central ring, like this," Yun said, raising and lowering the ring, causing the roof to open and close. "The other end attaches to each of the top spokes, here, with thread." She pointed one-fourth of the way along a spoke with the silk covering. "I stitched each strut to the supporting sticks with thread. See?" she pointed. "To finish the roof, I cut a narrow slice into one side of the shaft. It pops out to support the central ring when it goes past the cut. The wedge-shaped piece keeps the portable roof extended. When I want to close it, I just press the top of the protruding sliver like this; the ring slides back over the slice and closes." Yun opened and closed it again. She searched Lu Bān's face, waiting for a reaction.

Lu Bān held onto the portable roof, opening and closing it several times. "You designed and built this amazing thing by yourself?"

"Yes. Do you like it?"

"I am astonished! How did you get the idea?"

"A group of children at play caught my attention. They giggled as they carried broad lotus leaves over their heads. I tried to envision a way to make a lotus leaf stay on a stick. I realized they would be too brittle to fold up after a few days. It took several attempts before I found the right combination of sticks, silk, and proportion before I had a workable roof," she explained.

"You are a genuine inventor in your own right." Lu Bān examined the roof again. "These perfectly balanced inner sticks support the roof. The stitching holding everything together gives the sticks room to bend and fold. Remarkable!" he marveled before handing the portable roof back to Yun. His face lit with delight. "Yes, remarkable," he said again.

Lu Bān chuckled as Yun did an elfin dance with her portable roof before putting it away. "You should be proud of your work."

Yun bowed her head. She stared at her feet to avoid making

eye contact. "You should understand I am forbidden to consider pride," she said, her voice faint.

"Then I will be proud enough for both of us." Lu Bān wrapped his arms around her. "Now, I need to find your father to ask permission to use the room for a workshop."

魯班

Lu Bān walked to the room where Lord Huan conducted official business for the State of Lu. He found the lattice privacy screen open and his new father-in-law kneeling at an ebony table stacked with rolls of bamboo slips stitched together and tied with ribbons.

"May this humble son cross the threshold?" Lu Bān asked.

"Enter," barked Lord Huan's sharp voice.

Lu Bān passed through the opening and bowed. Before he could speak, Lord Huan bombarded him with questions.

"How did the wedding night go? Did my daughter please you? When will you produce a son for my family? Why did you not go to work this morning?"

Not expecting the barrage of more personal questions, Lu Bān's face flushed. He shuffled his feet. "Your daughter pleases me more than I can say . . ."

"Excellent. Tell Yun to study the dowry paintings, so she satisfies your every desire. I am afraid her mother failed in her duty to prepare her."

Lu Bān took a deep breath. "Going to work is why I am here. I would like your blessing to use the space off the back courtyard as a workshop. I would not need to travel to Master Sima's every day."

Lord Huan fingered his chin whiskers, contemplating the possibilities. *If Lu Bān invented something important, I would be the first to know and alert Duke Ai. I will enjoy even more of his favor.*

"I do not object." Lord Huan reclined on a stack of pillows. "You will have more time to work if you do not lose time walking that distance morning and night. When will you advise Master Sima of your plan?"

"I will tell him tomorrow when Yun and I go to pay our respects with tea. I will bring my drawings and tools back with me. Thank you." Lu Bān bowed and hurried to tell Yun his excellent news.

He passed Lady Huan in the courtyard. "Good morning," he said, bowing low.

She huffed, mumbling something that sounded like "worm," before retracing her steps to the inner hall.

鲁班

"Your mother glowers at me each time I pass. I do not know what I did to displease her. Is she always so hostile?" Lu Bān asked when he returned to the garden where Yun waited.

"I am not to speak ill of my parents," she said.

"I will try to avoid her. When she stares at me, I think she wishes she could make me disappear."

"I suspect she lacks happiness," Yun admitted.

"Perhaps," Lu Bān said with a sigh. "I am full of happiness. I have you and your father's blessing to create a workshop here.

Yun threw her arms around her husband. "Wonderful news!"

"I need to put my clothes away and ready the bamboo basket

I borrowed from Master Sima to go with us tomorrow."

魯班

On the third day after their marriage, Lu Bān and Yun prepared to go to Master Sima's home to serve him tea as a sign of respect. Yun packed the wedding basket she inherited from her mother with the items for tea service. *Mother is so opposed to our marriage,* she thought to herself. *I am surprised she gave this to me.*

"I am ready to go," Lu Bān said. He grabbed the sturdy, empty basket. "I will return this to Master Sima. Bring your tea-box."

Lu Bān began walking. Realizing Yun followed several paces behind him, he stopped. "What are you doing? Come here beside me."

Yun dipped her head, pausing before answering. "I may not walk beside you, my husband. It is disrespectful."

"Nonsense!" he shouted. "I want you next to me."

"My mother will be cross when she learns I break tradition."

"I am your husband. I want you here." He tugged her by her hand, hard enough to make her stumble. "Your mother must learn to adjust. Do you understand?"

Yun's eyes filled with tears. "Yes, my husband. I must obey you in all things. I will do as you say."

Lu Bān relaxed his shoulders and lowered his voice. "This is where you belong now." He flashed a gentle, reassuring glance. "We will face all of our challenges together, side-by-side. We are now each other's half. Our halves make a whole."

Yun agreed, remaining silent as they walked the final

distance to Master Sima's front gate. She glanced over her shoulder several times. *I hope none of my mother's neighbors recognized me. She will be furious if they tell her.*

鲁班

Lu Bān touched the carved peach blossoms and swimming fish on the east door. "I remember the first time I stood here, unsure of what lay ahead," Lu Bān said, waiting for a servant to answer his knock. "Now my life changes once more."

Lu Chi, Master Sima's faithful manservant, bowed, meeting them at the door.

"I am pleased to see you again, Lu Chi," Lu Bān said in greeting. "I am sure I know my way." He motioned toward Yun. "This is my new *Banqi*. We are here to take tea with Master Sima. Please bring us boiling water."

Lu Bān pushed open the carved door that ensured complete privacy into the tranquil courtyard. An elegant magnolia tree, covered with unopened buds, grew in one corner. A goldfish pond occupied another. The golden shower Chinese trumpet creeper flowers hung in full bloom as they clung to the wall behind Master Sima's bench. Lu Bān took a deep breath. "Their perfume makes me think they are good enough to eat."

Master Sima beamed as they entered the courtyard. The couple bowed.

"It appears marriage agrees with you," he said. "You both look jubilant."

"Yes," Lu Bān said. "I never knew such happiness could exist." He relaxed his posture. "She has changed my life in three short days. We are here to serve you tea."

"You may use this table." Master Sima gestured to one table beside Lu Bān.

Lu Bān sat on the other side of his mentor and friend.

Yun knelt on a mat and placed her tea-box on a small table. She opened her basket and took out her prized canister of Lu Shun tea, a tea scoop in the shape of an owl, two red dates, and lotus seeds. She rubbed her moist hands on a napkin.

Nervous, Yun's hand trembled. *Pouring tea is my first official duty as Lu Bān's wife.* She removed two seashells and set them on the table, along with two small, fragrant, sweet cakes. She positioned three porcelain cups, hand-painted with graceful pink orchids, on her serving tray, and placed the matching teapot on the bench.

After measuring the tea with the tea scoop, Yun positioned the tea, lotus seeds, and dates in the pot, tucked a silk napkin in her sash, and paused for the servant to deliver the boiling water. When it arrived, she filled the teapot, let the ingredients steep for several moments, and poured the tea into the cups.

Yun carried the tray to where Lu Bān and Master Sima sat. Kneeling in front of them, she first offered them the sweet cakes in the seashells before serving their beverage. Yun picked up the first cup with both hands and extended it to Master Sima. She presented Lu Bān's cup in the same manner.

"We pay homage to you, Master Sima," Lu Bān said. "I thank you for your kindness and for your blessing to marry."

Master Sima acknowledged Lu Bān's words with a warm smile. "I am glad you appear so content. Your faces radiate happiness."

"Is it possible to show Yun our workshop—I mean, your workshop?"

"Of course," Master Sima said. "Your drawing slate, sketches, and models are still there. You may take them if you wish, or you can come here anytime to continue your work. My door is always open."

"You are most kind," Lu Bān said, replacing his cup beside Master Sima's. "Lord Huan will permit me to create a workspace in an unused room. This arrangement will let me be close to Yun, and it will give her a place where she can also draw. I did not realize what a talented artist she is." He bragged. "She has designed several intricate tables. I am not yet sure how to build them; they are so complicated. As a team, I believe we can produce many exotic pieces."

"I would like to see her designs," Master Sima said with sincere interest. "Bring them the next time you come to visit."

When they finished their floral tea, Yun collected their cups and seashells. They made a faint tinkling sound when she placed them on her tray. She covered them with a folded silk napkin before packing the tea items back into her basket, replacing the lid.

Master Sima stood. "Are you ready to view the workshop?"

鲁班

They entered the familiar workroom. The welcoming scent of wood and ink greeted them. Lu Bān took the kite from a rafter and handed it to Yun. "Here is the wooden kite I made that caught your father's attention."

"It is magnificent," she said, admiring the bird. She ran her hand over its smooth surface. "The fine detail of its construction is perfect. No wonder my father thought you were a genius," she teased. "I am sorry I missed seeing it fly."

"It was quite a sight," Master Sima said. "It stayed in the air three days, tied to a stake in the ground."

Lu Bān scanned the workshop, remembering the way he felt the first time he stood there as a scared little boy. The days spent with his mentor flooded his mind.

"Would you like to take your drawing table?" Master Sima inquired, rubbing his hand over its slick surface.

"You honor me with this cherished gift. The table will remind me of our many happy hours together. With your patience, I learned to draw and sketch. Through your thoughts and words, the world has opened to me. Please accept my complete gratitude," he said, emotion filling his voice.

"My belief is it will continue to give you the inspiration to create more elegant buildings."

Lu Bān shuffled his feet, feeling sheepish. "Drawing has not been on my mind these past few days. My brain is elsewhere," he said, casting a glance toward Yun.

She lowered her eyes to conceal her joy.

Lu Bān bent to pick up the table. Daunted by its weight, he said, "It is too heavy. Could two of your servants carry it for me? I could borrow your basket again to take my tools and drawings, if you do not mind."

"Not at all," Master Sima said. With a wave of his hand, he sent Lu Chi to fetch two of his men. He placed his right hand over his breastbone. "I knew this day would come. However, I did not guess it would be so soon." He winced as memories surfaced. "I will miss your company. We have spent fifteen years together. Promise you will visit me from time to time. I want to keep up with your progress."

Lu Bān placed his tools at the bottom of the basket and arranged his drawings on top. He cleared his throat to dislodge the lump. "I will," he said. "The next time I come, I will bring Yun's sketches and take the kite."

When two servants arrived, one of them suggested, "What if we put the table, mat, and the reed basket in a cart?"

"Splendid idea," Master Sima said. "Lu Bān, you and Yun can start back. I will send your things behind you."

Lu Bān bowed. "May continued health follow you, my friend."

"I will take the tea basket with me," Yun said, clutching it to her chest. "I am concerned it would not travel well. It has been in our family for generations, and I need to protect it. If something happened to it, Mother would be furious." She stroked the basket with her fingers. "One day, I will pass it to our daughter."

鲁班

The couple waved goodbye to Master Sima and walked side-by-side back to their home. "Master Sima will realize how talented you are when I take him your drawings," said Lu Bān. "I will also show him your portable roof. Afterward, he will understand I am not the sole inventor of our family."

"Oh, no! You must not. My mother does not want me to receive praise for anything. She believes it is not my place to invent useful things. She complained to my father about my sketching. He told her drawing is acceptable," Yun said. "You must take credit for my invention. I am sure you will come up with a better name than a portable roof. What if you called it a movable house?"

Lu Bān stopped, glaring at her. "I love your cleverness and your charm, but I will not take praise for your idea. You deserve the recognition, regardless of your mother's opinions. I like your 'portable roof' name. If I found another name, *you* would still be the inventor, not me," he said, his voice edgy.

"You are too kind, my husband," Yun said. "My mother still believes a woman should not design furniture, let alone invent things. She has reminded me on more than one occasion, 'Those things are a man's work.' My job is to be your servant, make sons, and take care of my parents in their old age."

"You are not my slave," he snapped, grabbing her arm. "Remember, we will labor side-by-side and support each other until we succeed," Lu Bān said, determination in his voice. They walked in silence for a time. "Your mother *will* understand," he added, approaching Lord Huan's house.

魯班

Not far behind, the two servants struggled as they arrived with the cart, huffing and puffing, out of breath. "We noticed warriors leaving a house," Lu Chi said. "I trust they will not bring us trouble. Mount Lu is still away from the fighting."

"Perhaps they were just passing through town." Lu Bān scanned their surroundings. "In all likelihood, they were passing through," he said again, trying to convince himself.

Master Sima's servants put the table and the mat in the workshop. After they left, Yun remained while Lu Bān stacked his drawings on a stand against a wall and organized his tools into a wooden box.

He swooped Yun into his arms. "I can conquer the world now that you are by my side. I will draw plans for the most opulent buildings and sign them with my artist seal *chop* as my signature. Your love is a gift you give to me each day, and I give it back as my promise to you."

"I accept your love, my husband," Yun said, with a light kiss on his cheek. "I will check to see if there is soup left from the noon meal. Are you hungry?"

"Yes, I am always ready to eat."

Lu Bān knelt behind his drawing table. He released a slow breath of appreciation as he ran his hand over the surface and let his fingers trace the shapes of the turquoise stones inlaid around the edges, remembering that the ancient gems radiated peace, calm, and tranquility.

Lord Huan appeared in the doorway. His booming voice interrupted Lu Bān's thoughts. "Did I see two men with a cart? Were they with you?"

"Yes. Master Sima's servants brought my drawing table. I remember the first time I sat behind it. The wood reminded me of feathers. I am eager to use it to invent new things."

"What do you plan to create?" Lord Huan said, his tone casual.

"My task is to devise new tools to allow me to build Yun's elaborate table design." Lu Bān rubbed his chin whiskers. "I need to cut the dense, red sandalwood and find a way to remove the waves on its surface."

Yun returned with the bowls of food and served Lu Bān. She bowed to her father, who ignored her.

"I will work on an idea after eating," Lu Bān said. "Yun, even the soup's aroma stimulates my hunger."

Lord Huan's brow furrowed. "I want to examine this new tool as soon as you design it. You should begin right away." He started to leave, then paused. "I expect you to notify me at once. Do you understand?" He gathered his green silk robes and spun on his heels, disappearing through the doorway.

Lu Bān sucked in a quick breath to answer, but his father-in-law vanished before he could speak. He glanced at Yun. "Your father is different. Did I offend him?"

Yun furrowed her brow. "Sometimes he is abrupt. My mother often makes him ill-tempered when she displeases him. This will pass."

"Will it?" Lu Bān finished his soup. "I had better bring in more firewood while it is still light." He rubbed his arms. "I believe it is getting much colder."

魯班

It took longer for Lu Bān to get the wood than Yun expected. *I hope he is all right*, she worried. She fingered the ring he had gifted her. It remained warm, giving her a sense of calm. She scanned the courtyard to check on him. After a prolonged absence, he appeared with an armful of logs, out of breath and excited.

"My husband, you had me worried," she said when he returned.

"I know how to design a way to split the sandalwood," he replied with enthusiasm. "Examine my palm."

"Your hand is bleeding," she said, picking up a cloth to bind his wound. "What happened? How does a gash on your hand help you?"

"The firewood box had no wood. I climbed the hill to gather

sticks and slipped. I reached for the saw grass to break my fall. It sliced my hand. When I examined the blades of grass, I discovered the plant's edge had tiny teeth. I realized, if I could make a metal tool with an edge like the grass, it would be sharp and cut the wood."

"You are brilliant, my husband." Yun shook her head and finished his bandage. "But you must be more careful with your hands."

鲁班

Several weeks passed before Lu Bān showed his drawings to Yun. He scrutinized her reaction as she reviewed them. His eyes twinkled.

"I call it a Chinese saw, based on the saw grass. It has teeth on each side of this metal strip, which attaches to a wooden frame. Two men will sit on blocks holding the saw frame parallel to the floor with the wood braced on a table. Here is the drawing," he said, offering her a particular rendering. "This man will push the frame, and the other man will pull. This back-and-forth motion will crosscut the wood. The new chalk line device I made will mark a straight line to help them keep the cut straight."

Yun's eyes brightened. "Oh, yes. What a smart idea."

"I have other inventions." Lu Bān picked up a rectangular wood block with a metal piece sticking out at a slight angle. "I developed something else. I will call this a *plane*. It will make the surface of the wood flat." He showed how to use it by pushing the device along the wood's length in one direction. He repositioned it at the beginning of the board again and ran it to the end a second time. The plane made miniature wood curls as it left the tabletop even and smooth.

"Master Sima will be in awe when you show him these tools," Yun said.

Lu Bān wrapped his arms around her shoulders. "These new devices and improved methods to join wooden sections will make it possible to build your splendid table designs."

"You solved a hard problem. Now, with these implements, I can create more pieces of intricate furniture," Yun teased.

"My unbelievable wife," he said, pulling her into his embrace. "You make me happy every day. I thank the gods for you and live for your love and inspiration." He kissed her, swooping her up, carrying her to their bedroom. "I need a reward for my work," he said.

She giggled, putting her arms around his neck. "Yes, you do."

魯班

Hearing his daughter giggle, Lord Huan followed behind to ensure Lu Bān carried her into their room. He gave a satisfied smile. *They will be busy for a while. I will have time to search through his drawings to find out what Lu Bān is working on next.*

Entering the workspace, he stooped to pick up a roll of slips stitched together, untied the ribbon binding them, and stretched them out on the worktable. He pondered the symbols, rotated the sketch upside down, and wondered what the figures represented. Unable to decipher the drawings, he re-rolled the slips and retied the bindings, placing the cylinder as close to the position he found it as possible.

He examined a chalkboard drawing, circles, and lines connecting them with many numbers and equations. *At least he is working on something, but what? I hope it is as good an idea as the diagrams for the saw and the other woodworking tools. The drawings I took to Duke Ai proved beneficial for cutting timber, faster and cleaner than the old ax methods, but he failed to share much of his profits with me.*

Lord Huan replaced the chalkboard but failed to notice Lady Huan behind him.

"Snooping, are you?" she asked, causing him to jump.

"Damn you, woman, don't sneak up on me!"

"What did you find? Anything to sell to the duke or anyone else? You did not receive enough money for the other drawings. You must ask for more spade coins next time." She scanned the room. "All Lu Bān does is draw scribbles and eat."

"Those *scribbles* will one day give us prestige and wealth. Lu Bān desires to create beautiful, useful things. He is an asset to our family."

"Some asset . . . a few double-spade coins here and there, and one five-character knife money from Qi. A lot of good that would do unless you go to Qi."

"For your information," Lord Huan's face reddened, his eyes narrowed, "the knife money came from your father when, on that fateful day, I married you."

Unfazed, Lady Huan continued. "If you notice, he has been here long enough to give us a grandson. As a man, he is no more capable than you," she snarled. "Have you given your little mistress a son? You see her often enough."

Lord Huan grabbed his wife by the shoulders and shook her hard enough to knock the decorative hairpin from her topknot.

"You are an evil woman. I am sure you paid someone to abduct Lu Bān before the wedding. Somehow, no one found out, or we would all lose our lives. Your offense was grave enough to have killed us all. I should divorce you and send you back to your brother. You are a disgrace." He gave her a shove and stomped out of the room, leaving her in a heap.

He knows . . . but how?

Chapter 7

Late March usually heralded the rainy season, but the spring rains began a month earlier. A fierce storm pummeled Mount Lu for days. It caused roofs to leak and streets to become mini-rivers.

However, in June, these events were minor compared to the catastrophic flooding of the mighty Hanshui River in the low-lying town of Wuchang.

Faced with massive devastation, three Wuchang elders came to visit Lu Bān. The men wore soggy, long gray robes, their sandals stained with mud from their journey. They bowed when they approached him in his workshop.

Yun, seeing the visitors, bowed and left the room to prepare tea and food for the weary guests.

"May I introduce myself?" one guest inquired. "I am Chi Wei, from Wuchang. Your reputation for solving unique problems reached us in our time of need. We are here to tell our story and plead our case."

Lu Bān motioned for them to sit on the mat by a table. "What can I do for you?"

"We have suffered a devastating disaster. No one remembers this much rain pouring all at once. The swollen, raging river washed away our bridge. Several people lost their lives. Now we must depend on small ferryboats to cross. There are not enough boats to carry all the people with their tools and carts across in time for work," Chi Wei said.

Yun returned. She knelt at the table to pour tea from the steaming pot and serve the anise rice cakes.

"Thank you. I appreciate your kindness," Chi Wei said, accepting the hospitable tea. "Our haste pushed us to travel over muddy roads these past days."

Lu Bān reclined on a pile of emerald pillows. "How do you imagine I can help?"

"We want you to build a new bridge the floods cannot destroy. Will you design one for us? Of course, we will pay you," Chi Wei said, glancing at his two companions, both of whom acknowledged their agreement.

Do good deeds for your fellow man. Lu Bān remembered Master Sima's admonition. He recalled how they irrigated the fields. *There must be a way to build a better structure.* He pondered the challenge.

"I am sure I can find a solution to your problem," Lu Bān said. When the men's faces beamed and their shoulders relaxed, he added, "It is still the rainy season. I imagine it will be several weeks, maybe months, before the river is back within its banks and dry enough to make any assessments. Advise me when the conditions are right."

Chi Wei pressed his palm to his heart, exchanging relieved expressions with the other two men. "Thank you. We will send a message as soon as possible. We must do all we can to prevent future carnage."

"This is your good deed," Yun said, putting her arms around Lu Bān's neck after the elders made their polite exit from the workshop. "You are full of wonderful ideas. I am confident you will build a bridge that will defy the annual floods." Thinking of his absence, she stifled a tear. "I will miss you."

Yun pushed her sad thoughts from her mind while gathering the plates and empty teacups to take them to the kitchen. "I believe our cook is preparing chicken in red oil for tonight's dinner. It is one of your favorites."

"I cannot wait." Lu Bān rubbed his stomach.

He knelt at his drawing table, set aside a half-finished sketch of his earlier work, and reached for his slate tablet and chalk. Deep wrinkles appeared on his forehead. *I will make a few drawings of unique ways I might build it. Where do I begin? Someone built a bridge there before, so someone can do it. I will not know the river's width or what kind of construction materials exist—so many unknowns.*

鲁班

"A servant told me you had visitors today." Lord Huan leaned toward him with a furrowed brow as Lu Bān joined the family for the evening meal. "What did they want?" he barked.

"This chicken aroma makes my mouth water," Lu Bān said as he picked up his chopsticks. "The men came from Wuchang. The flooded Hanshui River has washed away their bridge, and several people lost their lives. They came to ask if I could design a new one."

A bridge? thought the father-in-law. *Duke Ai will be interested* in this news. Lord Huan relaxed his shoulders. "The disaster is on everyone's minds in town today. Do you know how to build it or how long it will take?"

"I have sketched an idea, but decided I needed to examine

several bridges and study their construction. That should give me clues to their weaknesses," Lu Bān said, chewing a mouthful of chicken.

Lord Huan crossed his arms over his chest. "Are they going to pay you?"

Lady Huan took a sip of tea. "Only if he can produce a bridge that will not collapse in the next storm." Her lips were straight and cruel. "So far, he has not even been able to erect a son for the family."

The room fell silent.

Lu Bān huffed, not wanting to respond to Lady Huan's insult. "Yes, they said they would pay for my services. I am sure I will stay with an elder while I am there. I will not know how long it will take until I examine the site."

Lord Huan asked, "When will you go to Wuchang? My sources told me today warriors occupy that area. You must be careful," warned Lord Huan.

"Warriors? Why would there be soldiers? The people of Wuchang are peaceful, aren't they?" Yun asked.

"It is none of your concern," snapped Lady Huan, her eyes flashing. "Be quiet and eat your chicken."

"General Yáng Jūn is always hunting for fresh territory to conquer," Lord Huan said. "We are fortunate to be so far away from those conflicts. Pray your paths never cross."

魯班

"I am afraid," Yun said when she and Lu Bān were alone in their bedroom. She undressed, took the hairpin from her hair, letting it cascade over her shoulders. "What if you encounter warriors?"

"Do not worry," he said. "My path will take me as far away from soldiers as possible. As a builder, I pose no threat." He wrapped her in his arms. "I will be careful. I promise."

Yun sat on the bed's edge, staring at the floor. "I regret my mother's comments. I believe she grows crueler each day. I do not understand why she hates you when you have been so respectful."

Lu Bān stretched out on the mattress, extended his arm, and patted the space for her to join him. "Your mother thinks you should have married someone equal to your father's station. She wished for a general's son."

"Yes, I heard her quarreling with my father before my Ji Li hairpin ceremony. She wanted me to marry the son of a family friend from her home state of Qi."

"Qi is a long way away," Lu Bān said, rubbing his chin.

"When my parents bicker, I learn many of their secrets. I believe neither had a choice, for my father serves at the pleasure of our duke, who arranged their union to fend off Qi's ruler's aggression. Mother, the daughter of the ruler's second wife, had feelings for a boy there, but she and my father became pawns in the political alliance." Yun chuckled. "I guess my father understands what it is like to have no voice in a decision. The tension between the two of them escalated when I arrived, disappointing my parents. Every time she catches sight of me, I believe I remind her of her failure to produce a male child. My father accuses her of being a *stone woman*. She retaliates, claiming my father to be impotent. Their arguments continue to increase. Mother thinks she married under her class because her father was the duke."

"According to my mother, my father, Xian, came from a noble family," Lu Bān said. "The warring factions killed all our relatives. I do not know their names, nor do I have any memories or proof of their existence."

"Tell me about your mother."

"I have vivid memories of her holding me, singing soft melodies, and working every day in the fields. I wish I knew more about my father and our ancestors. The day she left this world, everything turned upside down. Someone took our hut, and I had nothing to eat. The village elders came to my rescue, sending me to Master Sima."

"I cannot imagine how you felt. I have never experienced a mother's unselfish love." The jade ring warmed and tingled. She rolled it around her finger. "What can you tell me about the ring? I saw a faint vision of a verdant forest and majestic trees. It warms, vibrates, and gives me images I do not understand."

"I wish I knew. Our village elder told me it was magical. I, too, have experienced visions. I believe it is the magic that brought me to you."

"When my father gave the ring to me, I felt an immediate connection. I knew you were the right man."

"We must trust the jade ring's ancient wisdom to guide us."

Yun snuggled close to her husband. "Do you want children? Mother blames you for not producing a son." Yun wrapped a lock of her hair around her finger. "Doctor Tro assured me I should not worry, but I wonder if I am the infertile one, not you, for we lie together often."

Yun rolled her shoulders forward. "From the earliest time I can remember, my mother told me my destiny is to produce sons. What if I cannot produce a male child like my mother?

Will I too become a bitter old woman?"

"You should not fear. I would welcome any child we conceive. While your parents expect a son, I would love a daughter, for I am sure she would be your image, my love."

Lu Bān pulled Yun close, caressing her body. "Perhaps we need more practice."

魯班

The morning carried a needed break in the weather. Lu Bān traveled a half day's walk to assess a bridge near Guling, where he found a small, primitive structure of tree trunk planks stretched across a swollen stream in girder fashion. However, it could only carry pedestrians in a single file.

He mused. *No wonder this structure type washes away. There is no way to anchor it to the bank or support the center.*

Journeying another day, he found another span, made from ropes woven together to form a mat-like surface, crossing the turbulent Peach Blossom River. Swollen from the recent rain, the water's force made boulders tumble, crashing into each other, sounding like thunder. The bridge swung without restraint from the side of the hill, high above the water. He observed people needed to hold on to another rope, waist high, to cross the stream. *Carts or animals cannot travel on this type. It will not solve my problem for a prosperous, bustling town.*

Lu Bān tilted his head, rubbing his chin, mumbling, "I must return home with no answers. Lord Huan will want to know why I have no ideas." He arrived at nightfall, tired and hungry, in time for their evening meal.

魯班

Lord Huan pinched the skin at his throat and narrowed his eyes. "What did you learn today?"

"There were two unique examples," he told the family. "Neither is suitable as a model for the Wuchang Bridge. Yet, observing them, I understand why they wash away."

"Where will you go next?" Yun inquired.

"You should not ask such questions of your husband," scolded Lady Huan. "It is none of your concern."

Lu Bān made eye contact with his wife. "I plan to visit another river crossing construction to the north. I hope to find a better example there."

"Were there any signs of warriors on your journey today?" the father-in-law inquired with measured words.

"No, just a few travelers on their way to town. By the appearance of the rain effects on the fields, it might be several weeks before they are dry enough to plant crops."

Lord Huan picked at his food. *Duke Ai despises the Duke of Wu. I fear he would like to plan a war of his own if he had an army to command.*

魯班

Lady Huan slipped into her husband's official workroom to find him hunched over a set of bamboo slips stitched together, his ink brush making neat vertical rows of characters. He paused, collecting his thoughts. Her voice surprised him.

"I saw your reaction to Lu Bān's trip and observations. You also are aware Duke Ai despises the Duke of Wu."

Lord Huan slammed his ink brush on the table, splattering

ink as it rolled toward the slips. "You only think you understand what I think, woman. It is not your place to question me."

Lady Huan laughed. "You fear a bridge across the river will give Duke Ai an idea of how to wage war with Wu."

He sneered. "I fear all war. Duke Ai does not control the army; his chief minister does. And now he controls all the state's money. Lu lost some of its territories to Wu a few years ago. Duke Ai is correct in thinking they will want the rest of our state. Remember, bridges go both ways." Lord Huan exhaled an exasperated sigh. "King Fuchai of Wu is busy completing canals to join the major rivers, making travel by water faster than by land. They will be a force to heed."

"If Lu Bān completes this bridge, it will connect its neighbors to Wu," Lady Huan said.

"Woman, you know nothing of what you speak. You do not recognize up from down. Wu is to our south, Lu Bān's bridge is north. If the bridge helps any state, it will be your home state of Qi. Their duke is in a constant struggle with the all-powerful Tián Clan. It will not surprise me if your half-brother is not aiding them. They are a genuine threat to the entire region."

She thought, *If my brother is helping the Tián Clan, perhaps they would pay more than Duke Ai.*

Lady Huan leaned back against the wall. "I am aware you have secret meetings with the duke. You have become his running dog. He throws you table scraps compared to what he has gained from your information scrounged from Lu Bān's work."

"For your sake, you should hope my information helps Duke Ai, for if the duke weakens further, three states will vie to be our next ruler. One needs to be aligned with the winner to share in the spoils. It is prudent to protect oneself against loss by supporting more than one possible result."

魯班

Lu Bān awoke to the pitter-patter of raindrops on the roof. "I need the weather to improve before I can judge more bridges." He snuggled closer to Yun. "I will stay in the workshop today." He kissed behind her ear. "I have a wonderful idea," he rolled her over toward him. "Why not lie here with you all day?"

The jade ring tingled, its warm glow spreading through her. "Your ideas are always the best, my husband. I am sure tomorrow will bring sunshine."

魯班

Yun stayed silent as her husband dressed to continue his quest for the right bridge design. Still savoring their previous night's lovemaking, she stroked her abdomen. *When will I conceive a child? Doctor Tro, my healer, assured me everything was fine. I followed his advice and planted the seeds from the melon in the garden. A vine grew, yet no flowers . . . and no son.*

Her thoughts continued. *My best friend Dandan got married after I did, and she already has a boy child. The bridge quest will occupy Lu Bān all day. I think I will talk to her. Maybe we can take the baby for a walk around the lake.*

魯班

Yun dressed in a dark blue skirt under a pale-blue, knee-length lightweight robe, trimmed with white bands around the neck and sleeve's edges.

The shouts from her father's workroom attracted her attention. *They are fighting again.*

She caught a few words, something about cheating, Lu Bān's inventions, and money. Yun hurried to disappear through the festoon gate before they noticed her.

魯班

Dandan lived three compounds away with her new husband's family. The door stood open to let in the breeze, offsetting the heat of the day. Yun knocked and called, "Dandan, are you there?"

A servant recognized Yun at once. "Come in, Madam Huan. Madam will be happy to see you."

Dandan appeared, dressed in light green, holding a small bundle wrapped in swaddling clothes. Her grin spread from ear to ear when she reached the mat where Yun sat, but the smile faded to concern when she walked close enough to see Yun's pale face and red eyes.

"I thought we might be the little birds, flapping and singing again," Yun said, her voice low, trying to force a half-smile. "I am desperate to talk. Are you free to walk to the lake? The day is fair."

"Yes, give me time to tell mother where I am going."

"Is your mother here too?

"No, my husband's mother is my mother now. Does your husband not call your parents mother and father?

"Oh no. My husband calls them by their official names. My mother might kill him for sure if he called her 'mother.'"

"Sounds like she has not accepted him as her son. I am

sorry for you. I will be just a moment and return."

Yun surveyed the room. The décor was bright and airy, relaxed and inviting, not the cold, hostile atmosphere in her home. The aroma of soup bubbling over the open fire in the kitchen courtyard reminded Yun of the yellow noodles Lu Bān liked. *I hope he finds what he needs for the bridge today.*

"Are you ready?" Dandan said, her voice light. "I just finished nursing the baby, so we can have the time to ourselves."

They walked in silence, passing several houses on the way to the lake. Sitting on a small, grassy knoll where they often waited to see the cranes, Dandan broke the quiet. "Yun, what is wrong? Are you and Lu Bān unhappy? How can I help?"

"I love my husband, and he loves me." Tears streamed over her cheeks. "The problem is me. We lie together almost every night, but my moonblood returns with every moon. I asked Doctor Tro, but he gave me no answer, other than I am young and should not fear. But I do worry each day." Yun searched the sky, hoping for answers. "You married after I did, and you have a son. My mother is furious because I am not with child. She hates my husband, my father, her life, and me."

Yun stopped to search her friend's face. "What can I do?" she pleaded. "What if I am a 'stone woman,' unable to conceive? I wonder if the gods are angry with me for breaking tradition, walking beside my husband . . ."

"You walk next to him?" Dandan interrupted. "Why?"

"He insists. Or, perhaps my father annoyed the gods when he arranged my marriage, so I could take care of them, instead of marrying and living with my husband as you do. But why would they punish me?"

"I believe neither of those concerns is true," her friend

began. "When we disrespect our elders, the gods discipline us and fail to honor the earth, our ruler, ancestors, and Tsao-Chün, the kitchen god. If your aura is in the turmoil you describe, the fault is not yours. Remember, if one family member displeases the kitchen god, he reports the offense to the Jade Emperor in heaven, who, in turn, causes a year of bad luck to the entire household."

"The way my mother and father treat each other, we will never have good luck again."

Dandan gave Yun a reassuring smile and took Yun's hand. "You see, it is not your fault."

"I would like to believe you."

"Have you tried standing in water to increase your fertility? Or surrounding yourself with Chinese green roses and orchids? I wore orange often. Did your mother not give you this advice?"

"No, I believe my mother wants me to fail, but I do not understand why."

Dandan remained silent for a few breaths and lowered her voice. "Few people are aware, but my paternal grandmother is a *Wuism* . . ."

Yun caught her breath. "A sorcerer?"

"She is not evil, but she performs Chinese shamanism. Her religious practice interacts with the spirit world through trances for healing and fertility. Although she does not practice her craft openly any longer, I am sure she would help you if you desired assistance."

"When can I see her?"

鲁班

Better weather allowed Lu Bān to explore a village to the north. Over the fast-moving water of the Dejiang River, he found a primitive rock footbridge with simple arches made with flat stones laid on top of each other, with a slight offset until they met in the center. The water splashed against the base of the supports resting on the bottom of the waterway. The semicircles supported a wooden log floor.

Hmm, Lu Bān contemplated. *Stone is more durable than wood. Although I like the arches, the Hanshui River is too deep for this construction. Besides, there is not enough room under the arcs for an abundance of water or boats to pass.*

He replayed the bridge problems in his mind. *None of these examples solves my problem. Maybe tomorrow the answer will come.*

Chapter 8

A message arrived for Lord Huan the day Lu Bān went to the Dejiang Bridge. Lord Huan's face turned ashen. His heart thumped, seeing the summons. *What is my crime? Our meetings are always private.*

The messenger attracted Lady Huan's attention. She found her husband slumped over his table, his head in his hands.

"What is it?" she asked. "You are the color of the clouds."

"I am to appear in a court with officials who have displeased Duke Ai. I must go to the duke's palace right away. His reputation for ruthless punishment is widespread."

"What is your crime? Did you fail to collect the proper taxes from the merchants or keep part of the funds?"

"No!" he shouted, leaping to his feet. "Do you think me a fool? I would never cheat the chief minister. I do not know *why* the duke calls me to appear before him."

"Have you asked for more money or an elevated position of authority? You cannot risk making him angry. Our life, reputation, and status will be in jeopardy." Her eyes grew large as a coin as she gave voice to her thoughts. "You have risked our family's home with your hopes of Lu Bān's non-existent inventions."

"My standing with the duke and his friends has given you a luxurious life." Lord Huan raised his voice. "I did not notice you refusing any of the fine clothes you wear, your servants, this house, or the jewels on your hands. You do not realize how we have benefited from Lu Bān's work. Get out of my sight! I need to dress."

魯班

Duke Ai's palace and grounds occupied four square *Li* of the city. Lord Huan arrived on horseback. Its saddle, draped in black, displayed the color of his rank. A *Bo Le* took the reins of his horse as he dismounted.

Lord Huan and the other men who had been summoned shuffled as a group toward the entrance, a somber mood engulfing his peers. No one spoke as they approached the twenty-two-foot diameter scarlet panel of the eastern gate.

The red paint—usually a cheerful color—reminded him of blood today. Lord Huan presented his credentials to the sentinel.

A member of the "home guard of swordsmen" escorted him and the others to Duke Ai's court, held in a cavernous room filled with officials and visitors alike. Several paintings depicting palace life graced the wall to the left. A violent battle scene covered the entire right wall.

A palace attendant announced Lord Huan's arrival. The stench of fear permeated the gallery. He swallowed hard when he beheld Duke Ai sitting at his official desk, a rectangular pedestal draped with a scalloped, floor-length, brocade gold cloth on an elevated platform. Two dragon ornaments hung from a cord on each side of the tabletop. Subtle notes of a stringed instrument played in the background, giving a few defendants a false sense of tranquility.

With a carved dragon head, a high gilded throne towered over the duke, symbolizing his power and protection. The duke wore a thin mustache and long chin whiskers that moved with the dancing rhythm of his speech. Red-and-white piping trimmed his black robe, and the headdress of the State of Lu emphasized his position of authority. The duke's close-set eyes made him appear even more sinister as he administered verdict after verdict.

Two men flanked the duke's left side. One acted as a scribe. The other, dressed in green, grasped a roll of slips and served as the bailiff. Behind the transcriber stood a servant waving a woven fan on a pole to cool the duke.

Likewise, to the right side of the desk, one man held a blue glass tray with tiny cups, and a flask of *Water of History* should the duke need alcoholic refreshment. A second man remained at attention; his sword drawn.

"Execution!" the duke shouted, his decision directed to an emaciated figure of a man, naked to the waist, who screamed when two soldiers dragged him from the platform.

Duke Ai's declaration jolted Lord Huan's thoughts back to his reality. He averted his gaze in revulsion, not wanting to witness the man's removal from the room. Shuddering, he recognized the second man of status on his knees in front of Duke Ai, pleading for his life. Although the verdict remained unchanged, the duke offered the convicted official to choose suicide instead of public execution.

Lord Huan realized he was next. Trembling, he stepped forward when the bailiff called his name.

He prayed. *Let me live.*

The duke narrowed his eyes and stared at Lord Huan for

what felt like an eternity. The room fell silent as he fingered his long chin whiskers, giving Lord Huan ample time to squirm.

"What has your son designed that is useful?" he demanded, breaking the silence. "I am losing patience. The plan you promoted to me has borne little fruit. You promised me inventions of importance when you persuaded him to marry your daughter."

"He made three new tools for building furniture. The saw proved valuable to you, my lord, to cut logs for buildings. He continues to search for a suitable bridge plan to cross mighty rivers." Lord Huan held up-turned hands. "However, the existing passages still prove to be too small, and they exhibit no strength."

"You told me your son is an extraordinary builder and inventor."

"Yes, my lord. He is talented. Do you remember I told you about his idea to irrigate the fields? And what of his kite?" Lord Huan bowed. "I am respectful of reminding you how it stayed in the air for three days. I approached you after his success, suggesting he would be useful if handled with care. You agreed he would be valuable."

"Years have passed," the duke exaggerated. "What has your *son* produced since then?"

Lord Huan's neck withdrew like a turtle, disappearing into his robe at the duke's question. "I am positive he will build a fine bridge. Upon my word, you will be the first to know."

Duke Ai leapt to his feet. His nostrils flared, with eyes so bright the whites made his dark pupils appear even smaller. The duke's searing glare forced Lord Huan to lower his eyes.

"I expect more than *your word*. I want a bridge before my enemy gets one, or I will take your life. Get out!"

Chapter 9

Lu Bān traveled to a village in the east to examine a bridge suspended between two hills. Sticks, logs, and deciduous branches joined with long reeds and other harvested fibers, which bound them together to form a connective rope.

"Although it appears sturdy, a stiff wind or swift water would wash it away." The first raindrops of the day fell, morphing into a steady downpour. Lu Bān pursed his lips, viewing the structure. "This one will not work either." He rubbed his temples. "Maybe tomorrow. Time to go home."

鲁班

Lu Bān saw a feudal warrior on a giant black horse in the distance on the way home. Clad in a bronze helmet decorated with a demon mask and lamellar leather armor, the man galloped in his direction. For an instant, the horseman seemed familiar. His first instincts screamed, *Hide!*

Deciding not to take any chances, he dove into the soggy underbrush, pressing his elbows into his sides to make his body as small as possible. He remained as still as a stone while the rider galloped past, mud clods flying from the horse's hooves.

Lu Bān scampered from his place of safety. He pushed his drenched hair from his face, clutched his soiled wet robe, and checked for other warriors. He hurried through the rain to the security of his home's sanctuary.

His heart raced; a tight feeling gripped his chest. Exhausted, he entered the house, sagged against the protective walls of Lord Huan's home before hurrying to tell his father-in-law.

"A mounted warrior rode by me on my way home today," Lu Bān said, out of breath, his hair dripping water down his cheeks. "He did not see me. The emblem on his shield bore a pair of yellow dragons with red, yellow, and black bars."

"You are fortunate. Those are the colors of the State of Wu," Lord Huan said, pointing to a silk map. "My spies report more military activity in the east, toward Suzhou. One of my men is checking those rumors, even as we speak. From now on," his voice rose, "stay out of that territory."

Still trembling, Lu Bān focused on the drawing. "Yes," he promised. "I will not tell Yun. She would worry."

"Yes, I guess she might." Lord Huan cleared his throat. "What are your ideas for the bridge? We"—a flush of scarlet filled his cheeks—"*you* must find a solution soon. People are counting on you."

Lu Bān pursed his lips as his father-in-law swallowed hard. *Why did he say "we"? Lord Huan has nothing to do with my project.* Lu Bān backed away. "I will stay in my workshop for now. I will tell you when I have solved the problem."

魯班

Rain, lightning, and thunder hammered the area for the next four days, the gloomy weather sowing doubts in Lu Bān's mind. The constant drip from the leaky roof actuated the passing of time without a workable idea.

He pondered his promise to the elders. *Lord Huan is right; people are counting on me. Should I have pledged to solve their problem? I have no experience in bridge building. Each sketch is a failure. What made me think I could find an answer when others could not? I need to talk to Master Sima. I am sure he will have an idea.*

Lu Bān waited for the lightning and thunder to pass before assembling his straw rain cape, a two-piece covering woven from Chinese silver grass. The bottom circular apron piece, opened in the front, fastened around his waist, supported by two thin straps looped over his torso. The upper split circle draped over his shoulders and tied at his neck. Both pieces had fringed edges. With his sloped straw hat in place, he dashed out into the rain.

The muddy road slowed his progress as he picked his way through deep ruts, the mire caking his sandals and squishing between his toes. He encountered few people out on such a dreary day. Taking almost twice the time to cover the distance, he arrived at Master Sima's house and knocked on the door.

Lu Chi's eyebrows shot up in surprise when he saw the drenched Lu Bān.

"Good rainy day to you, Lu Chi," the soaked traveler said. "I need to talk with Master Sima."

"Come in. The master is in his workshop. I will bring water for you to wash your feet and will take your rain cape."

While removing his mud-encrusted sandals, the familiar incense met Lu Bān's nostrils, reminding him of the carefree days he spent with his mentor. The basin of water arrived, along with a towel. "Thank you, Lu Chi," Lu Bān said.

"I thought I heard voices," came a friendly voice. "What brings you out in such weather?

Lu Bān bowed to his dear master. "I need your help."

"Is something wrong? You know you are always welcome," Master Sima said, motioning for Lu Bān to enter the workshop. "I miss your company. Would you like tea? I am pouring tea for myself."

"I would appreciate a warm drink," Lu Bān said. He reached for the cup, inhaling the floral aroma, took a sip, and continued. "Although my life changes, and I am content, I miss working with you, too."

"Are you settled into Lord Huan's household?"

"Lady Huan continues to ignore me. I suppose she still believes Yun deserved to marry a man of higher standing. As far as I can tell, she resents Lord Huan's encouragement of Yun's unique talents. She often causes Lord Huan's ill-temper. However, he shows an interest in my work. He even said 'we' when talking about the bridge, as though it were 'our' project."

Master Sima touched his parted lips, leaning toward Lu Bān. "A bridge?"

"Yes, a bridge is why I am here." Lu Bān leaned forward, forearms resting on his knees. "Elders from Wuchang came to inquire if I could design a bridge to replace the one swept away by floodwaters."

"Yes, word travels fast. We heard there were many casualties."

"I made a hasty decision to accept the challenge, and now I regret it."

"Building a bridge is an ambitious project," Master Sima agreed.

Lu Bān drew in a breath and released it. "I know nothing

about bridge-building." He took another sip of tea. "I examined several structures within a half-day's walk. I investigated three distinct construction types, yet none appeared suitable for spanning the broad Hanshui River. The most intriguing one has arches," Lu Bān said, curving his hand into a semi-circle.

"Let's think about what you need to consider," Master Sima suggested. "First, water is an obvious concern. This year's excessive rain caused the collapse. If I am not mistaken, the Hanshui Bridge was a cantilever structure, with sizable logs extending from the river's edge to overlap and meet in the middle. The binding in the center could not match the uncontrollable raging river. I believe your interest in arches is worth pursuing."

He continued reviewing the situation. "Second consideration is the river's current, and perhaps your most formidable obstacle is the depth of the water."

Lu Bān replied, "The water's swiftness and its depth would not be a concern if I could eliminate the center column."

Master Sima pursed his lips. "I do not understand how you would put something in the riverbed to anchor a central support."

"Ah, yes, that is my dilemma. However, I still believe stone is superior to wood—if I can solve the middle support problem."

"Wind might be a factor," Master Sima suggested. "You will need to consult the locals."

"You make a good point," Lu Bān said. "I will not know the soil quality either until I arrive. The city's bridge carried people and carts with animals. My guess is the ground will support a structure, but the bridge's weight would require substantial anchorage."

"Three factors come to mind when you consider anchoring the bridge," Master Sima said. The dead weight of the bridge itself. Stone will add more weight than wood. Then the live weight: carts, animals, horses, and people. We discussed wind and rain, but we failed to identify snow, drainage, and shaking earth.

Lu Bān scratched the stubble of his chin whiskers. "I have tried to sketch, but so far, I have not found a suitable plan. What else would you suggest, Master?"

"Your understanding of building principles surpasses most people. Apply your knowledge to the bridge, but remember, not all ideas are successful. If you are sure you want to use stone, you could build a model of an arched bridge with a better structure to join the two sides," his mentor said. "You could test its strength with weights."

"An excellent suggestion," Lu Bān agreed. "I will try a model."

"When do you plan to go to Wuchang?"

"I need a workable idea first; then I need for this relentless rain to stop, and the water to recede to allow the riverbanks to be solid enough to support the bridge. I hope to be ready in a month or six weeks and to take advantage of the dry weather season in September."

"Your timeline is aggressive," the master noted. "I hear there are rumors of hostilities going in that direction. You must exercise caution, for General Yáng Jūn has his sights set on that territory. He is always a contemplator of war. A bridge capable of carrying men and equipment over the broad Hanshui would interest him or any other general."

"Thank you for your advice," Lu Bān said. "This is my second time to hear this general's name. I will stay as far away from him as possible." Lu Bān finished his tea. "I appreciate your time, my friend," he said, standing to leave. "I am grateful for your counsel. May you have a pleasant day."

"It appears the rain has stopped." Master Sima waved goodbye. "Safe travels. May your ancestors be with you on this project."

Lu Chi returned. "I cleaned your sandals for you," he said, holding the footwear. "You might have to rewash them when you arrive home. The roads are still muddy."

Lu Bān put them on and gathered his rain cape gear. "Thank you, Lu Chi."

鲁班

A light rain had begun a few houses away before reaching his workshop. He hung the rain cape, apron, and hat on a nail to dry.

"My husband," Yun said. "Where have you been? I see your soiled sandals. You disappeared without a word."

"I am sorry. My frustration drove me to visit Master Sima to discuss ideas for the bridge. He gave me many things to consider." He took Yun into his arms. "Forgive me? After your father reminded me people were counting on me; I began to have self-doubts. Master Sima helped restore my determination to solve the problems."

"You will be successful, my husband. Are you hungry? The evening meal will be ready soon."

"I could eat a buffalo," he said, chuckling.

"I believe we are all out of buffalo," she said, kissing his cheek.

鲁班

Lu Bān gathered some small sticks and pebbles to fashion a model bridge. The structure crashed, sending pieces flying.

"That will not work," he said, frustrated, pushing his damp hair from his forehead as the hot, humid air made his robe stick to his arms.

Yun entered the workshop. "I brought you these light-yellow hedge-tree flowers to brighten your spirits," she said, gazing at the pile of rubble on the floor. "Are you making progress?"

Lu Bān's shoulders sagged. He puffed out a blast of breath. "I understand what does not work. Stacking the stones, offset like the bridge over the Dejiang River, would still need center support, but the water is too deep. There must be a better plan that does not require the middle column. My models keep collapsing when I try different ways to use the twigs and small rocks to create a sweeping arc to span the river."

"Could the new metal, *Duàbtiě*, be used to secure the blocks?" Yun asked. "I overheard two men describing how they formed it into rods to add strength while repairing our rock wall in the garden. Or could you use wood to make a frame for the stones until they stick together?" she wondered. "Would that work?"

"I do not know." He scratched his head. "Yes, someone mentioned a new metal. I will pay a visit to the blacksmith shop in town to learn how they apply it—if it ever quits raining. Your idea of a support structure is intriguing. I will try your suggestion tomorrow. It might work on a dry surface, but I still have to find a way to span the river." Lu Bān rubbed his stomach. I am hungry. "Is the evening meal ready?"

"Soon," Yun said. "I will draw water to wash our hands." When she slipped her hand into the basin of water, her jade ring slid off her finger. She caught her breath when the water rippled, revealing an image of a bridge. "Come here!" she shrieked.

Lu Bān peered into the water. A vision of a gentle arch spanned a river. "That is the answer," he murmured, studying the likeness. He grabbed Yun; her lightweight robe billowed as he swung her in a circle. "How do I make it work?"

Yun threw her arms around him. Her eyes sparkled. "I am sure you will find a way. Do not tell my father yet. Wait until you are sure you have the solution." Yun slid the ring back on her finger. "Distract him with my idea of building a wooden support. I will meet you at the table. Pretend you are still trying ways to make it work. It will be our secret." Yun gave her husband a quick kiss before she disappeared through the door.

魯班

The family gathered for dinner. Lord Huan pressed Lu Bān while they ate: "How are you coming with the bridge?"

"It is slow," Lu Bān replied. "I built models from my sketches. They all failed to support weight. I am close, yet something is not correct. Yun had an idea to build a wooden structure under the center until the stones cured, or perhaps the use a new type of metal." He tilted his head to make intense eye contact in her direction. "I will try her model tomorrow."

Yun bowed her head. *I am confident this story will get my mother's attention. She will not be happy. I know Lu Bān is buying time.*

Lady Huan glared at Yun. "It is not your business to suggest anything to your husband. How many times do I need to remind you? What is 'metal'? How would you know about it?

When are you going to realize your place is not in his workshop? You only belong in his bed," she snarled.

Lord Huan huffed. "My daughter, your mother does not understand your intellect because she seldom has an original idea, and she has a hard time believing any woman could have a worthwhile thought."

Lady Huan scowled, shoving away her soup bowl, the broth sloshing on the table.

"Helping your husband is wise if he asks for your help," Lord Huan added.

Yun did not reply. She glanced at her father and lowered her eyes. She continued to eat without making eye contact with her mother. *At least Mother will be mad at both of us now, she thought.*

魯班

The couple entered their room, following the meal. "I am sorry. I put you in an awkward position with your mother," Lu Bān said.

"You are fortunate you are a man. She would not dare criticize you. Do not worry. When I am helpful or receive praise, my mother becomes furious. She believes in her old ideas." Yun sighed. "It will be an ideal distraction until you find a solution to build the perfect bridge. I annoy her most of the time, no matter what I do."

"She appears angry with me all the time. I seek no trouble between you and your mother." He pulled her closer. "You are, without a doubt, my other half. As I think, you are there to finish my thoughts. I bet you can read my mind," he said, kissing her.

The ring tingled, its green glow emitting the fragrance of the verdant forest. "I know. Let us go make our son," she murmured, guiding him to their bed.

魯班

Lu Bān mulled over potential solutions. He struggled to sleep, trying to find another way to stack the rocks. "I might as well go to the workshop," he whispered. "There must be a solution."

He lit candles to chase away the darkness. "A candle will shed fresh light on my problem."

By mid-morning, he threw up his hands, shoving the pebbles away in frustration. They tumbled in every direction across the floor.

"I give up," he muttered. "My back hurts, and so does my head. I might not be as gifted as I or everyone else thought." He envisioned the swirling water, the people being swept away in the torrents, and the promise he had made to the elders to build a bridge. "What if I fail?" Lu Bān closed his eyes, rubbing his temples. Master Sima's admonition replayed in his mind: "It does not matter how slow you go, so long as you do not stop." He exhaled a deep, measured breath.

"Yes, I must keep going. The people of Wuchang are counting on me," he said, stooping to gather the scattered stones from the floor. He closed his eyes again, trying to recreate the bridge's image, which appeared in the basin. "What am I missing?" He examined a variety of rock shapes again. "Could it be I am not choosing the right contour for the last course and the middle stone?" He built the model using several forms for the center. None proved satisfactory. He picked up one wedge-shaped stone, wider at the top than at the bottom, and placed it in the top space. "It fits. I cannot believe it. It is the key," he whooped, racing to find Yun.

"Come," he said, waving his arms. He grabbed Yun's hand. "Hurry, I found the answer. And it works!"

魯班

Yun gazed in awe as the graceful arch stood with a heavy plank on top. She flashed Lu Bān an excited grin. "You did it! I knew you could. How did you find the solution?" Yun knelt to study the model.

The commotion in the workshop attracted Lord Huan's attention. He arrived at the door in time to hear Lu Bān's explanation.

"I studied the contour of the stones to determine if a particular shape could wedge between the last two at the center." Lu Bān pointed to the stone. "A tapered stone slipped into the space with perfection. I will call it the 'keystone' because it is the key to holding the arch together." He folded his arms over his chest. "I am confident I can design a bridge like this for the people of Wuchang. As soon as the rainy season ends; I need pleasant weather to dry out the site."

魯班

Lord Huan disappeared from the workshop. Lady Huan caught sight of her husband sneaking into his official workroom. Curious, she stood silent as he selected a slip, prepared the inkstone, and rolled the brush between his fingers to make a fine point. His message requested a private meeting with the duke at their usual place and time. He paused for the ink to dry before placing it into an official courier pouch, sending it to Duke Ai by a government servant.

Lady Huan waited for the messenger to clear the festooned gate into the outer courtyard and find her in the shadows. She handed him two coins.

"It will cost you more than this paltry sum. The last time I did something for you, I nearly lost my life. If I had not used a double intermediary for the two men who messed up your job, the authorities would have traced the deed to me, and I would have led them to you." He smirked. "You must continue to pay, say, ten *jin nie* per moon for my silence, or I will use my secret channels to help the officials to solve the mystery of who attacked your son-in-law."

Lady Huan paled. "Robbery," she spat when she regained her composure.

"Take it or leave it. The choice is yours, Lady Huan."

She fumbled in her robe pocket, extracted the ten coins, and grunted. "Here, you scum," extending her hand to take the message.

"Not so fast. This slip will cost the usual spade coins." She complied, and he surrendered the slip after slipping the new coins into his robe.

Lady Huan read the note, then returned the slip to the courier. *I will be ready tonight*, she promised herself.

鲁班

At dusk, from her concealed position behind the screen, Lady Huan watched her husband dress in modest clothing under a long brown robe to conceal his identity. Lord Huan puffed out his chest, opening the festoon gate. *At last, I have something important to deliver to the duke,* he thought with great satisfaction. *I might even be in line for a promotion.* However, before he could make his way through the south door, his wife confronted him.

"I wondered what you were doing. Why do you wear peasant clothes?" she huffed. "Someone might recognize you. How will you explain your appearance? Consider your standing. You know how rumors travel; our entire town will talk about it before you return." She drew in a deep breath, her eyes reflecting her secret knowledge. "I will wager you are slipping off to meet the duke again, hoping to dangle Lu Bān's bridge news to garner favor. Have you thought that other state leaders would pay a handsome price for the plans? It should not matter who is in power, as long as you hold the information."

"Silence, woman! You go too far!" Lord Huan yelled; his face reddened. "It is none of your business, as you tell your daughter." He drew back his hand. "You will go this instant into the house and pretend you did not find me." He leaned in toward his wife. "Do you understand?"

Lady Huan raised her hands to protect her face, expecting Lord Huan to strike her. When he lowered his arm, she exhaled with relief. "Yes, The Respected One Above," she muttered.

Lord Huan waited for his wife to enter the house's sanctuary before calling the Bo Le to bring his horse. Under the cover of darkness and disguised in the hooded cloak, he traveled a circuitous route, making sure no one followed him.

He replayed his wife's toxic words. *If I sold the information for more money to an enemy, they would kill us all. She does not understand how these men think.*

The palace walls stretched before him, flames leaping from urns, illuminating the main entrances. A silhouette of the central palace stood in the center on a raised, pounded, earth mound surrounded by steps, a faint outline of the up-turned corners of the roof visible.

Lord Huan rode to the secluded servant's entrance in the south wall, where he often met the duke to deliver confidential information as payment for keeping his position and title. Then he slipped through an unmarked doorway.

Waiting in the pitch black, he rehearsed his news for the duke, waiting for another door to open. The latch clicked, releasing the door into another small, empty cubical. A single wall torch threw eerie shadows on the lintels' bright green-and-crimson carved dragon heads.

"What say you?" a voice on the other side of the room asked.

"Wei Gui." Lord Huan replied.

The door opened into a final small room with a tiny, wooden-fretwork opening covered with a scarlet silk cloth. Lord Huan stepped to the draped opening, bowing. "My Lord Duke. Your humble servant brings wishes for good health. I have excellent news, sure to please you and, perhaps, allow me to become one of your advisors. No one else is aware of this development. My son, Lu Bān, has solved the problem of the stone bridge over the Hanshui River. He will begin construction when the weather improves, and the banks are dry."

"This is superb news. Bring me word when Lu Bān leaves to do the work."

"Yes, My Lord Duke. You will be the first to know."

"Dismissed," the duke barked.

魯班

He affords me no respect, thought Lady Huan. *My husband doesn't think past this tiny State of Lu. If he is correct, we had better think of the two or three states who would most likely take out territory—the Wu state for sure. Why else would Duke Ai hate him so, along with the Qi State? They have already taken part of the land on our border. I cannot risk sending a complete letter to my brother in Qi. Someone might intercept it. I must find someone with a Qi connection I can trust. Ha, in these terrible times, who can you trust?*

She knelt at her husband's short table, selected a slip, and prepared the ink on the inkstone. Holding the ink brush, she contemplated her words.

Dear brother. When I left Qi, you told me to send word if I needed help. Please send a courier to collect my message. I do not want it to fall into the wrong hands.

—your sister

Chapter 10

Another moon passed before a note from Chi Wei arrived for Lu Bān. It read, "The flooding is over. The banks are dry. Please come."

"Chi Wei's cousin and I will travel together tomorrow," Lu Bān said to Yun, gathering his drawing canvas, slate board, chalk, tools, and clothing to journey to Wuchang. "It will be safer. We will stop in Huangchuan to spend the night with Chi Wei's relatives."

"I will ask our cook to pack a food basket to take with you," Yun said, holding back tears.

"Do not cry, my love." He cupped her face in his hands, brushed her cheeks with his thumbs, and kissed her. "It should not be more than a week. I will return as soon as I can, I promise." His eyes twinkled. "We still have tonight."

魯班

Lu Bān awoke at dawn to fair weather. When he reached for Yun, she was not there. His heart raced. Bolting upright, he discovered her kneeling before the dragon candles.

She twisted her jade ring around her finger and prayed: *May your mother's spirit protect you, my husband. May you build a magnificent bridge and come home to me unharmed.*

Yun blew out the flames and stood. When she faced Lu Bān, he took her in his arms.

"I know you must go, yet my heart is full of sorrow. What if the evil men of war cause trouble?" Yun sobbed.

"As a builder, I am not a threat to them. A bridge is useful to everyone." He brushed the tears from her cheeks. "You are too lovely to cry. Chi Wei's cousin knows the way. I will not take chances." He kissed her again, dressed, and left.

魯班

Yun crossed her arms, holding her shoulders, pretending they were Lu Bān's arms embracing her. She stood frozen at the door long after she could no longer glimpse her husband and Chi Wei's cousin, descending the mountain path. She lifted red puffy eyes toward her mother when her mother called her name.

"Yun, why do you cry?" Lady Huan gave a quick, disgusted snort. "You should be glad to be free of that cramped workshop." She narrowed her eyes and spoke with a slow, steady cadence to emphasize her words. "You might be fortunate. Perhaps Lu Bān will not come back. You could marry someone who can produce sons. It is obvious he is unfruitful."

An icy sensation filled Yun. *How can she be so cruel?* she thought. *Why does she hate my husband? I know I must be silent. If only I could fly away like a bird.* Yun swallowed hard, trying to suppress the nauseous feeling in her stomach.

She ran past her mother to her room, collapsing on their bed, drawing up into a fetal position, and sobbed. She rolled the jade ring around her finger. Lu Bān and I lie together often. *Why am I not with a child? Perhaps I am the one who can bear no fruit.*

Yun woke with a throbbing headache and nausea. She rubbed her chest and stomach to ease the queasy sensation. When she touched her breasts, she felt tenderness. A child? she wondered, making a quick calculation. My moonblood is just four days overdue. Could I have these sensations this soon? She kissed the jade ring and beamed. "Thank you," she said, and then she realized, Lu Bān will be so excited!

鲁班

"Where is our daughter?" Lord Huan inquired at the evening meal. "Is she ill?"

"She refuses to come out of her room and claims she is not hungry." Lady Huan lowered her eyes and picked at her rice cake. "It is possible she worries her useless husband will not return. It has been a week."

"She should not fret. If something happened to him, I would know. I have contacts in Wuchang to keep him under observation." *Perhaps it would be wise to send a message to get a report from my spy watching Lu Bān,* he decided.

"If he did not come back, Yun could marry someone else." Lady Huan scowled. "Then she would produce a son."

Lord Huan huffed. He pointed his chopsticks at his wife. "If you had fulfilled your duty and prepared Yun for marriage, she would already have a son by now. If it is anyone's fault, it is yours."

鲁班

Yun refused to come out of her room for meals. Even though she lost her appetite, her abdomen continued to appear round like a compact ball. *The new moon has passed,* she contemplated. *Where is Lu Bān? He promised he would be back in a few days.*

She ambled to the ancestral altar, lit candles, closed her eyes, and prayed for a sign of her husband's safe return. Her jade ring tingled and warmed.

A vision appeared, revealing a bustling worksite within a walled city alongside a river—massive blocks of stone, carts, animals, and hundreds of workers erecting scaffolding and pulleys. A man resembling Lu Bān stooped to talk to a boy, drawing on the ground with a stick. He laughed, ruffling the child's hair. Other boys carried water to the laborers.

A slow, satisfying smile filled Yun's face. She breathed a sigh of relief, knowing her husband was busy working on his bridge. She relaxed her shoulders, confident of her secret knowledge. "Hurry home, my love. I have wonderful news."

鲁班

Yun snuck out to visit Doctor Tro, convinced she carried their son. She slipped into the tiny room, filled with shelves holding glass bottles of colorful herbs and liquids. The astringent potions and incense permeated the room and made her stomach even more queasy.

Doctor Tro motioned for her to come sit on a stool. She fidgeted with the collar of her robe. "Please do not tell my mother I came here. I do not want to tell her yet. I want my husband to be the first to know I am with his child."

The doctor acknowledged her request. Uncrossing his

arms, he examined her tongue. "When did you have your last moonblood?"

She stared at her feet. "Less than a new moon ago."

Doctor Tro noted the dark circles under her eyes. "It is not unusual to experience a delay. Are you upset or worried?"

"Yes," she said. "My husband is away longer than he expected."

"Let me say this as gently as I can." The doctor took her hand in his. "I do not believe you are carrying a child."

Yun caught her breath. "Why do I feel sickness here?" She placed her hand on her stomach. "I gain weight, and my breasts are tender?"

"It is difficult to explain. Sometimes when you want something enough, your body wants it too. I would wish this for you as well." Doctor Tro sighed. "Alas, you must wait."

"No, no." Tears streamed down Yun's cheeks. "I want a son more than anything." She pressed her hand on her abdomen. "What is the matter with me?"

"Nothing is wrong." Doctor Tro assured her. "You are still young. In due time, you will conceive a handsome son."

Yun bowed her head in silence. She felt several inches shorter when she found the strength to stand.

鲁班

What do I tell my husband? He will believe I am a fool. Yun walked with labored steps back to her home and tiptoed through the hall to avoid attracting attention. She slipped into her room, slumped in a corner, leaning her back on a wall. She rolled the jade ring around her finger. "What are you trying to tell me?"

she asked.

Yun thought about her friend Dandan's offer to meet her Wuism grandmother to help Yun to conceive a child. *Can I benefit from her skill? I am willing to try.*

魯班

Dressed in an orange robe with oversized, billowy sleeves trimmed in white, Yun met Dandan at her Wuism grandmother's house, where Dandan lived before she married.

"I am nervous," Yun said, seeing her friend. "My husband is away. I did not tell him I intended to come today."

"You will like my grandmother. She is kind and soft-spoken. She is eager to meet you."

Yun swallowed hard, took a deep breath, and followed Dandan into the bright sunshine of the inner hall of the house where they waited.

A stooped woman with a red shui-sa walking stick appeared. Her weathered oval face, the color of parchment, reflected the wisdom of her years, but her hooded, almond-shaped, slate-gray eyes twinkled. Wispy strands of silvery hair escaped from her upswept hairstyle tucked under a fabric-wrapped, violet-colored turban, matching the robe covering her thin frame. A hawk-feather mantle draped over her shoulders. She sat.

"Dandan tells me you seek my help, and you live under a cloud of bad luck because of your parents' discord. Have you discussed this idea with them?"

"My mother angrily dismissed the idea of the Kitchen God reporting the strife in our house and causing us bad luck," Yun said, rolling her shoulders forward, her voice a whisper.

"She keeps the picture of Zao Jun on the wall above the stove because my father believes in his power, but she pays no attention to him."

"Not a good sign," the grandmother said, her thin lips curled over her toothless gums. "Is it your desire to have a baby?"

"Oh, yes, Grandmother Wuism. I have tried everything. My husband wants a child as much as I do. I have prayed to the goddesses Péigu Niāngniáng and Kuan Yin," she plucked at her sleeve, "but they are silent."

"Perhaps they are testing your worthiness," suggested the grandmother.

"What must I do to be worthy?"

The grandmother rang a tiny bell. After a brief pause, a servant arrived with a tray containing a porcelain cup decorated with butterflies.

"If you wish to proceed with my help. You must drink this."

Yun accepted the cup and peered into the amber liquid. Without hesitation, she sipped the earthy, floral-tasting, warm drink.

"The drink is green rose tea, something to calm your anxieties and relax you for your journey," the grandmother said. "If you pass the spirits' test, this September day will bring you a new power. You must trust yourself to be ready for a new mold. Talk to your fears, then choose to let them go. Pay attention to what you see and hear, even if you do not understand."

Yun and Dandan followed the grandmother Wuism, who carried a small drum and mallet, into the lush grassy garden, devoid of all other sounds, bathed in bright sunlight and a gentle breeze.

"Lie on the grass and close your eyes, Yun. Dandan will

beat the drum on my signal," she said, handing Dandan the drum and mallet.

Dandan received the signal to begin the soft regular rhythm, like Yun's heartbeat. The Wuism knelt beside Yun, extending her hand over Yun's abdomen. Without touching her, she drew a symbol with her finger to open Yun's sacral chakra, then moved to her third-eye chakra, tracing another symbol over Yun's forehead, just above the skin. The air between her finger and Yun's skin wavered. Then the woman took Yun's hand, prickling Yun's palm, awakening her spirit to fly.

Yun's body lurched as her spirit tumbled into a tunnel-like dark void, falling faster and faster, the blackness so intense she felt her heart might burst. After some time, she came to rest in a cold, dim forest, disoriented, her eyes adjusting from total darkness to the daylight. She walked toward the brightness when The White Tiger of Autumn appeared. Terrified at first, she remembered the Wuism's words. "Talk to your fears. Trust yourself." She stared at the animal, a secret knowledge passing to her, and followed him into a space of peaceful light leading to a crystal-clear lake.

They drew closer. Yun realized sacred white lotus blossoms—the flower of life, the womb of the world—covered the water. She knelt to pick a blossom when a giant whirring, mechanical bird swooped over the lake, causing a flower to open, revealing a baby. The bird made another pass, snatched the infant, and flew away, its shrill *karrooo* call fading into the distance.

"No, no, come back," Yun cried, unable to understand the bird. She focused her attention on another flower, extending her hand to touch it. The snow-white petals opened, revealing another infant. She tried to grasp it, but some invisible force blocked her effort. She tried again. "It is so close. What prevents me from taking my baby?"

The drumbeats faded. "Understand, you are not to blame," the Wuism said. "Your mother's ambition and your father's selfishness cloud your pregnancy. They must see they are the impediments to your bearing a son."

Yun opened her mouth to ask, "How do I make them see it is their fault?"

As though yanked from a vital dream, the spirit flight ended. Yun found herself curled in a ball on the soft grass, exhausted and cold, still clutching the grandmother Wuism's hand. "Tell me what I must do?"

"Alas, your parents must assume responsibility for the discord, or they will never hold their grandchild."

Chapter 11

Lord Huan again clothed himself in his peasant disguise to travel in the darkness to give Duke Ai an update on Lu Bān's plans.

A guard stood at the spot where Lord Huan usually entered the secret passageway. *This is unusual,* he thought. *The duke is expecting me.*

He approached the sentry, but before he could speak, the sentinel barked his orders. "You are to enter through the south door tonight."

Not wanting to ask questions, Lord Huan retraced his path to an unimposing arched entrance, piercing the fortified wall. Flames from two urns on either side illuminated the red door, leading into a two-story square pagoda building with a green tile roof. Another sentry asked his name, opened the door, and escorted him into a receiving hall.

Perhaps I am now going to enjoy an elevated status, he hoped.

The escort and Lord Huan passed through a moon gate opening to a roofed walkway leading to the central palace. Ascending twelve steps to the landing, they entered an enclosed reception room without furniture. The man withdrew, leaving Lord Huan alone. He glanced from side to side. Green-and-red painted paneling covered the walls, and a small candle lantern hung from the ceiling, gold tassels suspended from its upturned tips.

As the moments passed, Lord Huan noticed a lump forming in his stomach, his mouth dry. Gripping his hands together, he took several deep breaths to stay calm. He tried counting the swirls of the carved dragon scales on the lintels to occupy his thoughts.

More time passed. Beads of sweat began to pool on his forehead. *What could go wrong? I have good news to deliver. The duke must have other important business.* The seeds of dread crept into his mind. *Perhaps Lady Huan is correct; the duke is weakening. Am I mistaken for not cultivating other alliances . . .*

The latch clicked, causing Lord Huan to jump as Duke Ai swept into the room.

"My Lord," he said, bowing. "I bring you excellent news. My son is on his way to build a great stone bridge in Wuchang."

"When I consulted my palace builders, they scoffed. It is folly to assemble something that colossal over a mighty river." Duke Ai spat in Lord Huan's direction. His voice reverberated off the walls and ceiling. "You deceived me."

Lord Huan stumbled backward. His mind swirled, trying to figure out a way to diffuse the duke's anger. "No, my lord. Lu Bān built a model. It supported an enormous weight. He assures me it will work." The duke leaned so close, Lord Huan could detect alcohol on the duke's breath.

"I should take both of your heads for making me sound foolish," Duke Ai said. "I need a bridge before my enemies build one."

Sweat trickled down Lord Huan's back; his shoulders slumped. "If it does not stand, my lord, it is Lu Bān's fault, not mine." He held up his hands, palms raised, toward the duke and swallowed hard. "I beg you, give him time to prove he can erect the span. If you kill us now, you will not know if the design is sound."

Duke Ai took a heavy breath and folded his arms across his chest. "My trusted man in Wuchang will send me reports. For your sake, I will give Lu Bān two moons."

Chapter 12

Lu Bān took the food basket, while the cousin carried the container of tools, drawings, and clothes. They wound their way down the rugged mountain. Lu Bān inhaled a deep breath. "The last time I traveled this path, I arrived in Lu as a child. My journey loomed insurmountable, much like building this bridge."

"Our families of Wuchang are excited to once again have access to cross the river."

"How many people lost their lives when the crossover fell?" Lu Bān asked.

"We recovered twenty-five bodies," the cousin replied. "Ten people are still missing. The search continues downstream, with no luck yet." He winced as the memories flooded his mind. "I lost a friend and a neighbor. It is a tragedy."

"Yes—one I hope I can help avoid in the future."

Clanging sounds from a nearby building site attracted Lu Bān's attention to the edge of Baliu. He spotted a bench and a suitable shade tree, its branches beckoning them to rest.

"This is an ideal place for our midday meal. I wonder what my wife gave us." Lu Bān opened their food basket. "Oh, my favorites: spiced rice cakes, dried fish, and tea. It is still warm," he said, holding a golden bottle gourd.

"Your wife is caring," the cousin said, biting one cake.

"Umm, these ginger cakes contain just the right spice. My wife only sends a hard biscuit or two with me. Otherwise, I would be on my own. Be sure to thank your wife for me. She is kind."

"I shall," Lu Bān said, packing the leftovers in the basket. "We had better move on before I want to take a nap."

Descending from the mountains into smaller hills, the men continued toward the flat terrain, making their walk pleasant. Lu Bān and the cousin shared the road with travelers on horseback. Several others rode in farm carts or walked. Oxen pulled slow-moving carts loaded with vegetables toward Huangchuan; their drivers cracked whips to urge the beasts onward. The pungent odor of the many pig farms reminded them they were still in the countryside.

They covered the remaining distance with no signs of warriors. Huangchuan lay before them by late afternoon.

"The village has a reputation for its many rivers and lakes. Cihu Lake covers the most landmass in this area. It reminds me of a shimmering, luminescent pearl. It will come into view before long. I know the way to Chi Wei's uncle's house. We should be there soon. Search for a blue tile roof. It is the only one in town."

魯班

Huangchuan bustled with activity. Merchants pushed carts over stone-covered streets, their wheels making rhythmic, clattering sounds. Two dogs ran past them, chasing a stray cat. Children's giggles filled the air when they passed a park, and the cauldrons of rice noodles in beef broth in front of a shop sent pangs of hunger through Lu Bān.

"These fruit trees are a good landmark. The house is around this next corner," the cousin said. "You will find my uncle is a pleasant man."

"Yes, I see the blue roof beyond the treetops." Lu Bān said. "I am one step closer to building my bridge."

魯班

A high wall surrounded Chi Li's three-bay house. Positioned on the right side of the south enclosure, they waited at a wooden door carved with dragons.

Chi Li, a tall man with a round stomach, bowed to his guest, and the cousin mirrored his bow as a sign of respect. "Welcome to my home," he said. "We have prepared a rare feast in your honor. I am sure you want to wash after your long, dusty trip. My manservant will show you the way."

"Thank you," Lu Bān responded with a bow. He patted his belly. "I find I am hungry all the time, and as for my appearance," he pointed to his soiled clothes, "I need to remove some dust."

魯班

Refreshed, Lu Bān followed a servant to an inner hall to join three generations of Chi Li's family. He sat cross-legged on a thick mat at the low table as the honored guest, surrounded by ten relatives. Candles, a vase filled with spikes of forsythia, and light green willow leaves adorned the table. A musician played soft music on a *Qin*. Everyone spoke in hushed tones.

"We give honor to our ancestors," Chi Li said, holding a

bowl of rice toward heaven. "May our departed family rejoice with the safety of our recent friend, Lu Bān. May his good deeds please his ancestors."

Lu Bān's thoughts flashed to his mother. *I hope my actions pleased you.*

An aroma of sweet soy, ginger, anise, cinnamon, and *Cao Guo* filled Lu Bān's nostrils. When the bowl of savory crimson sauce arrived, he reacted with enthusiasm.

"Chicken in red oil—my favorite." He picked up his chopsticks, waiting for Chi Li to take the first bite. "Walking all day has left me ravenous."

"My brother, Chi Wei, is eager for you to begin the new bridge. With all our rivers and lakes here, we experienced flooding, but it pales in comparison to Wuchang."

"I plan to produce the drawings in a few days, after I determine the conditions of the site and gather materials. I am ready to begin."

鲁班

After the meal, Lu Bān stretched out on his sleeping mat. *Tonight is the first night to sleep without Yun since our wedding. I miss her warmth and closeness.* His eyes drooped, then snapped open. *What will I find in Wuchang tomorrow? Can I solve the challenges awaiting me? Will my bridge idea become a reality?*

鲁班

"We packed your food basket for your trip," Chi Li said after they finished breakfast. He gestured toward the sky. "The weather is fair. You should arrive in Wuchang well before nightfall. Give my regards to my brother. Good luck with the bridge. I hope to visit you when you finish, and we will expect you again on your way back to Mount Lu."

"Thank you for gracious hospitality," Lu Bān said, bowing to Chi Li. "It is time to depart."

鲁班

"I wanted to wait until we were on our way," Chi Wei's cousin told Lu Bān. He glanced from side to side and over his shoulder. "I did not want to worry our host. Last night, several servants said they saw warriors ahead. Should we try to avoid Sanshan Lake, in case?"

The news made the hairs on the back of Lu Bān's neck stand. "Yes," he said. "I want no part of a dispute between two warlords. That is how I lost my father and my relatives. Only my mother and I, as a baby, escaped. I do not remember any of the details."

The cousin checked behind them and searched the sides of the road for signs of hostile warriors. He shifted his basket. "I worry the neighboring state of Wu's conflict will spill over into our town one day. Rumors of war abound."

They walked several hours, always alert, but encountered no soldiers.

The shadow clock showed the noon hour when they passed a pagoda. "Are you ready to eat? A majestic magnolia tree stands on the other side of the road."

"It is perfect," Lu Bān agreed.

He and the cousin enjoyed their lunch and a brief rest. The tree's fragrant lemon blossoms filled the air. Satisfied, they continued their journey.

"The smooth path makes for an enjoyable walk with no warriors or war uniforms," said Lu Bān. "What a relief. Our fellow travelers are regular people, going and coming from the market. We've also walked alongside a flock of sheep, their shepherd whistling instructions to the dogs guiding the animals."

The cousin's eyes searched the cloudless sky to calculate the sun's position. "I believe we will reach Wuchang well before dark. We are near," he said, pointing to a towering stone wall looming before them. "We are passing through a series of cemeteries, graded according to status, including an altar dating back a thousand years. Legends tell us the people wore headdresses made of feathers. They are responsible for our knowledge of water—how to use the waterway and its forks as a perfect base for growing rice. It is our city's great wealth."

"I would like to examine the river's edge where the bridge fell as soon as possible," Lu Bān said. "Will you take me there?"

"Of course, we are close."

They passed field workers knee-deep in water, harvesting rice, their work songs echoing across the shallow water, while raucous birds circled overhead, trying to spot fish dislodged from the plants. They folded their wings, resembling arrows, and shot into the water after their prey, unconcerned with the men waving their arms to shoo them away.

Lu Bān heard the water tumbling along its banks before the river came into view. The mighty Hanshui river still swollen but contained within its banks, surprised him. *Master Sima said the river was immense. My project will tax every skill I have*, he thought.

The cousin's words refocused Lu Bān's attention. "I will hurry to tell my uncle you have arrived. I am sure he will want to join you right away." The cousin bowed his goodbyes. "I will come tomorrow. My wife expects me home tonight."

魯班

The odor of the debris mounds, left by the flood's high water on the riverbanks, filled Lu Bān's nostrils. He viewed workers who were in the last stages of clearing the fallen bridge's remaining rubble.

Several fishermen stood at the river's edge, hoping to catch their dinner. Lu Bān opened his tool bag, stooping to examine the soil.

A young boy spotted Lu Bān and ran to meet him. "What are you doing?" the child asked.

"I am digging holes in the bank to take samples," he said. "I can rub the soil between my fingers to test its stability."

"What is 'stability'?" the boy asked, raising his eyebrows.

"We will build a replacement bridge here. I need to be certain the ground is dry and solid enough to support its weight."

"Can I help you?"

Chi Wei ran toward them, his robe trailing behind. He arrived, out of breath. "We are thankful you are here," he said, "and eager for you to begin. Our building supervisor will meet you in the morning. You will stay with my family while you are here. I hope you will be comfortable."

Lu Bān bowed to his host. "Thank you. I am ready to start."

He put his hand on the boy's shoulder. "I suppose this is my new junior assistant," he chuckled.

"We can use everyone's help," the elder said.

"We would like to examine the bank on the other side while it is still light. Can you arrange a ferry for us? I want to compare the soil over there to this site."

"I can get my father to take you," the boy offered. He put his two fingers in his mouth and whistled. "He is there," pointing toward a small craft at the river's edge. "Come on."

"The fisherman's boat is convenient. It would take some time before I could find a volunteer," Chi Wei said. "I will wait for you here."

Lu Bān climbed into the boat. "I am Chi Ah," the boy said. "This is my father, Chi Son. Everyone is excited about the new bridge."

Arriving at the opposite bank, Lu Bān continued his lesson with Chi Ah. "The dirt appears rock-solid, and the shore is flat. This is a good sign. It should make anchoring the bridge easier." Lu Bān paced up and down the river to determine the perfect spot for the footings. He poked a stick in the ground for a reference point, took a few rough measurements, and made notes on his chalkboard. They returned to where Chi Wei waited.

"Thank you for your help, Chi Ah," said Lu Bān. "I will meet you here tomorrow after school. I believe I understand where to locate the bridge," he reported to Chi Wei. "We will need to dig many feet into the ground next to the river to measure its anchoring depth and determine the makeup of the earth." He grabbed his tool bag and soil samples. "I will discuss my plan with your man tomorrow."

Chi Wei led the way to his house. "I hope you are hungry," he said. "There is an exceptional meal in your honor."

魯班

Lu Bān joined the elder's extended family in their inner hall—a spacious, well-appointed room with tables, seating mats, chests, and bamboo plants in pots. A painting of an elegant branch of crepe myrtle blossoms, bursting with vivid pink and magenta flowers, appeared like dense strands of silk-forming tassels, the petals folded into delicate crinkles of oval-shaped buds. It covered an entire wall.

Chi Wei pointed to a thick mat. "Please sit here," he said. "You are our honored guest."

After Chi Wei invited his ancestors to their feast, a servant poured tea, while another man presented Lu Bān with an extraordinary meal. Its familiar aroma brought memories of home—*chicken in red oil.*

"This is one of my favorites," he said. "Your honor humbles me. I hope to design a magnificent bridge for you and your town."

魯班

A welcome, cool fall wind greeted Lu Bān when he met the building supervisor at the river's edge the next day. "Can you access rocks and substantial stones other than the rubble from the bridge?" he asked the supervisor.

"Wuchang has an abundance of stone," the superintendent offered. "I believe their quality will please you. My men are gathering it now."

"I will need the precise measurement of the width of the river from this point," Lu Bān stuck a stick in the mark in the bank, "to seven paces past the stake I placed in the soil yesterday on the other side. I need this dimension to complete my drawings and calculations. Are you able to get that figure?"

"Yes. Someone will take the measurement right away," the superintendent said. "Please come this way. Our stone reserves will delight you. I have collected several sizable rocks. We have more if you need them."

"These are perfect," Lu Bān said, examining the stones. "Are there masons who can shape them?"

The supervisor expanded his chest. "Yes. Artisans representing the five elements are available to contour them," he said with pride. "Will you be working with those fundamentals?"

"Yes, we need the blessings of fire, water, earth, metal, and wood for our project. My sketches should be ready for the elders to approve in a day or two. I will complete them with your measurements."

Lu Bān continued: "Task your men to collect long log-poles for bracing, ladders, and scaffolding. We will need poles for carrying buckets and oxen carts to help move the materials into place. Ask the men to bring their tools. To shelter the artisans working with the *duābtiĕ* rods, we will need a lean-to-lodge, and we will require a doctor. How many ferryboats will be available to transfer supplies from one bank to the other?"

The supervisor flashed an air of superiority, straightening his back. "I expected your needs and assembled most of your requests in advance. The new furnace, to make the *duābtiĕ* iron rods, is new to our city. Its construction is near completion.

We are fortunate to have an abundant deposit of black earth nearby. The miners will work overtime to gather enough of the material. Our men who worked at the *bloomery* will apply their skills to forge the new metal."

"Excellent," Lu Bān said. "We will need a massive number of rocks and boulders. Start collecting ten thousand times the number of stones you have. We will construct the entire structure out of stone."

"Impossible," the supervisor snapped, his voice elevated. He sneered. "The river is too deep. It will never work." He flapped his hand to dismiss the idea. "I cannot build such a bridge. We have tried stone." He gestured toward the rubble. "This is the result. How many bridges have you built?"

A knowing smile filled Lu Bān's face. He put his hand on the supervisor's shoulder. "I figured out how to make it work."

The supervisor frowned, slapping the air with his hand. "It is a waste of time. It will not stand."

"Trust me." Lu Bān said. "I found a way. The key is a wedge-shaped stone for the center."

The supervisor scoffed. "I will believe it when I see it."

魯班

A courier arrived with a message for Lord Huan's wife. She took the message, retreating to her dressing room.

> My sister. What a surprise! I have an envoy coming to Lu in a few weeks. Please send your information with him. He will have a black-and-yellow band on his right arm. Pretend he is a cousin. These are perilous times.

The balance of power hangs with the wind.

I am thankful my husband is not home; she thought. *He will not be aware of my brother's message.* A slow smile crept across her thin lips. *My plan continues. One of us must plan for the future.*

魯班

Lu Bān received the critical measurements a few hours later. He pondered them and thought; *I guessed the river was 150 feet wide at its narrowest spot.* He set up a table, spread a canvas sheet over it, and gathered a bamboo pen, ink, and a bronze ruler to create his scale drawing. Lu Bān completed the diagram in a day and a half, along with notes and figures, then called the elder Chi Wei.

"I finished the illustration, and I am ready to present my plan," Lu Bān said.

"We are eager to view your idea. The elders will be here this afternoon."

Lu Bān and the wise men of the town gathered at Chi Wei's inner hall table. Lu Bān spread out the drawing. They stood in a semi-circle around him. "This is my sketch to solve your problem. I invented a masonry arch in the shape of a new moon rising above the clouds. There is a central arc and two smaller ones on either side. The bridge's total length will need 164 feet to put the footings on solid ground, and the center span will be 122 feet."

A man called out, "Is there enough room for boats to pass below when the river is high like before?"

"I calculated the height of the arch at twenty-four feet." Lu Bān separated his hand, gesturing to show the elevation. "It will allow many types of vessels to glide under the arch when the water level is above average. I designed it broad enough for two people to cross in opposite directions to help families traveling and workers to get their tools and carts to their jobs on time."

"This design is magnificent," Chi Wei said, admiring the drawing. "How can you build a stone arch this wide? No one could ever attempt such a project. It is impossible. Our supervisor could never build this."

Lu Bān longed to go home. He had produced the bridge plans as promised. However, Master Sima's teachings reminded him: "Faced with what is right, to leave it undone shows a lack of courage."

He focused on the elders' faces, understanding their fears were correct. They knew their supervisor could not build this new plan alone.

"I will stay to oversee the bridge foundation and teach the workers and their supervisors how to form the arch." Lu Bān faced the elders. "When they need other bridges, your workforce will understand how to construct them." Lu Bān rolled up his drawing. "I have spoken with your supervisor about starting the footings and collecting the needed materials. Give me three hundred men, and we will complete the project in a few months."

"I will give you six hundred men if you believe you can erect this bridge," Chi Wei said, a tinge of sarcasm in his voice.

"This project will need as many men as you can muster. We have plenty of jobs for everyone."

"They will be ready to start work tomorrow," Chi Wei promised.

"Would you lend me a runner and a slip? I would like to let my wife know of my delay," Lu Bān said.

"Yes, of course," the elder answered.

Lu Bān wrote a quick note and gave it to the envoy. "I will leave at once," he said. "I also carry urgent news to Wu."

He furrowed his brow. *What is so pressing? Is this about war?*

魯班

The messenger, wearing a badge signifying his neutrality, placed Lu Bān's slip in his courier pouch and set off on the well-traveled road toward Huangchuan, where he would head southeast to Lu and then to Wu, his destination.

Two men disguised as spiritual wayfarers in wind coats with hoods trailed behind the envoy, walking among the travelers until the courier passed through city walls into the countryside bordered by trees as evening approached. The two pilgrims kept their distance but followed the go-between's path.

Convinced they were alone on the deserted road, the two men closed the gap, attacking the agent from behind, knocking him to the ground, face down.

"Give us the message you carry," came a gruff voice.

"I am a neutral carrier. I have the protection of this state.

"Where is your protection tonight? Give me the message," the man in brown said, jerking the pouch from the dirt.

The heavier man sat on top of his victim while the brown-coat searched the pouch. He extracted Lu Bān's slip.

"What is this?" he growled.

"It is from the bridge builder to his wife."

"Where is your dispatch for Wu?"

"What you hold is the only one in the bag," he moaned, trying to breathe through the dirt with the man sitting on his back.

Brown-coat jerked the man to his feet and punched him in the stomach, causing the courier to double in pain.

"Where are the Wu slips?

"I do not know if the sack is empty."

"Hold him," ordered the brown-coat.

The heavy man pulled the victim's arms behind while the other assailant hit the courier's jaw. A cracking sound preceded another painful howl.

"Am I going to have to kill you?" he asked, taking another swing at the man's midsection.

The message-bearer crumpled; the heavier man let him fall to the ground.

"I think he is out," the brown-coat said. "Search him."

They went through his coat.

"Nothing," said the larger man.

"Check again. There must be a secret pocket somewhere."

"I found it," the heavy man said, handing the stitched roll of slips to his partner, who unrolled the missive.

"It is strange symbols I cannot make out. Can you?" the brown-coat asked.

"No, but I bet this guy can. Wake him up."

After some shaking and slapping, the messenger awoke blurry-eyed.

"Read this," he ordered, thrusting the slips in his hand at the courier.

"It is code. It always is. I do not know its contents."

The brown-coat huffed. "What about the other one? Do you know what is in it?"

"I did not read it after Lu Bān gave it to me."

The heavy partner picked up the slip from the dust, pushing it into the man's hands.

"Yes, it says, 'The plans are complete, but the supervisor will need help to build the project. The timetable will delay me, but the bridge will rise on time, and we will surprise them all. I love you.'"

"What is the surprise?"

"He did not tell me. He wrote the hasty note, and I went on my way.

"You have one more chance to read the other slip. If not, I am going to kill you," he said, drawing a dagger from his belt.

"If you kill me, you still will not understand its meaning."

The brown-coat moved toward the man, pressing the blade on his throat. "Last chance."

"Alright, I am a spy, planted by General Yāng Jūn of Wu. I am delivering the message about the completion of the great stone bridge and the date it will be open."

The brown-coat smirked. "That is more like it," he said, knocking the man unconscious. "Leave him for the wolves."

鲁班

The supervisor met with Lu Bān to study the ultimate bridge plan. "It is picturesque," he agreed. "I still do not believe it will stand. My men's safety is my concern. You need to find another design."

Lu Bān tapped the drawing center with his finger. "This

wedge-shaped stone is the key to the structure. The other stones push against it to hold it in place. We will begin one stone at a time. You will understand after we start. It will be your greatest project ever. People will remember your name forever," Lu Bān said.

Chapter 13

Build-the-bridge fever swept through the city of Wuchang in a collective effort to replace the bridge, washed away from the torrential rain. Excitement ran high on this, the first building day.

Chi Ah found Lu Bān surrounded by workers and equipment. "I am here to help."

"You should be in school," Lu Bān said.

"But I want to work," the boy protested. His face beamed, tucking his thumbs in his armpits. "Remember, I am your assistant."

"My assistant needs to be in school. My teacher taught me, 'One cannot become useful without learning. If they do not cut and polish jade, they cannot make it into anything.' Come back after class. Do not worry. There will be work for you."

Chi Ah's heart sank. He lowered his head, knowing he must obey his elders. "I will be back after school."

The construction action on both sides of the river brought many of the town's people to watch the flurry of activity, the building site resembling an anthill. Sounds of carts, animals, shouting of orders, and laborers added to the cacophony of noise.

Workers assigned to gather and sort stones toiled in similar areas on each side of the river. The men, charged with cutting the stones for the arch, worked nearby under the lean-to lodges, shaping the rocks according to the drawing and measurements. The *clang-clang* of their hammers echoed through the site while carpenters busied themselves constructing scaffolds, supports, and pulley towers.

Enormous cauldrons hung over cooking fires, smoke billowing toward the sky. Their bubbling contents filled the air with the savory aromas of roast pork and soups for the noon meal, along with pots of molten sticky rice, an ingredient in the slacked lime mortar.

Farmers herded their oxen to help haul materials from the staging zones to the worksite. Men with carts and artisans with tools came from all parts of the town, plus a few from neighboring towns, eager to have a sturdy bridge again. An armada of small boats ferried supplies and men across the river.

Chi Ah ran straight to Lu Bān, who was supervising the stones' setting when school recessed. "What are they doing?" he asked, out of breath.

"Do you remember when I dug holes to determine where to build the bridge?"

"Yes," the boy said. "It needed to be dry and solid for the found . . . something."

"Right, the foundation. The excavation crew went deep enough to find rock-hard ground to begin the footings," Lu Bān said, pounding his hand to emphasize the hardness. "Next, the men levered these massive stones into place to sit on the rock. This way, the bridge will be solid enough to support its weight. I wanted you in school today so you could build a good foundation for new knowledge. Without it, you would not be useful."

"What is that stuff? It looks like gray porridge?"

Lu Bān chuckled. "It resembles something you might have for breakfast, but you would not want to eat it. We call it 'mortar.' It is sticky because we use ground sweet rice, lime and water. It bonds the blocks together, and when dry, it is hard as a rock."

"What is this other thing?" Chi Ah asked, forming his hand into an A-shape.

"Builders have been using this for years. We use it to make sure the stones are level," Lu Bān said, placing one leg of the A on one block and the other leg on the adjacent one.

"If the weight hanging on this string lines up with this mark on the crossbar, it is even on both sides. If not, the next course will be off too. So, the mason taps one stone until the string hangs in the center." Lu Bān checked the string. "If you skip this step, the entire wall will slant. By the time we built the structure to its desired height, it would lean so far off center, it would fall over in no time."

The boy's eyes grew wide. "Is that why the other one fell?"

"The power of the water pushed the old one over." Lu Bān ruffled Chi Ah's hair. "Enough of today's lesson. I need to get to work. Let me see your arm muscles."

Chi Ah puffed out his chest, showing off his right arm.

"With your strength, the men sorting stones can use your help. We will talk again."

鲁班

Qianliyan, the spy Lord Huan had sent to monitor Lu Bān, blended into the throng. He started asking the locals about the flood and how the passage's loss impacted their daily routines.

His report began:

My Lord, I found the city's hopes to return their lives to normal hung on Lu Bān's success, and everyone I spoke to wanted to help. Workers from the neighboring towns came with their tools and skills, for they all missed the bridge.

I have never seen so many rocks sorted into piles by size . . . some so massive, no single man could move.

They built several tri-pole structures fitted with a device they call a "pulley" to lift stones. And in their bloomery, they are forging rods from *duābtiĕ*, a new substance, to cramp the stones together for strength.

Lu Bān has an invention for digging, something he calls a "shovel." It has a long wooden handle attached to a square metal scoop, shaped like our spade coins, about the width of your foot.

I mingled among the children, asking how they planned to help. Chi Ah, Lu Bān's self-appointed assistant, told me how Lu Bān tested the soil for stability and his plans to make the bridge's arc out of stone.

My efforts to talk to the supervisor failed. He is skeptical of the stone concept and leery of unfamiliar visitors.

Lu Bān has assimilated into Chi Wei, the village elder's extended family home, with two sons and their wives and small children.

The region is uneasy, with war rumors rippling throughout the land. I heard reports of fighting several hundred *Lis* to the northwest of the river toward the borders of Nie or Wey with Qi.

He concluded his first report:

The citizens of Wuchang are enthusiastic. At least six hundred people volunteered to help. The organization is impressive. Barring any additional problems, Lu Bān's bridge will be a reality.

魯班

On the fourth day of construction, several of the crew in charge of the footings and abutments fell ill with high fever and upset bowels. The rest of the team presented with the same symptoms the following day.

Murmurs of doubt rippled among the workers, each concerned they would be next to fall prey to the illness.

Alarmed, Lu Bān called the doctor.

The doctor's conclusion after he examined the men came as a surprise. "The spirits of the people who left this world when the bridge collapsed contaminated the ground and caused their sickness," he said. He consulted his medicine book, burned incense, and used several parts of a pear tree to mix a potion to cure their ailments.

A week later, most of the men were back on the job. However, four refused to return to work, frightened by the spirits. The supervisor sent a runner to a nearby town to recruit more skilled laborers.

With the foundations complete, the townsfolk marveled at how fast the bridge started taking shape. Residents volunteered to labor with the builders. They carried rocks, mixed mortar, and helped pull ropes to set the massive stones to speed production.

An unexpected slowdown occurred when the supervisor overestimated the stonemasons' ability to keep pace with construction. This delay coincided with an unseasonal storm lasting six days of intermittent rain, allowing the stonemasons to work through their backlog.

Although these events extended the scheduled completion, everyone's commitment moved the bridge toward its conclusion. It became a community project, one in which everyone took pride. People streamed into town from the surrounding cities to see if the rumors of a great stone bridge were true.

鲁班

Lord Huan's heart pounded when he received another report from his spy in Wuchang: "I hope Qianliyan has uncovered more new tools. The shovel idea so delighted Duke Ai he reduced the taxes on my field." He tucked the slips into his robe pocket to conceal them from his wife. Then he disappeared into his official workroom and closed the screen with a *swoosh*. His thoughts were feverish: *Now, what news do you send me? Tell me Lu Bān's bridge is a reality.*

My Lord, the work progresses after a mysterious illness struck the foundation workers, causing a one-week delay. All workers recovered.

The unseasonal rain halted work for another six days. However, the structure is taking shape. It is remarkable, as if some divine being were intervening.

Lu Bān has taken an interest in one of the local town boys he calls his "junior assistant." Lu Bān is patient with the child, answering his questions and explaining the building process.

If nothing goes wrong, they expect to dedicate the bridge in a few days. It is a marvel.

There may be a spy here from Wu. No one is sure of his name, but he is not a local.

As word has spread, more people come to see the structure daily. Among the visitors is a man and an assistant from Duke Ai's court. I am unsure of their names, but they are familiar. There may be other emissaries from other states too.

I fear one of the elder's sons recognized me, but I cannot be sure.

Lord Huan folded his arms across his chest. *I may sleep better tonight. Duke Ai's time allotment is running out. It is going to be close.*

鲁班

Chi Wei approached Lu Bān with a wrinkled brow. He lowered his voice. "One of my sons identified a notorious spy for Duke Ai's court among the strangers yesterday. His presence could be trouble."

"Duke Ai of Lu? Why would our work interest him?"

"I am not sure. It makes me uneasy with warfare rumors spreading from town to town."

"Do you think Duke Ai has war plans?" Lu Bān asked.

鲁班

Chi Wei's brother, Chi Li, came to the construction site. "I had to check out the progress of your project for myself. Stories of this great stone bridge have spread throughout the region." His mouth slackened, studying the structure before him. "It is grand beyond belief, and it will save many lives," he said.

A massive cheer ascended from the workers and the citizens.

"You arrived at the right time," Lu Bān said, gesturing to the graceful arch. "The keystone just settled into place. The completed bridge stands before us as a testimony to the towns-people's cooperation and arduous work."

Chi Wei announced, "Next week, we will celebrate the bridge's completion."

魯班

Bright sunshine, blue skies, and white puffy clouds greeted the citizens of Wuchang for the bridge-opening ceremony. The slight nip in the air did not diminish the throng of people who came to see the building marvel.

Colorful banners fluttered in the light breeze at each end of the bridge. Cinnamon and spice aromas drifted through the air from food vendors who set up stalls in a nearby park. Lu Bān's mouth fell open when he saw two men flying kites by the river, remembering his excitement when his magpie kite flew for the first time. Now that seemed like a distant memory.

Spectators clapped and sang while jugglers, gong players, and actors dressed as dancing lions entertained the crowds, adding to the swelling sounds. Loud merriment echoed through the audience, who awaited the bridge's official opening, their enthusiasm building in a crescendo of anticipation.

Locals and visitors lined the riverbanks. A crowd of men and boys shouted and jockeyed for a position at each end of the span, pushing to be the first ones to cross.

Chi Wei pulled Lu Bān aside, pointing out an emissary he knew from Duke Ai's inner circle. The man did not wear the splendid garb often seen in the duke's court. Today, he appeared dressed in peasant clothes. "My younger cousin has followed him among the merchants and heard him mention Lord Huan and ask questions of the bridge. Pushing past him in the market, I glanced at the slip he'd written to Duke Ai stating the project is a reality."

Lu Bān's mind reeled. "What did he do with this slip?"

Chi Wei shook his head. "He handed it to another man with him. I tried to follow, but the man lost me in the crowd. I suspect the message is going to Duke Ai."

魯班

Lu Bān, dressed in an orange robe with a bright blue sash, followed Chi Wei and the three elders, clothed in white, to the bridge's center. Chi Wei raised his hands, signaling silence.

"We have waited for this day," he began. "Lu Bān, our supervisor, the workers, and our neighbors have erected the most elegant structure ever built. It reminds me of a rainbow hanging over a mountain waterfall. We will name it 'The Rainbow in the Sky Bridge' in honor of Lu Bān, the finest builder in China," he said. The crowd whistled, applauded, and cheered. "The Hanshui River will never threaten us again!"

Lu Bān bowed to Chi Wei and the elders. "This bridge is my gift to you and the people of Wuchang. It is now your job to help other towns up-and-down the river to build new bridges."

"We shall!" Chi Wei bowed to Lu Bān. "Your design is splendid."

Lu Bān tilted his head. For a fleeting moment, somewhere in his mind, he recognized a familiar voice saying, "You will do magnificent work in China."

The crowd's noise refocused his attention on Chi Wei, who gave the signal to light the firecrackers to ward off evil spirits. Drums and gongs added to the pandemonium. The elder faced the multitude again. "I now declare The Rainbow in the Sky Bridge—*open!*"

More cheers and applause erupted from the crowd, people rushing to cross the span from each end for the first time.

Lu Bān bowed to Chi Wei. "My task is complete," he said. "I will return to Mount Lu in the morning. I miss my wife."

魯班

The celebrations continued into the late afternoon. Lu Bān accompanied Chi Wei back to his home. "We will celebrate your accomplishments and my brother Chi Li's arrival with a wonderful feast tonight," the elder said, patting his belly.

Chi Wei, his family, and Lu Bān knelt together that evening at long tables in the inner hall. Candlelight covered the room in a warm glow. A sweet fragrance of Lushan tubular white flowers perfumed the air and decorated the tables. A meticulous painting of a peach tree in full bloom graced a wall-screen.

The meal began with black tea, served in orange porcelain cups, presented first to Chi Li, the eldest family member, then Chi Wei and Lu Bān. Roasted pig followed the noodle soup first course.

"May you enjoy a long life, and may your ancestors be pleased," Chi Wei said, raising his cup of tea to Lu Bān. "We bid you a fond farewell and safe travels to your home tomorrow. Our cook will pack your food basket for your trip," Chi Wei offered. "We would not want you to be hungry on your journey home."

"I too will go back to Huangchuan in the morning," said Chi Li. "Lu Bān, I will enjoy your pleasant company. It always makes the day go by faster. You are, again, welcome to my home overnight."

"Thank you for your hospitality," Lu Bān said, raising his cup toward his host. "You treated me like a member of your family these past weeks."

Lu Bān faced Chi Li. "I am eager to share your companionship tomorrow, too. I suppose we should get an early start." Lu Bān bowed to his host. "I will say goodnight."

Lu Bān prepared for bed, letting his thoughts drift to Yun. *I cannot wait to sleep beside my love. I wonder if there will be warriors along the way. As a builder, I have nothing to fear, for I hold no anger toward anyone.*

鲁班

Lu Bān stood in the bright morning sunshine, gazing the last time at his bridge. It bustled with workers pushing filled carts, travelers with bundles, horses and riders, and men herding sheep. Underneath, boats slid through the water with ease, clearing the central arch.

"Thank you, Chi Wei, for the use of your woolen travel tunic to ward off the plummeting temperatures. I did not expect to be here when the weather turned cold," Lu Bān said. "Farewell to you and your family." He picked up his basket of tools, drawings, and a food bucket to join Chi Li, who waited to accompany him on their journey.

The road to Huangchuan teemed with barking dogs and raucous travelers returning to their homes after the ceremonies and celebration.

"The design of the bridge is unbelievable," Chi Li shouted over the racket. "How did you know it would stand?"

"I examined several spans. I tried to make a model using small stones. It took many tries to understand how to shape the center stone," he recalled. "Although the work is hard, I had to be successful."

"You are a master builder," Chi Li said. "I am sure many people will come to you for help. You will be a rich man soon."

"Thank you for your confidence," Lu Bān said. "So far, I have made no money. My father-in-law will be angry when he discovers the elders offered to pay me, and I refused. Realizing how much the town needed the bridge, I knew gifting it to the people of Wuchang was my only choice. It is my obligation to assist my fellow man."

"Your generosity is commendable," Chi Li said. "My brother said you required the workers to promise they would teach others what they learned."

"Yes. New bridges will help save lives," Lu Bān said.

"You will enjoy many rewards in your afterlife. Your ancestors will be proud."

A cloud of dust rising ahead on the horizon alarmed Lu Bān

and his companion. Fellow travelers shouted warnings, most running from the road toward the fields. Suspecting trouble, shepherds drove their sheep off into the ditch to safety.

The oxcart drivers pulled as far off the path as possible, climbing down and hiding beneath the carts, hoping the war party would pass without stopping.

Warriors on horseback and all the chariots flying the yellow-bear banner closed the gap rapidly. With little time to react, pandemonium broke out; people scattered, trying to avoid the shouting riders. Swinging their swords at random, the men hit innocent travelers who fell in the path of the oncoming horde.

"Run!" Chi Li yelled.

Lu Bān stumbled, trying to retreat to the safety of the ditch, dropping his tools and bridge plans.

Chi Li grabbed Lu Bān's arm, dragging him off the road at the last moment before a chariot wheel rolled over the footprints where they last stood. The yellow bear group continued whooping and hollering as they disappeared.

"Thanks," Lu Bān said, lifting a shaky hand to a cut on his head. "Did you escape injury?"

"I have a few scrapes on my knees and elbow, but nothing life threatening. We are fortunate. Let's see if we can help those injured."

People who took refuge in the tall grass returned to the road to aid the wounded. The horses left six mangled figures mutilated beyond recognition. Four others with cuts and bruises were alive, with varying wounds, moaning in pain.

A group of the men loaded the dead bodies into a cart to return to Wuchang. With no doctor available, another drayman took the unconscious—but still breathing—casualties.

"Are you able to continue to my home?" asked Chi Wei, retrieving their food bucket.

"Yes," Lu Bān answered, his voice still shaking. "We are lucky." He plucked his tools from the dirt and dusted off the bridge plans, putting them back in the basket.

They walked in silence, reflecting how close they came to leaving this life. After some time, Lu Bān motioned toward the opposite side of the road. "I would like to rest. I recognize the shade tree there," he said. "Your cousin and I had lunch under it when we traveled to Wuchang." Its branches were teeming with open buds. "It has added fragrant pink blossoms since we were here." Pulling his cloak tighter, he knew the blooms would soon fall off with this cold snap. "Are you ready to eat?"

"Yes, I am not as young as I used to be. After diving off the road as we did, I am sure I will be sore tomorrow—as will you," Chi Li said, leaning against the trunk. "My stomach is rumbling, too. What did my brother send?"

Lu Bān occupied the bench. Opening the basket, an aroma of spiced rice cakes met them. "Umm . . . delicious."

A stray dog wandering in the road trotted over, hoping there might be a morsel for him, too. The dog waited, drool dripping from his mouth. Tipping his head, he whined, pleading for a scrap.

Lu Bān took care to unwrap their food. Pleased, he mumbled, "Dried pears, biscuits, and tea."

After they finished lunch, Lu Bān tossed a small piece of biscuit to the dog. He gobbled it down and took the offering as an invitation to join their journey.

Lu Bān pointed to their dog companion. "It would appear you may have an extra member of your family," he chuckled.

They continued to Huangchuan, arriving at Chi Li's home at dark, weary from the morning's brush with the slaughter and glad to be alive.

魯班

After a hot bath to ease their tired muscles and remove the dust, Chi Li and Lu Bān dressed for dinner.

According to custom, Chi Li invited their ancestors to the evening meal of a savory pork stew and gave thanks for their safety and Lu Bān's success.

"The bridge is beyond belief," Chi Li told his sons. He spread out his arms to their full length. "You cannot imagine its breath. Two people can pass in opposite directions. The entire structure is stone. I saw it with my own eyes. It is unbelievable!"

"Tell us about the attack," the youngest son said.

"We were among the travelers departing after the dedication ceremony, about halfway between Wuchang and Huangchuan, when a cloud of dust rose in the distance," Chi Li began. "'Trouble!' someone shouted. People screamed and scattered, running to hide among the silver grass fields along the road." He continued recounting the event:

Shepherds' whistles and their dogs barking urged their sheep off the thoroughfare, their bleating cries signaling panic. Likewise, we heard the low, deep *moooo* of the frightened oxen as their cart drivers cracked their whips to drive their beasts to the edge of the road to make way for what lay ahead.

We had little time to think. Before we knew it, the

warriors were upon us, swinging their swords at anyone in their path. Cries of pain from the attack, mixed with the whooping and yelling, made the hairs on my neck stand.

Lu Bān rubbed his shoulders, reliving the sensation. "Your father grabbed my arm, pulling me to safety, just as a rider passed so close, I could hear the snorts of the horse, see its wild eyes, and feel its hot breath. I dropped everything and dove with him into the ditch, tumbling down the bank. I have never been so frightened. My heart pounded with such fury; I feared it might burst."

"From our hiding place, we watched the chariots roll over our footprints where we had stood moments before, flying the flag of the yellow bear," Chi Li said.

"Chu?" the middle son gasped. "What are they doing here?"

"My friends who have relatives in Chu say it is a matter of time until they control all of our states," the youngest son answered. "Our quiet life may be over."

"My father-in-law fears Wu," Lu Bān said. "These war rumors are worrisome."

"Were people injured?" asked the youngest.

"There were many injuries; the survivors sent them in carts to go back to Wuchang. Six lost their lives. The mangled bodies made my stomach churn," Chi Li said.

"Lu Bān," Chi Li continued, addressing his guest. "You are welcome to stay here as long as you need to rest."

"Thank you for your kindness. But I have been away for too long. My wife might forget my face if I do not return soon," Lu Bān chuckled. "I plan to leave at first light." *Just a half-day more. I will be safe when I am on the mountain path. Mount*

Lu is above the fighting. To hold Yun in my arms again will be my greatest pleasure.

魯班

Exhausted from her doctor's visit, Yun fell asleep in her room. When she awoke at twilight, shadows surrounded her. Yun lit dragon candles on a side table and knelt before them. She wrapped her hand around her jade ring, letting her fingers caress the smoothness of the stone. *Oh, my husband, where are you?* she thought. *Two moons have passed. I wanted to give you wonderful news. Now my only gift is sorrow. I cannot bear to confess my failure to conceive your son.* Salty tears fell in a constant stream.

The flames flickering in the evening breeze mesmerized Yun. A vision of a woman appeared, her skin tan and wrinkled. Her eyes gleamed. The ring on Yun's finger tingled and warmed, its green jade glowing.

"Remember the basin of water," the woman said before her image disappeared.

Yun repeated the words, "Basin of water. Yes, the water."

Yun blew out the candles and raced to the workshop. She lit a candle, placed the jade ring into the washbasin, and poured in the liquid. The water rippled. In the swirling water, Lu Bān carried his food basket and tools. "He is coming home," she said, breathing a sigh of relief. "He *is* coming home."

魯班

Lu Bān said goodbye at daybreak to begin the trip back to Mount Lu. When he arrived in Baliu, he spotted two warriors riding through town. Their shields bore a symbol of two yellow dragons. The riders did not stop.

Where are they going, and why? Lu Bān wondered. He pulled his hood low over his eyes and clutched his cloak tighter. *After our encounter yesterday with the Chu, I must be careful and alert. I am glad Chi Wei's tunic is a drab color. Perhaps they will mistake me for a local.*

Lu Bān let his thoughts revisit his bridge. His lungs filled with deep, satisfying breaths. He could not wait to show Yun his sketches and details of the ultimate design. He was excited to tell her how well the project had progressed with the workers' help. How could he begin to describe the excitement and the opening ceremony's splendor?

A satisfied smile crossed his lips when he recalled the supervisor's thanks for teaching him how to build the bridge. He pondered telling Yun about yesterday's attack, but he thought better of the idea, knowing it would frighten her.

The closer Lu Bān came to his home, the faster he walked. When the house came into view, he broke into a run the last few *chi.*

鲁班

Lu Bān found Yun in the courtyard, sitting by the fire, playing a qin melancholy tune.

"The bridge is complete, my love," he called, sweeping her off the ground and into his arms. "I hurried to finish, so I could hold you like this."

Yun's squeals of delight alerted Lady Huan. "I had hoped he would not return," she muttered.

Still holding onto her husband, Yun cooed, "I missed you too. I know you were successful."

"Impossible. How could you know?"

"Two days ago, my ring made my finger tingle. I did not understand its meaning. I prayed before the dragon candles. A woman's face, tan and wrinkled, told me, 'Remember the basin.'"

"My mother's face," Lu Bān said.

"I remembered the washbasin when my jade ring slipped off into the water, and we saw a bridge reflected in the water."

"Yes."

"When I slid the ring into the water, I saw your reflection. I took it as a sign you were coming home today. I am thankful you are back and safe."

Lu Bān reached for his drawings. Yun noticed the cut on his forehead illuminated by the fire's light.

"What happened to your head?" Yun asked, reaching to touch the wound.

"Nothing to worry you." He brushed off the question, unrolling the plans.

Yun bent to examine the drawing. "What of these hoofprints that mar your canvas and this dirt?"

"Just hazards of the construction site," he said, clearing the smudges, hoping Yun would accept his casual answer. "This bridge is my most successful project so far. The elders liked the finished product so much, they named it 'The Rainbow in the Sky Bridge' in my honor."

"You performed an outstanding deed, my husband. I am so proud of you. You can tell me more later," she said, a twinkle in her eye. She took his hand. "Come this way. I missed you."

Chapter 14

News of Lu Bān's bridge and his building skill reached a high-ranking military general of Wu through a spy who had attended the grand opening. Impressed by Lu Bān's abilities, the general traveled with an aide to meet him unannounced.

When the general arrived at Lord Huan's house, he told a servant, "I am General Yáng Jūn. Summon Lord Huan's son, Lu Bān. I want him here without delay."

The attendant bowed and took the visitor to the well-appointed inner hall to wait.

Lady Huan, overhearing the general's demand, concealed herself behind the screen to listen. *So, this is the general from Wu, whom everyone fears. My husband warned Lu Bān to be careful if he met him. Perhaps he has an interest in Lu Bān's bridge or his other inventions.*

Lord Huan and Lu Bān appeared together to receive their guest. They bowed.

The general's snow-white hair, pulled taut into a hair-knot, revealed several deep creases in his face, yet his bushy eye-brows and beard remained coal black. He wore a gray patterned robe with an orange cape of silk brocade, decorated with yellow, green, and blue circles, which he draped over his shoulders. The general's hand, resting on a slender dagger with two red tassels on the handle, sticking out behind a silver belt buckle, attracted Lu Bān's attention.

"Welcome. You honor us with your presence," Lord Huan said, bowing. "General Yáng Jūn, may I present my son, Lu Bān. I understand you wanted to talk to him."

"Yes." He ignored Lord Huan. His eyes bored into Lu Bān's gaze. "I need to scale the walls of an enemy city. You will invent something for me to use." The general crossed his arms over his chest with a grunt of superiority. "It must be easy to move and sturdy enough to carry the weight of many men."

"I design buildings, bridges, and new tools, not war implements," Lu Bān argued, lifting his hands, palms upward.

"You misunderstand. I want it finished by next week," the general said, poking his finger at Lu Bān's chest. "You will build it. The choice is not yours. You will regret any decision to ignore my commands. You have seven days," he snarled, glaring at Lu Bān. He gathered his robes with a commanding flourish of color, whirled on his heels, and departed.

Stunned by the general's words, Lu Bān stood in silence. "Lord Huan, I cannot design something so destructive. It will cause many to lose their lives. I will not do what he asks."

Lord Huan paced across the room, his arms locked behind his back. "The states in our region are in a constant war for power, like a game of Go, each trying to capture territory. Our State of Lu is weak. It may be a matter of time before Wu rules us. If that happens, I would be in a better position if you cooperate. General Yáng Jūn is a ruthless man, and the trusted advisor to King Fuchai of Wu. He possesses the full authority of the king," warned Lord Huan. "You would be wise to stay on his good side and do what he wants. Disobedience could bring much sorrow to you—and my family."

Am I not part of your family? Lu Bān wondered.

鲁班

Lord Huan returned to his official workroom, mulling over the general's demands and his options to defuse the blame if Lu Bān refused or failed to design the war machine when, without warning, Lady Huan swept into the room.

"This may be your opportunity to garner the general's favor," she announced. "He has an army and influential allies. This situation might be a good time to cultivate the general's trust if our duke is as weak as you think. He may be interested in the worm's other inventions. I suspect he will pay more for them than Duke Ai."

Lord Huan's face reddened, his anger growing. He leapt to his feet. "You are a confused 'worm,' woman. You do not know how powerful and ruthless this general is. He would slit his mother's throat to get what he wanted. He pays for nothing; he *takes* it."

Lady Huan did not speak for a few moments, mulling over her husband's harsh words.

"I know what you are thinking," he said. "You think you can contact him. All you think about is money and your *status.* You do not understand how things work in this realm. Your first mistake is that no woman may connect to anyone, military or otherwise. It is a man's world; remember your place. If Lu Bān does not give General Yáng Jūn what he wants, he might kill all of us in retribution." Lord Huan sank to his mat. "My concern is Duke Ai. When he finds out Lu Bān is working for the general, he will explode. *He* might kill us. I am caught in the middle of two dire possibilities."

魯班

Uncertain of his options and unable to focus on a solution, Lu Bān threw on his wind coat to visit Master Sima. Feeling the world's weight on his shoulders, Lu Bān did not wait for the servant. He pushed through the door, entering as though he still lived there.

He surprised Master Sima in the workshop, blurting out his words: "General Yáng Jūn is forcing me to design something to conquer enemy cities," Lu Bān said. "Lord Huan warned me if I do not cooperate, Yun and the family could be in significant danger. Help me!" He paced to a wall and back and stared at Master Sima. "What am I to do?"

Master Sima caught his breath, not believing he heard Lu Bān correctly. "When did this happen?"

"Today. It seems one of the general's men attended the bridge opening last week. He told his superior. Now the general commands me to build a war machine. Lord Huan warns me he might kill Yun if I do not complete the task. I cannot take such a chance. I could not live with myself if something happened to her."

"Lu Bān, if you are asking permission to create something to help General Yáng Jūn destroy people, you know I cannot. However, I agree with Lord Huan. It is unwise to make this ruthless man angry. You might go to another state where he has no jurisdiction."

Lu Bān threw his hands up and let them fall. "The general has posted a guard outside of Lord Huan's house to monitor my movements at all times. We have no way of escaping. If I had not agreed to build the bridge, I would not need to make this decision."

"You must remember, you built your bridge to save many lives. News reached us about your success. I am proud of your tenacity and your skill."

"I am afraid," Lu Bān confessed. "How did your master teacher counsel you on fear?"

"Master Kong would say, 'If you search your heart, and you find nothing wrong there, why worry? What is there to fear?'"

"You know I hold no malice in my heart toward anyone."

"The decision you must make is difficult," Master Sima said, putting his hand on Lu Bān's shoulder.

Lu Bān inclined his head, his shoulders slumped. "I must protect Yun, Lord, and even Lady Huan. I fight knowing what I have to do." He opened his mouth. The words stuck in his throat. He muttered, "The general leaves me no choice."

魯班

Returning to Lord Huan's house, a damp breeze engulfed him, appearing as an omen for his next week. Lu Bān mulled over solutions in his mind. *What if I make it so complicated, the builders cannot follow the blueprint? No, that idea will not work. The general would make me start again.*

Lu Bān went straight to his workshop, determined to produce something to appease the commander. As a rule, his favorite place, today he found it an uncomfortable stranger. He stared at his table, hoping the turquoise stones along the table's edge would help clear his thinking. He sketched. *Impossible.* He leaned forward on his table, throwing a bamboo slip across the room. It rebounded off the wall with a thud. Two more attempts ended the same way.

Yun heard the crash and came into the workshop to check on her husband. She knelt beside him, putting her hand on his shoulder. "Any ideas yet? I recognize this project is difficult for you."

"Yun, you do not understand." Lu Bān raised his voice. "I must do this to protect you and your family. I do not want my work to kill people." His face reddened. "Just go away. If you want to help, bring me something to eat."

"As you wish, my husband," Yun said. She left him with his head buried in his hands.

When Yun returned with a bowl of fragrant lemongrass soup, she noticed several more bamboo slips littering the floor. She stooped to pick up the pieces.

"Leave them!" Lu Bān bellowed. "Go away." His arm slashed the air, motioning for her to disappear.

Tears filled Yun's eyes. She bowed before walking to the door.

"Yun, I am sorry," Lu Bān called after her. "I am a foolish man. I should not make you cry."

He followed her and reached for her hand. Without hesitation, she moved closer.

"You will find an answer," she said. Yun put her arms around her husband. "I am confident you will succeed. When you are ready to talk, I will listen."

鲁班

Yun disappeared from the workshop. She knelt at the family altar to plead with her ancestors to help her husband find a solution. Yun held the jade ring, calling on Lu Bān's departed family to send him inspiration. The warm ring went cold. *This is not the sign I wanted.*

"Yun," Lady Huan said, startling her daughter, "I believe there is something you should understand." She hesitated. "Your father is in a precarious spot. He serves at the pleasure of our duke. This general is powerful and commands the army of Wu. They have captured part of our state already and they want more. Our duke is weak, with no warriors to command."

"But we have soldiers. I see them on the roads."

"Someone else controls them, not the duke. You must try to convince your husband to appease the general and design the war machine. If he fails to give the general what he demands," Lady Huan sneered, "General Yáng Jūn will kill him and our family. We will then be free of the blight your father has brought upon us."

鲁班

A chilly wind whistled through the gaps between window screens. Lu Bān stoked the fire in a brazier to drive away the chill. *Maybe my favorite sandalwood incense will inspire me,* he thought. He erased sketch after sketch throughout the day. The pile of broken bamboo slips reminded him of his failure to produce one useful idea by nightfall.

The following morning began as the day before had ended. Lu Bān's drawing slate held a few lines and calculations. He cringed, hearing Lord Huan march through the door to check on his progress. Arms crossed over his chest, Lord Huan elevated his voice. "What is your plan?"

"I cannot think of one yet," he said, louder than he intended. His father-in-law stepped backward.

Lu Bān ran his hands through his hair. "It is an impossible task."

Lord Huan pounded the table with his fist. "You have four more days." He narrowed his eyes and squinted at the few lines on the chalk tablet. "Do you expect these scribbles to save *my family?* I am in severe jeopardy if you fail."

A blank stare filled Lu Bān's face. His mouth gaped. A sudden coldness rose in his core. He shivered from cold and anger. *You believe you are in grave danger? What about me? Do you only consider yourself? Am I not part of* your family?

"Work harder. Concentrate," Lord Huan bellowed as his face reddened. His lips quivering, he turned and stormed out.

"Concentrate, indeed," Lu Bān mouthed. "If everyone would leave me alone, I might find a solution."

By the fourth day, sleep and food were not priorities. Lu Bān remained in the workshop day and night. His wrinkled clothes hung on his unwashed body. He headed for the door, hoping an intermission and fresh air might renew his focus.

Lu Bān walked into the courtyard, took a deep breath, and cringed when the storm clouds gathered overhead. *It does not rain this time of year.* Remembering the roof leaked, he shook his head. He raised his arms to the sky, crying out, "What else can go wrong?" *I need to hurry and move the drawing table.* The first raindrops ended his brief break. Abandoning his recess, letting his head droop, he trudged back to his self-imposed seclusion.

On the fifth day, the blank slate still tormented Lu Bān. A servant peeked in the door late in the afternoon. He bowed. "I am sorry to disturb you," he said, his voice tentative. "General

Yáng Jūn's envoy is here. He carries a message."

Lu Bān took the slip and grimaced when he read the words: "I wait for your design. I will come tomorrow at noon, and I expect great things!"

鲁班

Lu Bān grabbed his wind coat before following their servant to the inner hall. He glimpsed a shadow outside the room divider and suspected from its size that Lord Huan was hiding, listening to the conversation. The messenger appeared uneasy, shifting his weight from one foot to the other.

"Tell the general I will meet him tomorrow at the appointed time." Lu Bān's voice wavered. "I need to make a few more refinements before it is ready, but I trust the design will not disappoint him."

"I will convey your answer," the go-between said.

鲁班

Lu Bān followed the general's envoy out of the house, acknowledged the soldier on guard outside, and proceeded through the outer wall's door and onto the street. He inhaled a deep breath of cold air to clear his head before walking toward the park where children played tag, welcoming the chilly weather. Their gleeful squeals lifted his spirits for a few moments. *It would be wonderful to be carefree again,* he thought. His shoulders drooped, remembering his urgent work.

Lu Bān ambled toward the house, his gaze unfocused until an unwieldy handcart, overflowing with a family's possessions, spilled out on all sides. A ladder rocking on its side caught his attention.

What if I used a cart? he wondered. *Yes, that is my answer.* He sped back to his workshop, picked up the drawing chalk, and sketched as fast as he could. "It is so simple," he shouted to the empty room.

For the first time in a week, Lu Bān drew with purpose throughout the night. He added dimensions and building instructions to the sketch. By late morning, he transferred the completed design to a canvas-type roll, finishing the plan at the last breath before the general arrived.

Lu Bān emerged from the workshop. He stretched his arms to the sky, rolled his shoulders back to ease his tension from hours of sitting. He massaged the back of his neck and his leg muscles, tired from kneeling. His only thought was, *I cannot wait to bathe, eat a hot meal, and once again sleep alongside my wife's warm body.*

鲁班

Lu Bān waited in the courtyard with Lord Huan arriving at the last second. They received General Yáng Jūn and his aide in the inner hall.

He spread a canvas out on the rosewood table for the general's inspection. The afternoon sunlight illuminated the sketch.

Lord Huan fanned his fingers out against his breastbone when he eyed the drawing. *At last, something essential to give Duke Ai. Another bargaining chip.*

"I call it a 'cloud ladder.' The device is a mobile cart with a counterweighted siege ladder attached. It will extend to the top of a wall, then fold in half for transport," Lu Bān explained, mimicking the ladder's movements with his hands.

The general squinted. His eyes lit with an inner glow as he scrutinized the plans. "This is ingenious." A sinister look filled his face as he clenched his fist. "The enemy is mine!"

Lu Bān shuddered. A cold sensation he had never before experienced engulfed him.

The general rubbed his hands together. His nose wrinkled when he snarled. He grabbed the drawing, rolled it up, and held it high above his head. "No one will stop me now."

Exiting the front door, he promised, "I will return when I need more designs!" He took the guard posted at the door with him.

Lu Bān stood speechless, unable to protest. Still stunned, he returned to his drawing table, collapsing behind it, head in his hands.

Lord Huan found Lu Bān in the same position later in the day. "True, the general removed the sentinel, but he forced me to employ a new gardener to keep track of you before he left."

Lu Bān shook his head and stood. "The good general keeps a guard on his new trophy."

Lord Huan's posture straightened. "Did you keep a copy of your design?"

"No," answered Lu Bān in a daze. "I did not want to remember the method I created to cause so many people to lose their lives."

"Most unfortunate. No drawings," Lord Huan muttered, walking away. *Lu Bān is so naïve. Those plans would make me wealthy.* He tapped his cheek with his index finger. *I believe*

I recall enough of the design to create a sketch of my own for Duke Ai. The apparatus will impress him and keep me in his good graces.

A second icy wave overwhelmed Lu Bān. Woozy, he needed to sit, fearing his legs would not hold him. The general's words still rang in his ears: *The enemy is mine. The enemy is mine.* Although the general offered him no choice, he regretted putting such a lethal weapon in the hands of a man devoted to killing his enemies. *I need to find Yun.*

Lu Bān struggled to his feet, walked to the kitchen, picked up a tray with a teapot and two black lacquered cups, and searched for his wife.

He found her in the inner hall, sketching a bouquet of yellow flowers in a green vase along with pine branches, its needles growing in pairs, symbolizing longevity, steadfastness, and marital bliss. He knelt at her feet, placing the platter on a low table. Lu Bān poured a cup of tea and handed it to Yun with both hands.

The sight of Lu Bān carrying a tea tray caught her off guard. Yun offered a timid smile, accepting the cup. She took a sip before setting it on the seat, still trying to understand his actions.

"Yun, my love." He took her hands in his and whispered, "Please forgive me. The general gave me no choice. I regret my behavior, for I am an unpleasant husband these days. You know I did not want to design a war machine. The general snatched my drawing to use it for slaughter and destruction. Though it surpassed his expectations, it is not enough. Now, he expects me to continue to create more weapons." Lu Bān pressed his lips together in a slight grimace. "Master Sima taught me to do noble deeds or suffer in my next life. I will produce nothing so destructive again."

"I know you have struggled with this task. May our ancestors appreciate your motives." Yun took his hands. "We will go away. My father will have to understand. We can go to my wealthy uncle's home in Yingqiu in the state of Qi. He visited us two years ago. He is loyal to the ruling Tián clan. They are powerful and unyielding. We will find safety with him." Yun drew a quick breath. "My uncle says they have many bronze works there. Perhaps you could be of service to him with your inventions."

"It must be at least five hundred miles away. Getting there will be a challenge. Remember, we have no money."

"Would Master Sima lend us some? My uncle would repay him, I am sure. He is like a surrogate parent; if something were to happen to my parents, he would step in."

"I will visit Master Sima tomorrow," Lu Bān assured her.

魯班

Lu Bān slipped out without the gardener-spy noticing him, he thought. Master Sima agreed to Lu Bān's request, urging him to keep a low profile in Qi.

Armed with their strategy, Lu Bān and Yun intended to leave the following day.

The general's men stormed into the house before they could flee. They knocked over tables, flowers, and candles on their way to the workshop. Soldiers grabbed Lu Bān, overpowering him, as he struggled to escape.

"You cannot take him!" Yun pleaded. "Please, do not take him!"

Yun's screams alarmed Lord Huan. He realized at once the men were there to arrest Lu Bān. Ignoring his son-in-law, Lord Huan hid to prevent his capture.

Yun pulled against one man. "Let him go."

The officer paid no attention and pushed her aside. Yun fell to the floor. Rising, she chased after them in horror when they wrestled Lu Bān to the street, shoved him into a wagon with bars, and took him away.

"No!" she screamed. The men ignored her, not listening to her cries.

鲁班

Lady Huan heard Yun's screams, arriving in time to see Lu Bān hauled away. She smirked, watching him disappear. "Come inside at once," she demanded. "Our neighbors will witness your shameful actions, begging on the street like a criminal."

Yun spun around and glared at her mother. "They took my husband. I tried to stop them. No one would help me," Yun sobbed, unable to catch her breath.

Lady Huan lifted her nose with an air of superiority. "They took the guilty one. I hope, this time, he does not come back."

Yun's face flushed. She lunged toward her mother without considering or caring about the consequences. Her words spilled out like a flood. "You delight in making my life unhappy. May your ancestors be ashamed and turn their backs on you . . . *forever!*"

鲁班

Yun entered the safety of the family's walled compound. Her eyes lacked focus. Returning to her room, she slumped motionless, wondering if her mother already knew he would not return.

What if Lu Bān does not come back? She fled to the workshop, knelt behind Lu Bān's drawing table, stroking its surface and the turquoise stones, hoping to absorb his essence and communicate with her husband's spirit. Her almond-shaped eyes caught sight of his magpie kite hanging in the rafters. "If you were a bird, you could fly away from your captors." Yun buried her head in her hands.

"The basin," she said. Yun filled the washbasin with water. She slipped her jade ring into the shimmering liquid. The ring emitted a faint glow. "Please let my husband return."

Chapter 15

Lu Bān found himself in a dank prison cell reeking of urine, complete with rats and three emaciated prisoners huddled along a corner wall.

"Why are you here?" probed one man with matted hair and a long beard. His tattered clothes hung on his frame like a scarecrow. "You do not resemble a criminal."

"I refused to make new war machines for General Yáng Jūn. Although I tried to escape, they arrested me before I could get away," Lu Bān said. He held the brocade hem of his cream-colored robe up off the slimy floor, soaked with urine and feces. "How do you stand this putrid stench?"

"Get used to the ground. Someone scrapes it once a month. Like us, you will rot here."

"There is no escape," said another prisoner, missing his left leg.

"Quiet, someone is coming," a third man said. He pointed past the bars. "It is the general," he mouthed, scrambling to his feet.

The general stood outside the cell, glaring at Lu Bān.

"How do you like your new accommodations?" The general sneered. "If you want out, you will do what I say. If not, you will stay here until you rot. Decide. I give you one hour."

Lu Bān grimaced. The general spun on his heels, leaving him, a prisoner, to contemplate his answer.

鲁班

Laughter and music drifted out of General Yáng Jūn's lavish apartment in the headquarters building adjacent to the jail. He opened the door to find five of his favorite *ladies,* each dressed in a different color of translucent garments revealing their supple bodies, lounging on benches, waiting for his arrival. The music continued, as did the conversations around the room.

A woman in blue crossed to him, rubbed his chest in a slow circular motion, and handed him a wine goblet.

With the drink in one hand, he grabbed her by her neck with the other hand and drew her close, kissing her hard before letting her go. She stepped back, wiped the back of her hand to her lip to catch the blood, and then licked her lips. The general laughed, going to the table ladened with fruit, ginger rice cakes, roasted meat, and sweets. He grabbed a peach and took a bite; the juice dribbled down his chin before he ate the rest.

"I only have an hour with you, ladies." He selected some meat and rice cakes and sat. "Let me see you dance while I have lunch."

The women's bodies undulated to the music with sensual movements, taking turns dancing close to their host, teasing him to join them.

Their temptation proved too great. General Yáng Jūn pulled the lady in purple to his bedroom and closed the sliding screen.

鲁班

Lu Bān took several deep breaths to dislodge the tightness in his chest. He held out his hands, pretending to weigh his decisions on an imaginary scale. "I can design war machines or stay here with my new cellmates."

"You have a way out of here. You are foolish if you do not take it," the man with one leg said.

"I do not want to make structures to kill more people," Lu Bān said, holding onto the cell bars. "I agreed to invent one destructive device so General Yáng Jūn would not hurt my wife and my in-laws."

"You are not doing them much good now, are you? You have a way out. I would call a guard and tell him you agree to the general's demands. The longer you stay here, the more you will wreak like us."

Grunts of agreement passed between the other cellmates.

Lu Bān paced the slippery floor, trying to keep his footing. After almost an hour of soul searching and facing the prospect of sitting on the repulsive surface, he called to a watchman. "Tell General Yáng Jūn I will do what he asks."

魯班

"You made a wise choice." The general motioned for a guard to open the cell. "I knew you would come to my point of view. Follow me. I arranged for you to have individual quarters with a workspace. Everything you need to succeed will be at your disposal if you promise not to run away. Will you give me your word? I will not provide a second chance. The next time, I will kill you and your family."

"You have my pledge. I am a man of my word," Lu Bān said, glancing at the ragged men who remained behind bars.

魯班

Lu Bān followed the general through a tunnel carved into a rocky hillside, emerging on the opposite side of a knoll. Lu Bān relaxed as they left the jail, returning to the light of the sky above. He inhaled a deep lungful of fresh air, not realizing he had held quick breaths to avoid the jail's stench.

A three-ring, concentric, circular warrior camp occupied an open field below them. It resembled an anthill with warriors, cooks, boys exercising the horses, and service workers doing their assigned tasks. Walking closer, Lu Bān could hear the grunts of soldiers practicing their combat moves. The dull thuds of their long poles and axes pierced the quiet countryside. He noted the crossbowmen set up targets to hone their accuracy. Carpenters were hard at work, pounding their hammers on chariot frames, preparing them for their next battle.

"The outer-ring tents house our warriors and workers. I am pleased they are busy. I do not tolerate laziness," the general said. They passed guards posted at an opening to a second ring.

The evening meal's aroma coming from hefty pots hanging over cooking fires stoked Lu Bān's appetite. Makeshift tables dotted a section of the left half of the gap between the outer and middle rings. Horses, other livestock, and chariots occupied the right side.

"The center ring tents house the duty officers." General Yáng continued his camp orientation. "You will find them helpful when you need answers."

They passed two yurt-type structures inside the circle, covered with animal skins on either side of an elaborate building.

The general drew himself to his full height, gesturing to his right. "This is my new portable command pavilion."

Like his quarters near the jail, rich tapestries and a decorative screen enclosed each side of the transportable war room. A pagoda-style textile roof hung from a carved dragon, a wooden support. Two yellow-dragon banners on long poles projected at an upward angle from the structure's rear, suggesting the best things come in pairs.

Lu Bān pondered its construction. "Impressive," he said.

A late afternoon sun cast long shadows on a dirt path leading to a tiny hut on the camp's outskirts. Lu Bān followed his captor into a small, musty room with a mat for sleeping, a washbasin, a brazier, and a candle-lit table.

Kneeling at a table, General Yáng Jūn spread out a long roll of tattered canvas. It contained drawings with labels, dimensions, and notations.

"Here are boat plans for our fledgling navy. We stole them from an enemy courier. You will design something to give me naval superiority, something to do severe damage to these rival ships."

"I have no knowledge about boats or how one would fight on water. I am just a builder and inventor," he reminded his captor.

General Yáng Jūn gritted his teeth, his jaw tight. "That does not matter." He glared at Lu Bān. "Find a way. Our adversaries will use these four unique vessels to wage war on our rivers and the new canal connecting the Yellow River to the Yangtze." He pointed to a set of crude plans. "The largest ones are seventy-five-feet long, with twenty-five oarsmen on each side. We expect them to play a major role in skirmishes. The smaller crafts act as support vessels. This one is a massive, slow ship with crossbowmen. The other one will cut off the opponent's retreat," the general pointed out.

"Study these plans. Make whatever changes you need to improve my ability to attack them and win. Begin now!" the general ordered, moving toward the door.

"Will you free me when I complete the task?" Lu Bān asked.

General Yáng Jūn pursed his lips. "If I am pleased."

Lu Bān capitulated. "I will need materials to build models: hand tools, four chalkboards, chalk to sketch, a drawing canvas, glue, ink, and a fine bamboo brush."

The commander straightened his posture, hesitating at the door. "I will send these things right away." He departed, leaving Lu Bān to make sense of the crude drawings.

A short time later, a junior officer appeared with his requested supplies and military clothing. Lu Bān opened his mouth to protest. The official held up his hand as a signal for silence. "General's orders. You will wear this uniform while you are in our camp. The gong will sound when it is time to eat."

Lu Bān stood motionless. *First, I made war machines, and now I must resemble a warrior. Again, the general gives me no choice.* He stared at the garments before he exchanged his comfortable silk clothing for a soiled, knee-length, heavy olive-green robe, blousy trousers to tuck into high-top leather boots, a three-quarter-length padded, belted coat, and a helmet.

He tried to cross his arms over his chest. "How am I supposed to move, wearing this uncomfortable thing?"

鲁班

The next three weeks brought frenzied activity within the camp as warriors and officers prepared for minor battles with their enemies in the nearby countryside. Stockpiles of weapons—swords, daggers, and shields—lay in neat rows. Iron-headed clubs—five- to six-feet long, weighing ten to fifteen pounds—stood in barrels alongside huge iron hooks and ropes. Drums, cymbals, gongs, horns, banners, and streamers flew, all pieces of the equipment and the din of war.

A select group of slaves responsible for keeping a stockpile of wolf dung, was part of an advance party dispatched to the expected battle-line to light beacon-fires for signaling the enemy's approach.

No one bothered Lu Bān as he worked to conceive ways to improve the boat's functions. Try as he might, he produced no workable ideas.

Lu Bān spent time outside each night, studying the stars, trying to calculate the direction of home. Remembering his lessons with Master Sima, he located the evening star, Jinxing, the yellow dragon, and the seven dukes. *We must be south of Mount Lu, but how far? I rode in the cart most of the day. Too far to walk. How will I ever return to Yun?*

魯班

Unsure of the cause, Lu Bān lost weight. "Is it the terrible food, the burden to invent more war machines, or extreme sadness?" He paced, talking to himself. His world coiled at a snail-like speed toward his demise.

"I miss Yun," he said. "Designing a cloud ladder came easy compared to this challenge." He walked the eight steps on the earthen floor from wall to wall. "I must go to her. But how? It is too far to walk. I need to fly like a bird." He scratched his chin whiskers. "That is it—a bird. Could I design a bird to take me home?"

Remembering his original magpie kite plan, he reasoned, *It would need to support my weight and be long enough to hold my body lengthwise under its belly. Gliding downhill will be easy. To "fly" back up, I will need to propel the bird.*

Lu Bān sketched with determination. Satisfied with his workable idea, he gathered the materials to build his escape.

If things go awry, and they catch me, I will tell them, "The flying bird is my recent invention to spy on an enemy." I am certain General Yáng Jūn would like the concept. I need to consider a way to improve the boats while I work on my bird. He drew four crude boat pictures with cryptic comments in case the general or his aides checked on him.

鲁班

At night, Lu Bān worked on his design, scrounging the scrap heap's material while everyone slept. His initial attempt to fly failed. He and his creation crashed to the ground, wrenching his left ankle. Collecting the salvageable pieces of the bird, he hobbled back to his hut to rebuild.

Over the following weeks, recalling the wing structures of the birds he discovered as a child, he built the bird's wings to replicate an up-and-down flapping motion. He found he could generate enough lift with three silent strokes to glide on the wind currents.

魯班

While the garrison's men were asleep, Lu Bān made his second try. He flew a short distance from the compound, flapped the wings, and returned. *Success. Tomorrow, if the weather is fair, I will go home, surprise Yun, and return before the men wake. Flying in a straight line will make the trip faster.* He hid the bird behind the camp's rubbish pile. The stench and the amount of rotting garbage proved a perfect place few people would want to explore.

Inspired by the hope of seeing his wife, Lu Bān worked on boat designs the entire day. His remote workshop location by the river separated him from the daily hustle and bustle, allowing him to work without interruption or surveillance.

魯班

The next night, Lu Bān added an extra layer of clothing for warmth, uncovered his bird concealed by the trash pile, and flew out. He didn't allow himself to entertain thoughts of getting caught. He fixed his eyes on the Jinxing star, setting his course north into the night sky.

Lu Bān and the flying machine made their way on the wind currents. A dim view from above gave him a faint perspective of the landscape's hills and valleys. Walled enclosures of the villages reminded him of the board game Go, with the "stones" surrounding their territory. Their cooking fires provided pale dots of light and a smorgasbord of aromas.

It is so peaceful here, away from the turmoil on the ground, he mused. *I wish I could swoop down, pick up Yun, and soar away together to her uncle's safe place far, far away.*

鲁班

Lu Bān landed in a clearing near Lord Huan's house without a sound. He hid his bird as best he could behind the north wall in the overgrown privet hedge and the undergrowth, and he tiptoed into their room. He put his hand over Yun's mouth and awoke her with a gentle kiss.

Startled, Yun opened her eyes. Lu Bān stood before her dressed in warrior's clothes. She whispered, "How did you get here, my husband?" Throwing her arms around him, she inquired, "Are you hurt?" She felt his bony shoulders. "You are so thin. Do they not feed you?"

He held her close. "I missed you so much. You are the only food I need." He kissed her with the passion and thirst of a man in need of water.

They made passionate love for the first time in many weeks.

鲁班

After they caught their breath, Yun stared into his eyes. "How did you escape? Why do you wear soldier clothes?"

"This is my slave uniform. I invented a flying bird, capable of carrying a man. It will let me visit you while I work on General Yáng Jūn's project."

Yun smiled a secret smile. "Where is this bird now?"

"I hid it near the house."

"Come home every night," Yun urged. "I miss you so."

"I am not sure how often I can get away, but I will return when I believe it is safe, perhaps on a new moon when it is darker, or on the seventh day of the week. The men drink too much at night after their skirmishes. Their drunkenness will give me a better chance of avoiding capture," he said. "Tonight, I need to be back before the sun rises." He kissed her again before retrieving the bird, disappearing into the black midnight sky.

"Hurry home," she whispered as he disappeared. Yun kissed her jade ring. "Thank you."

魯班

The quiet warrior camp came into Lu Bān's view. *Almost there.*

He prepared to descend into the deserted field outside the camp's tent perimeter when he detected movement by a fire. *Someone is awake,* he realized. *Did he see me?* A sudden, overwhelming sense of dread gripped him before shifting his mind into survival mode. *I need to circle again and wait until the guard returns to his interior post.*

With two flaps of the bird's wings, he regained altitude and began a wide arc away from the camp. He strained to see if the figure had disappeared, but the darkness obscured his view. After circling again to buy more time, Lu Bān decided to land if he detected no movement. He rehearsed his story of designing something for the general to spy on the enemy in case the guard found him.

The bird carrying Lu Bān landed with a slight *whoosh.* To his relief, the sentinel had returned to his post, leaving the field deserted. Lu Bān wiggled out of the harness, stowed the bird behind the rubbish pile, and slipped into his hut. Tingling all over and walking on weak knees, Lu Bān sank onto his sleeping mat, relieved. *All is well. To see Yun again, the risk was worth it.*

鲁班

The breakfast gong sounded. Lu Bān passed three men in a heated argument.

"I tell you; I saw a bird carrying a man to its nest," the guard said. "I am not mad."

"Then you were drunk again," the taller man said. "No bird alive could transport a human."

"Perhaps you had a bad dream," the third man suggested.

Lu Bān dipped his head, not wanting to hear the rest of the discussion. *I think I will wait before flying again.*

鲁班

Rejuvenated by his trip home to see Yun, Lu Bān worked on the boat plans in earnest. He consulted one of the field commanders, Wu Bao, to help him understand field battle strategies to apply land concepts to warships.

Wu Bao explained, "We base warfare on deception. When we can attack, we must seem unable; when using our forces, we must appear inactive. When near, we must make the enemy believe we are far away; when far away, we must make him think we are near."

"How is that possible?" Lu Bān asked.

"We have code words for strategies," Wu Bao explained.

"Deceive the sky to cross the ocean."

"Meaning what? I do not understand." Lu Bān said.

"Disguise your intentions with everyday activities. The next point is, surround Wei to attack Zhao; meaning, if the opponent is too strong, strike something he loves. This weakens his mind and resolve."

"The enemy would damage troop morale for sure." Lu Bān said, tapping the side of his jaw.

"Kill with a borrowed knife—"

"Let me try to guess this one. Trick an ally into striking your opponent."

"You are correct," affirmed the commander. "The next few are straightforward. Make the enemy wear himself out; save your energy and wait until he has other internal distractions, then begin your assault."

"My father-in-law told me about one state so intent on attacking a neighbor, they left their home state vulnerable to attack."

Wu Bao nodded and said, "Make the enemy think you are in one place, but strike somewhere else."

"Another idea which makes sense," Lu Bān said.

"There are three more. Employ the same tactic three times, with the third one as the actual assault. Second, the beauty trap—use a woman to enslave the man."

"I have that one," Lu Bān said, grinning. "Do not let your crotch do your thinking."

Wu Bao stifled a chuckle. "Yes, many battles were lost when the woman distracted the man. And the last one: send your trusted men to poison the opponent with lies."

"These principles are interesting," Lu Bān said, scratching

his chin whiskers, "but I am having trouble understanding how these land philosophies could transfer to water battles."

"These nine strategies are all concepts, a foundation to give you a sense of how the generals think," answered the commander.

"If you are going to attack, how do you plan the strike?"

"We have four groups: the heavy chariots for combat; the smaller chariots to avoid direct contact—we deploy them in skirmishes; and the mobile assault towers."

Lu Bān grimaced when he heard his cloud ladder had become an integral part of the military's arsenal.

"And our light cavalry is used to cut off retreat. The straight battle line puts the bowmen on the left, the spearmen on the right, and the chariots with three or four horses abreast in the center, with the lightweight chariots behind them, protecting the rear."

"Your armed forces would strike fear in the hearts of any army," said Lu Bān. "Thank you. Your information helps me think of ways to alter the designs."

鲁班

Lu Bān's flying bird carried him undetected to sleep with Yun many times in the coming weeks. One night, when he slipped into their house unnoticed, Yun greeted him with her exciting news. She threw her arms around him and kissed him. "My husband, we will have a son."

"This is amazing. Are you sure? When?" Lu Bān wondered in disbelief. "Have you told your parents?" He put his hand on her belly. They perched on the bed's ledge. "How are you feeling?"

"I have told no one about the baby yet. I did not tell Doctor

Tro for fear someone would find out," she said. "I wanted to keep it a surprise for you. My moonblood stopped over two moons ago. My stomach experiences milk sickness in the mornings. I prayed you could get away from your camp tonight to share our splendid news." She curled up in his arms. "It has been so hard waiting for you."

"How can you be sure it is a son?"

"I use a chart to calculate my lunar age and the moon of conception. It is never wrong," she said, rubbing her hand over her abdomen. She held up her fingers. "It will be six moons before he arrives. We are most fortunate. He will have the luck of leap year."

"I should finish my boat designs by then, maybe before the last part of this moon."

"Oh, your news is wonderful." Yun's eyes brightened. She walked to the end of their bed. "I am taking precautions." She lifted the mat's edge. "According to tradition, I put a knife under my mat to ward off evil spirits. No construction work occurs here at our house. I am mindful not to face south or east while bathing for fear of angering the Sun god," she said.

"Yun." Lu Bān took her into his embrace. "I love you. I am the happiest man alive. Our ancestors are rejoicing with us, too." He kissed her again. He paused at the door. "Please be careful. Take excellent care of our son."

"I promise." Yun patted her belly. "We will wait for you next week, my husband."

鲁班

The weather turned frigid. A rare, light dusting of snow changed the landscape to an endless white ocean, lasting a short time before the winter rain returned.

Yun tried to conceal her morning sickness from her mother in the days that followed. The aroma of food made her nauseous. She took early morning walks when she could. She loosened the sash on her robe, drank Sheng Jiang tea, and avoided as much contact with her mother as possible. Nothing worked. Lady Huan eyed Yun with suspicion, drawing on a mother's sixth sense.

"Is something wrong, *xiǎonǚ?*" Lady Huan inspected Yun from the top of her head to her toes. "Your face is thin and pale. You should visit Doctor Tro."

"Oh no, I am feeling better. My yin and yang may be out of balance," Yun offered with a shrug.

"Show me your tongue," Lady Huan demanded. Yun complied. "Is your Earth in disharmony?"

Yun hesitated. "Yes," she said, avoiding her mother's stare. She cringed when her mother stormed out and returned with her father. He stared at Yun with a scowl.

Lady Huan glared at her. "Are you with child?"

Tears flooded Yun's face. "Yes. I did not want to tell you."

"How can you be when your husband is missing?" her father shouted, waving his arms.

"Everyone will dishonor us." Her mother wailed. "How could you do this?"

Faced with repeated inquiries, Yun confessed, "Lu Bān invented a secret flying machine. He flies home and returns to his camp the next day."

Lady Huan drew her lips into a fine line. "What camp?"

"He is being held by a general while he designs new war boats," Yun answered.

"Show us this device," Yun's father demanded.

"It will surprise you tonight when he arrives after dark," Yun reassured them.

鲁班

The family dressed in heavy-wind coats at nightfall, huddling in the vacant land, waiting for Lu Bān and the apparatus.

"There he is," Yun said, bouncing from one foot to another. She drew in a deep, relieved breath. "I said he would come on the wings of a bird."

Lord Huan took a step back. His eyelids blinked several times, trying to process the image of Lu Bān and a bird. Lady Huan froze in place, her mouth opening and closing, gasping for words.

A sudden icy feeling engulfed Lu Bān to his core. He spotted the group below waiting for him.

After Lu Bān landed, his father-in-law charged at him, shouting, his nostrils flaring, his warm breath making steam puffs. "How could you take such a chance?" he demanded, grabbing Lu Bān's shoulders, giving him a vicious shake. "You position me in a terrible spot. If General Yáng Jūn finds out, I will be in a lot of trouble." He straightened his hat. "I told you about the *Lianzuo System* in place for hundreds of years. If one family member breaks the law, the punishment extends to the entire family. The ruthless general will kill us all."

"I did not intend to flee my job. I missed Yun so much. You cannot tell anyone," Lu Bān pleaded. "The general will have me in jail forever . . ."

"Only if you are lucky," Lord Huan spat.

"My ship designs are near completion. I will deliver my drawings next week and explain the changes to the boats. The general agreed to release me. I want to be with Yun as she waits for our son. You cannot mention the flying machine to anyone or, as you say, they will kill us all."

"I will keep your secret," Lord Huan said, "if you promise not to return until you complete your work. The risk is too great. I understand this general. My daughter needs her husband when your son arrives."

"I pledge my word. I will stay until I finish the plans."

Lu Bān faced Yun. "Do not worry. I will be back soon." He kissed Yun. "I will give the general what he wants."

鲁班

The vision from the air on his return flight gave Lu Bān an unobstructed view of the fires of another warrior's encampment a day's walk away. *This must be the enemy camp the scouts found last week. I cannot warn General Yáng Jūn. He would ask how I learned this and discover the bird—more bloodshed on my hands.*

Again, he circled the field, searching for anyone who might see him. *If I can land without detection, I will not use the bird again.*

He landed without incident. The tightness in his chest increased while he struggled to remain focused on his task. *Just do my work and go home to Yun. I will deliver the naval*

*designs and return home. But what if the general changes his
mind and makes me his prisoner?*

魯班

Lord Huan reclined on a stack of pillows in his official workroom, daydreaming about how the bird could be valuable. *I will
be wealthy when Duke Ai learns of this ingenious invention.
However, I need to wait until Lu Bān returns. If I tell the duke
now, he might not believe me. I wager Duke Ai could use it to
spy on his enemy. Or send messages without being detected.
Lu Bān continues—*

Lady Huan swept into the office, interrupting her husband's
solitude. "I know the perfect way to increase your influence
with the general," she began. "If you tell him about the flying
machine, he will kill Lu Bān for us, then Yun could marry
someone important."

Lord Huan's head snapped up from his papers, believing
he misheard Lady Huan's suggestion. Surprise accelerated
to anger. He jumped to his feet. A flush of heat engulfed his
body. Spittle escaped his mouth. "Woman, do you hate Lu Bān
enough to risk our *demise?*" He pounded his fist on his desk.
"You do not understand how this general's mind works! You
did not listen when I reminded Lu Bān of the Lianzuo System.
He will punish us, not reward us! Disaster comes from such
careless talk."

Lord Huan paused, relaxing his fists. "Lu Bān is more
useful to us alive than in the ground. If we are to profit from
his genius, I must keep his trust. His inventions and fame add
stature to our family." He relaxed his posture, sinking into the

pillows. "Besides, we have more practical things to consider. If Lu Bān left this earth, Yun's child would be without a father. If she married someone else, she would live with his family, and we still would have no one to take care of us. You are a *confused worm!*"

Lady Huan rolled her eyes. "We would not face these problems if you had not brought this peasant among us to marry our daughter." She curled her arms over her chest after her husband called her an idiot. She glanced around for a way to escape his angry words. After several moments of silence, Lady Huan bowed. "You, The Respected One Above, are correct, as usual."

魯班

Yun's belly continued to grow as the days progressed. Sickness in the mornings plagued her. As a last resort, she approached her mother to ask for her advice.

Lady Huan crossed her arms over her chest and directed an icy stare at Yun. "In the beginning, you did not share your condition." Her words spewed out as toxic as a snake's venom. "You forgot the virtue of *filial piety*. You are a disrespectful daughter." Lady Huan huffed, storming out of the room.

Yun hugged herself, yearning for her husband's arms to enfold her, while tears filled her eyes, spilling over her cheeks. She closed her eyes and rubbed her jade ring for comfort, praying for Lu Bān's return. She listened. Could it be Lu Bān's voice?

Go to Doctor Tro. He will help you.

Chapter 16

General Yáng Jūn left no stone unturned. Days before the proposed assault, he called the diviners to study the omens, observe the movements of the celestial bodies, gauge the meanings of natural phenomena, and consult their calendars to determine the most auspicious time and place to engage the enemy. They determined the signs were right to attack the following day.

In the evening, the general called the troops to a campfire meeting, addressing his men: "I regard you warriors as my children. I favor you as beloved sons. Our victories bring us neither reputation for wisdom nor credit for courage. Our preparation will win the victory. The diviners believe the omens are in our favor, and our spies confirm the Chu army has not yet organized their ranks. You are well prepared. We will march in silence to aid our advantage of surprise. Remember, drums command you to advance, cymbals signal to engage the enemy, and the bell to retreat. I have faith you will give your full measure to King Fuchai and our State of Wu."

The men stood in a collective ovation, shouting the pledge of their lives to the general.

鲁班

A single thump from a massive war drum signaled the order for Wu's army to begin their advance. The warrior's meat ration from the previous night's dinner buoyed their spirits. The pandemonium of horses, chariots, and whooping warriors broke the predawn morning's silence the day before Lu Bān's scheduled meeting to deliver his alternative plans for the general's navy.

Walking toward the noise, he grimaced as he viewed the soldiers preparing to march toward the enemy's camp he had discovered from the air. *Many will not survive*, he knew.

Lu Bān eased back into his hut to check his last changes to the ship's project. A handful of warriors, the cooks, and carpenters were all that remained in their encampment. The absence of the usual cadence of the base created an eerie silence. He checked and rechecked his calculations, leaving nothing to chance, expecting to meet the general when he returned after the battle.

魯班

The breeze blew the directional standard to mark the course to the enemy camp. "We will march in the wind's direction," the general commanded.

Wu's army advanced, divided into five divisions, comprising hundreds of five-man infantry units—two archers and three spearmen, each designated by a pennon color.

The red-bird flag represented the vanguard. The left-wing group flew the green-dragon banner, while the white tiger identified the right-wing. The rear guard marched under the yellow-dragon standard. A Great Bear constellation banner marked General Yáng Jūn and his bodyguard's position.

At the top of a rise, the silent army assembled to view the Chu camp unprepared for the attack. All the warriors held their collective breaths, waiting for the signal for the battle to start.

The war drum sounded.

The units broke into two flanks, sending a hoard of yelling and whooping men attacking from the north and advancing from the south to engage their foe, ready for fierce combat.

Chu sentinels saw the enemy begin their descent and shouted the alarm. The unprepared Chu warriors scrambled to grab their weapons and shields and to form their defensive ranks.

Wu's bowmen sent volley after volley into the defenders, killing the front linesmen. Others took their places.

The flank with the spears attacked the north soldiers. Horses drawing chariots whinnied, kicking dust into the sky as they charged the enemy's midsection. The deafening din of the fighting swallowed any vocal commands. Two gongs signaled the army to advance again. The drums beat out the cadence of attack. Screams of the fallen men filled the air while the odor of blood, fear, and carnage tested every man's resolve, regardless of their allegiance.

The battle wave swayed first in Wu's favor, but the Chu warriors, being greater in numbers and better trained, rose to defend their camp, each commander believing they had the upper hand, only to see their advantage sip away. The crashing cymbal signaled another assault.

With a final push, the Wu's army overwhelmed the Chu camp. Their fire arrows ignited structures, sending billows of acrid smoke springing from their huts, embers flying into the clear blue morning sky. The cavalry slayed anyone in their path.

Chu's tattered army retreated to the woods. Wu's chariots

gave chase, killing some soldiers before they slipped into the safety of the trees.

Chu's general, realizing the encounter lost, committed suicide, unwilling to return home in disgrace.

One of the field commanders grabbed Chu's battle standard and presented it to General Yáng Jūn, who held it high, sending a great cheer rising from his warriors. "We secured our victory!" he declared above the din of celebration.

The casualties of war and destruction lay before them. Designated soldiers assigned to the execution squad honed in on the cries of the suffering Chu to end their misery. They also collected all the left ears of the dead, sending them with the victors back to camp to count, record, and use them in a sacrificial rite, believing the ear provided some spiritual protection for the next battle.

Slaves attached to the Wu forces gathered their fallen comrades, loading them into wagons to be buried near the campground.

The Wu army bells signaled their men to return to camp. Those too weak, unable to walk the distance back to camp, rode in the chariots. Foot soldiers helped the other injured men.

鲁班

Doctors tended their mangled warriors and several guards returning midmorning, realizing these would not be the only casualties of the day. Most injuries were puncture wounds from spears and swords. A myrrh and herb mixture combined with *The Water of History* helped dull the pain. After cleaning the gash, the doctor put Greek Fire powder in the lesion and lit the powder with a burning twig to cauterize and stop the bleeding.

Splints served to set broken bones.

Moxibustion involved igniting a moxa stick or other herbs to produce a warm sensation and moxa smoke inhaled. Belly injuries were most often terminal, the patients succumbing to massive infection in a short time. The sight made Lu Bān's stomach turn.

Is the fight finished? Lu Bān wondered, seeking someone to ask.

The garrison remained quiet until early afternoon, when General Yáng Jūn led the victorious army back to celebrate. Gongs, horns, and cheers of victory announced their arrival.

"The general will be in an agreeable mood," Lu Bān said when the men entered, dragging an enemy's banner in the dust. He thought, *I hope my boat plans will please him tomorrow.*

魯班

"Today is the day," Lu Bān said, gathering his drawings. He paced his hut's damp floor, waiting in the pre-dawn glow for his escort to take him to the general.

Wu Bao, the ranking officer, walked with Lu Bān past a makeshift infirmary he had passed the night before. A doctor tended to the suffering. Their cries of pain rang in Lu Bān's ears, causing his stomach to roil.

"How many men lost their lives yesterday?" Lu Bān asked.

"We brought back over one hundred of our brave warriors," Wu Bao said, his voice low. "We were fortunate to have lost so few. The credit goes to our divinators and the surprise attack plan. The Chu State is mourning three times that number based on the count of the left ears."

"You cut off their left ears? What happened to the rest of them? Did you abandon them to rot?"

"Victorious armies leave the dead of their enemies. It is both a courtesy and a war tactic. Those skilled in warfare withdraw a day's march to allow the enemy to gather their corpses, chariots, and armor, battered in the conflict. The state then uses some of its wealth and precious resources to collect and bury the dead. They call it 'attacking from within.'" Wu Bao explained.

"If the vanquished do not gather their dead, they have committed three crimes. First, they fought and lost. Second, they departed with all their men but did not return with all of them, and third, we gave them their corpses, but they did not take them. The citizens would hate the superiors. The superiors could not recruit. Thus, we call it, 'attacking them twice.'"

They arrived at the portable command center in the camp's inner ring. The envoy announced Lu Bān's arrival and withdrew.

鲁班

Stacks of maps and rolls of canvas littered both sides of the general's desk. His full suit of armor hung on a T-pole, while war implements (including a sixteen-inch bronze sword with a gemstone hilt) rested by a shield.

General Yáng Jūn narrowed his eyes, scrutinizing Lu Bān, as he unrolled his drawings. "What ingenious plan have you created to make our navy unstoppable?" the general demanded. He pored over Lu Bān's plans, tilting his head, puzzled. "What is this?" He twisted his lips.

"I designed this unusual four-pronged bronze hook," said Lu Bān. "Each hook holds an end barb. I call it a grappling hook. Like these, it mounts on long poles on the Great Wing ships to grab an opposing vessel and hold it in place. If you tie one of these hooks on a long rope and throw it onto an enemy's vessel, the hooks will catch the railing and grasp it, preventing its escape."

General Yáng Jūn considered the diagrams. "It might work. However, we need to be close enough to reach the adversarial vessels." He stroked his beard. "How do you suggest we do that?"

Lu Bān unrolled the first boat sketch. "I redesigned your immense wing ships to add two distinct features. I fitted one vessel with two huge, V-shaped metal protrusions mounted on the bow and stern. Because these boats are so massive, you can now use them as battering rams going forward or backward. I named this one a 'Stomach Sticker' because it will pierce the belly of the opposing ship."

"Astonishing," the general said, his mind racing with possibilities. "Explain this second one."

"I labeled it the 'Tower Ship.' It will carry mobile assault ladders like the cloud ladder I gave you for scaling walls. It will be useful after the 'Little Wing' ships clear the opponent's decks with their crossbows."

"Yes, I understand how it might work," agreed the general, knitting his brow.

"The 'Bridge Ship' you have will cut off the enemy's retreat. I consulted with one of your field commanders to understand strategies of fighting on land and designed ships to serve the same functions," Lu Bān said. He added in a more contrite tone, "I did what you required. I want to go home. Will you release me?"

"You gave me the full measure of what I wanted and more. I will honor my word and let you go back to your family," General Yáng Jūn said, still admiring the drawings. "I am confident these ships will give the State of Wu a superior navy." Unfocused, he smiled, adding, "Yes, you may go."

Lu Bān bowed and backed out of the general's tent. His mind raced. *What do I do with my bird? There is no way to fly it home. It would attract too much notice in the daylight.* He considered leaving a bamboo slip on the invention, explaining how he designed it to spy on an enemy, but reconsidered. He rushed to where the bird lay hidden and broke it into pieces, scattering them among the debris in the camp's rubbish heap while breakfast held everyone's attention.

With the evidence destroyed, Lu Bān wasted no time. He exchanged his uniform for his civilian clothes and gathered his drawing instruments and tools before the general changed his mind.

鲁班

Lu Bān considered his equipment. *My long journey on foot with these things is impossible. I arrived in a wagon. A horse or a chariot is my only hope of travel. I think I will ask Officer Wu Bao, who helped me before.*

He found Wu Bao dressed in torso, arm, and leg armor of bronze and leather lamellar scales, and a spiked metal helmet topped with a plume of black feathers. He checked his chariot harnesses of a pair of barrel-chested, stocky brown horses protected by tiger skins and chest plates. White feather headdresses decorated their bronze face armor.

"Without your knowledge of military land tactics, I could not have understood how to design the boats," Lu Bān began. "I want to thank you, and ask a favor."

"Oh?" Wu Bao raised his eyebrows, continuing his inspection of the chariot's frame and twenty-four spokes on the five-foot diameter wheels. "What do you need?"

"General Yáng Jūn released me from service." Lu Bān said. "I live a significant distance away. Is it possible to ride with you to your next assignment if you are going north?"

Wu Bao wrinkled his brow. "I would need the general's permission," he said with caution, fastening a belt around his middle, securing his padded waist cushion.

"I understand." Lu Bān's shoulders slumped, shuffling his feet. "I miss my wife and want to go home. Will you help me?"

"I can identify with you. The fighting separates my wife and me for months at a time. I will see what I can do." Wu Bao looped the reins around a hitching rail three times in a clove hitch to secure the stallions and walked toward the general's command center.

Lu Bān waited by the chariot, admiring the horses, while Wu Bao consulted the commander.

Wu Bao returned, amused. "The general's spirits are soaring. Your work must please him. He is agreeable. If you come with me, you must wear a warrior's uniform," Wu Bao handed Lu Bān a bronze dagger, "and be prepared to fight if we fall under attack."

Prepared to fight? Lu Bān swallowed hard, examined the weapon, and protested, "I possess no combat skills."

"We won a major battle. Our enemies are retreating, and our warriors will soon return. I do not expect any further trouble.

But, as a precaution, we must stay vigilant. No one understands what lies ahead. You will need this, too." He handed Lu Bān a bronze spherical helmet topped with a small, simple crest to protect the edges of his ears and the back of his neck.

Lu Bān changed back into his uniform and secured the helmet on his head. Its heaviness surprised him, but the soft material inside cushioned its weight. He tucked the bronze dagger into his waist-sash and grabbed his tools and drawings.

Wu Bao gestured toward the chariot's wooden, rectangular basket platform. "You cannot take so many things. There is not enough room."

Lu Bān affirmed his understanding. Not wanting to miss his opportunity to go home, he strapped the roll of sketches to his back, discarded his tools in a heap under a tree, and mounted the crimson-painted chariot. The State of Wu's yellow-dragon banner hung atop a standard attached to the chariot box's back. Its streamers fluttered in the cool breeze.

Wu Bao snapped the reins. The horses lunged forward.

"Balance is a skill you learn," Wu Bao said with a chuckle, watching his passenger struggle to stay upright. "I think I was born in a chariot," he shouted over the thunderous pounding of the horse's hooves, throwing clods of dirt behind them.

Lu Bān grasped the chariot's crossbar with a white-knuckle grip. "It is a talent I do not care to master. I prefer my drawing table seat. However, I am grateful for the ride."

鲁班

"Our warriors are coming back from battle," Wu Bao said, motioning toward the cloud of dust heading their way. He pulled off the road to let a mounted army and officers in two- and four-horse-drawn chariots pass, their deafening hooves beating the hard ground.

Wu Bao urged his horses to continue up the hill to its crest. Signs of the fight littered the landscape. Lu Bān caught his breath when he recognized his cloud ladder invention against the walled village ruins. Smoke billowed from its houses. Destroyed rice fields, broken wagons, and the stench of bodies of horses and men, not yet claimed or buried, made Lu Bān nauseous. He covered his face, not wanting to accept the possibility that he'd contributed to this destruction.

Wu Bao acknowledged Lu Bān's reaction. "You will become immune to the carnage. It is the cost of maintaining our way of life."

"I hope I never become accustomed to seeing this war-ravaged landscape. My goal is to do *good* deeds, not kill people. I wish I had not given the general those lethal boat designs or the cloud ladder."

"If you had not drawn the plans, General Yáng Jūn would have found someone else."

Lu Bān crouched behind the chariot's front wall to block his view of dead bodies, the sounds and scent of slaughtered men, and the destruction on both sides of the thoroughfare.

The compressed dirt road stretched before them, now devoid of war signs. Oncoming mounted archers and an occasional chariot passed beside them. Each carried a yellow-dragon standard.

They stopped at the army's left-flank camp at midday. Lu Bān stayed with the chariot while Wu Bao went for food and to secure fresh horses. He poked his fingers in his ears to try to drown out the wounded and blood-curdling cries, but to no avail.

Climbing down from the chariot box, Lu Bān decided to stretch his legs while he waited, striking up a conversation with some warriors standing by the corral.

"Were you part of the battle we passed to the south?" Lu Bān asked.

"Yes, we escaped with our lives, a few cuts, and bruises. We were some of the lucky ones today," the tall man said.

"Our recent mêlée diminished our ranks," related the shorter man. "We lost almost two-thirds of our warriors and three senior commanders. Our mercy squad relieved our injured and hopeless comrades of their agonies." The shorter man took a deep breath to regain his composure. "We brought their bodies back to bury. At least they did not lose their ears."

"I am sorry for your losing your friends," Lu Bān said as Wu Bao returned with dried fish and rice cakes for their lunch.

Wu Bo climbed into the chariot, extending his hand to help Lu Bān. "We need to take advantage of the daylight."

"Safe travels," the tall man called after them.

"Thanks," Lu Bān shouted over the rattle of the chariot wheels and pounding hooves.

"Their battle did not go well," Wu Bao said. "We are fortunate they had fresh horses available."

The hairs on Lu Bān's neck stood up when Wu Bao said, "Keep your ears open for trouble. Keep your eyes sharp. We must be vigilant while traveling north. We may encounter enemy warriors separated from their units."

魯班

The rested horses brought Lu Bān and Wu Bao to the

three-quarter point of their journey. Smoke billowed from a walled city's ruins in the coming distance, yet the yellow-dragon banner remained.

"We missed the battle. The flag of Wu still flies, even though the enemy battered the city. Failure is a delay, not a defeat."

"Why must neighbors kill each other?" inquired Lu Bān. "Are we all not equal? My master teacher taught me they base moral conduct on individual rules of mutual respect, ethical behavior, and family ties," Lu Bān said. "I hold a basic philosophy of how to be a flawless gentleman on the simple ideology of love and tolerance."

"No 'perfect gentlemen' engage in war any longer," Wu Bao scoffed. "Your scholarly education is mere platitudes, not reality. Men's hearts are evil. My eyes witness their wicked deeds every day. We recognize King Yuan of Zhou is weak. His reign will soon end, and the individual states will wage battle with each other for dominance. Our golden-dragon state lost part of our northern territory to Yue last year. Their metalworking skills are superior to ours. Our swords and shields are no match for theirs."

"I overheard General Yáng Jūn and the other officers discussing the loss," Lu Bān said.

"The Chu State is growing in strength. They annexed Chen four years ago," Wu Bao said. "I worry they will help Yue take our remaining territory."

Lu Bān stopped listening. He searched the cloudy sky, hoping to guess the time. His spirits fell. *Will there be enemy warriors? What if they kill me? I will never again see Yun—or my child.*

鲁班

Lu Bān's journey with Wu Bao took them over rough terrain. The gray sky darkened; the chilly wind and rain pelted them. The horses whinnied, struggling to pull their chariot through deep-rutted roads. Lu Bān searched the angry heavens. *Will I ever hold Yun in my arms again or play with the son she carries?*

Despite the weather and the dangers, they arrived at Mount Lu's base in the late afternoon after a long day's ride. The skies cleared in time to catch the orange-colored sun sinking toward the western horizon, a few raucous birds clamoring for space on a nearby tree branch.

Lu Bān dismounted the chariot and returned his helmet to Wu Bao. "Again, thank you for my safety," he said. "I hope you go home to your wife before long."

"I cannot wait to hold her in my arms," Wu Bao said with a sly smile. "It will not be soon enough."

The chariot disappeared, slinging mud in the air from its wheels. Lu Bān began his ascent up the mountain's open stone path. Although he savored his new freedom from the army's camp and General Yáng Jūn, two worries plagued him. One, his uniform might cause someone to mistake him for an enemy. And second, Lord Huan's angry diatribe concerning his flying machine. He hoped to make it home before someone recognized him. He knew Yun would understand his motives.

Lu Bān's fear became a reality when a mounted warrior dressed in full armor of lamellar lacquered leather scales stopped him. His helmet, decorated with fanciful turtle designs in part, covered his face. He carried a shield bearing a black turtle and pointed a long sword at Lu Bān's chest.

Lu Bān recognized the turtle symbol from the stolen boat

plans of the enemy's army. His thrashing heartbeat surged in his ears.

The rider glared at Lu Bān. "Why are you on foot in this territory dressed as a Wu warrior? Where are your other group members?"

"I am Lu Bān from Lu. I am going home, and I travel alone." He thrust his hands in the air. "General Yáng Jūn took me prisoner, forced me to wear this uniform and work for him. They let me go when I finished my task."

The warrior's eyebrows shot up in surprise when he heard Lu Bān's name. He straightened his spine.

"Lu Bān? The great stone-bridge builder?"

"Yes, I am," he said, his voice muted.

"My own eyes beheld the bridge. It is unbelievable."

A rush of adrenaline tingled through Lu Bān's body. He was not sure if his recognition was for good or evil.

The rider dismounted and walked with determined steps toward Lu Bān, still holding his sword in a hostile position. He tilted his head and narrowed his coal-black eyes.

"And what did the greatest builder in Zhou do for this general?"

Lu Bān's mind raced. If he told the truth and General Yáng Jūn found out, he would execute him. When this scout learns what he did for the general, the horseman will take him prisoner. Both choices lead to the same horrific outcome. Lu Bān shuffled backward.

"I just reviewed a few boat ideas," he said in a calm, measured voice.

"Boats?" the warrior's shrill voice repeated. "Does Wu have a fleet of boats now?"

The man's response made him flinch. "I do not know.

I glanced at a few rough sketches," Lu Bān said in a shaky voice. He could feel the sweat following his backbone under the padded jacket.

"What are you carrying?" The warrior waved his sword toward the rolls of canvas strapped to Lu Bān's back.

Lu Bān's mouth moved several times, trying to conceive an idea of something to say to get him out of this situation. "Just preliminary drawings."

"Move toward that broad, flat boulder beside the path." His captor motioned with his weapon. "I will examine your *drawings*. Perhaps you are a courier."

"No." Lu Bān assured him, "I am going home."

Lu Bān untied the bindings holding his plans and surrendered them to his captor. He followed the warrior to the rock. With the inevitable realization of doom, his thoughts flew like lightning when the soldier recognized the boat designs and the flying machine. *I have no means to escape. I must kill him before he kills me.* He remembered the bronze dagger fingering it in his sash.

Distracted by his intense interest in the plans, the warrior ignored Lu Bān as he moved behind the soldier. When he unrolled the tubes, Lu Bān grasped the dagger and thrust it into the warrior's neck in one swift motion, killing him in an instant.

The soldier fell without making a sound. Blood squirted from his wound in the rhythm of his dying heartbeat, forming a pool of scarlet on the ground around Lu Bān's feet. He dropped the dagger, scanning his surroundings. No one. Grabbing his drawings, he ran up the mountain path as far as possible to collapse in a place of safety behind a pile of enormous boulders on wet leaves—with a lizard for company.

His chest ached from running as he gasped for air. The exertion made his leg muscles shake. He raised trembling hands to his hide his face when the reality of what had happened gripped his mind.

He had just killed a man.

Chapter 17

Lu Bān took a brief rest to calm his jangled nerves before resuming his climb up the mountain trail. He peered over his shoulder several times. No one followed him. Sinister shadows, long and dark, stretched across his path. He struggled with his mental picture of the warrior falling to the ground and the metallic odor of his blood.

He gave me no choice; he reasoned. *General Yáng Jūn would execute me if he learned the Black Turtle Army knew the boat drawings. If the warrior took me prisoner, I would never see Yun again. I saved myself.*

鲁班

Lu Bān arrived at dusk with the familiar sound of crickets. He hesitated at the south door of Lord Huan's house, feeling the weight of his ancestors. *Freedom at last from the camp. At what price? A man's life.*

Lu Bān entered the door and passed the servant's quarters, the aroma of the evening meal drifting from the kitchen. No one in sight. He crossed to the festooned gate into the family's enclosure, his heart yearning for Yun.

Sweet notes of his favorite song echoed from the garden. In the courtyard, Yun played her *qin*, fire-thrown shadows dancing around her. He marveled at her loveliness.

Yun cried out when Lu Bān stepped into sight. "My husband."

She ran to his arms before he could close the gate. "I have been out of my mind with worry. Our ancestors heard my prayers."

Yun's shriek caught Lady Huan's attention. From the latticed window, she viewed Lu Bān's embrace with her daughter. She spat. "I thought we were rid of that worm for good. No such good luck."

"My ring told me you were coming home," Yun said. "I asked for your protection and safe travels. Why do you still wear stinking, dirty warrior's clothes?"

"They required me to dress in them to ride in a chariot. It is a faster way to travel. If not, I would still be walking." He paused and swallowed hard, trying to ease the pain in the back of his throat. *I will not tell her about the warrior. I need to bear my guilt alone.* His eyes focused on the ground to avoid Yun's gaze. "I did so many things I regret."

"What did they do to you?" She took his face in her hands. "Did they hurt you?"

Lu Bān tossed the roll of plans on a bench, before ripping the warrior uniform from his body, leaving it in a mound. The cool evening air made him shiver.

Taking an ember from the crackling cooking fire, he ignited the garments, reminding him of his warrior camp time, then soaked in a wooden tub of hot water, hoping to wash off the last few months' actions and purge his feeling of shame.

As the last act, he dressed in the orange silk robe, complete with a blue sash worn at the bridge dedication ceremony to remind him of his good deeds. Lu Bān took Yun into his embrace.

Yun could feel the tension in her husband relax as she held him close. She decided not to ask about boats or what he did in the camp. *I will wait for him to tell me if he ever does.* "I am thankful you are home alive," she said. "All is well now."

"How are you? You are radiant."

"I am much better after my visit with Doctor Tro. The herbs he gave me helped settle my stomach."

"Is your father still angry with me?"

"I try to avoid contact with both of my parents. Father acts as though I have a disease instead of carrying his grandson. Mother still fumes because I kept our son a secret. My parents are not content with each other, and neither is happy with you." Yun frowned. "I do not understand. All my father talks about is your flying machine and how you should have told him about it before anyone else. I am sure he will question you tonight."

"Although I wish to avoid your parents, it is the price I pay for a fine meal."

"You are so thin; I feared they did not feed you," Yun said. "Our cook will fatten you up in no time."

鲁班

Soft notes of music drifted from the inner hall and the ring of a ceramic dinner bell signaled the meal's beginning.

Lu Bān savored the aroma of the long, narrow, yellow-noodle soup served in black lacquer bowls placed in front of him. He wiped his sweaty palms on his robe, sensing Lord Huan's eyes watching his every move.

Lord Huan can't know about the warrior's murder. I should not worry. He took a sidelong glance at Lady Huan while keeping his head still. *If looks could take my life, I would no longer be in this world. Not the homecoming I desired.*

Yun took her place at the table last, hoping to quell the constant uneasiness in her stomach. She glanced at her mother and lowered her eyes. The prolonged quiet made her fidget. Yun hoped their life would return to normal after the awkwardness of the first meal.

Lord Huan broke the silence. He raised his eyebrows. "Tell me how you designed these *boats.*"

Lu Bān took a sharp breath to calm his nerves. "There are four distinct types. Each with a different use." He spread his hands shoulder-width. "One uses twenty-five sets of oars."

Lord Huan's mouth flew open. "What do you know about boats?" His voice was incredulous.

"Nothing when General Yáng Jūn gave me the task. Someone in his command stole the original plans from one of their enemies with the black turtle symbol."

"The black turtle." Lord Huan's eyes widened. "It belongs to the Yue state. Their power is growing along with the State of Chu. They are a dragon's pool."

"It became my job to find their weaknesses and design better crafts." Lu Bān relaxed his shoulders. *At least Lord Huan is asking questions and not taking me to task.* "A field commander helped me to understand land-battle strategies. I applied them to the water. The same officer allowed me to ride in his chariot to the base of the mountain today."

Lord Huan leaned an elbow on one of the lounging pillows. "What did you do with the flying machine?" he asked, his tone casual.

"Alas, I left it behind. I could not take a chance to fly it in the daytime. I kept my drawings."

Lord Huan bolted upright, wondering if these diagrams could give him something new for Duke Ai. His voice elevated. "You brought back plans?"

"Yes," Lu Bān said, surprised at his father-in-law's sudden interest in his work for the general. "I have both my flying machine and boat plans."

A sly smile crossed Lord Huan's face. His pulse quickened. "I am eager for you to explain them to me tomorrow."

Lady Huan narrowed her eyes, staring at him, a cunning smile growing at the corners of her lips.

Lu Bān no longer felt Lord Huan's hostility, but wondered what made Lady Huan smile. He bobbed his head. "I will be glad to show them to you," he said with a mouthful of noodles.

The meal concluded without further questions. Lu Bān offered a gaze of reassurance to Yun. She responded with one of her smiles that always melted his heart.

Yes, all is well now, he thought.

鲁班

"Although there is a chill in the air, with a wrap, it is still a pleasant evening." Lu Bān said, taking Yun's hand, leading her through the courtyard. "I would like to sit here in the garden to enjoy the peacefulness and freedom from the noisy camp and the general." He nuzzled her neck. "I missed you so." Seated, he continued with a loud exhale. "At least your father did not appear angry at dinner."

"No, he is more interested in your drawings than anything else."

"Yes, I wonder why."

They enjoyed the moonrise, spreading its soft glow across their tranquil garden. Crickets serenaded them. A welcoming owl chimed into the chorus with an occasional baritone hoot.

Lu Bān put his hand on Yun's growing belly. "I dreamed of you every night and day. My thoughts were always of you and our son. I will never again leave your side," he vowed. "We will teach our son kindness and obedience. We should name him Lu Zhong, meaning 'loyal and steadfast,' just as we are loyal toward each other, our hearts entwined for eternity."

"Yes. In our hearts and our souls, forever." Happiness flooded her face. She kissed him. "I am so thankful you are safe."

魯班

Over the next two days, Lu Bān realized a change in Yun. She tossed and turned as she slept. She complained of a stiff neck, backache, and swollen feet. He attributed it in part to her pregnancy. Yun remained motionless with her husband in the workshop, her gaze unfocused, her thoughts lost in another place.

"My love," Lu Bān said, his voice tentative, "you are quiet this morning." He abandoned his drawing table and knelt beside Yun's thick mat. She reclined on dark-yellow-and-chartreuse silk pillows. "Is something wrong?"

"I am fatigued." She put her hand on her chest's left side. "It is hard to take in my breath. I want to sleep. I see the majestic trees." She moved her hand to her forehead. "I am hot." She took Lu Bān's hand, placing it on her face.

"You are burning!" he shouted. "Lord Huan, come at once!" he shrieked, scooping Yun into his arms to carry her to bed. By the time he reached the bedroom, she had lost consciousness.

"Yun, wake up. Wake up!" he pleaded, patting her face, holding her hand.

Lord Huan ran into their room, breathless. "What is the problem?"

"Yun's face is hot. I will find Doctor Tro. Stay with her."

鲁班

When Lu Bān entered the house, he lowered the shades to their room and lit Phoenix candles, kneeling beside the bed.

Lord Huan paced the floor, grumbling. "What is keeping the doctor?" He peered out a window. "Ah-ha, here he comes now. I will meet him."

Doctor Tro rushed to Yun's side, followed by Lord Huan. Lady Huan arrived and stood in the doorway. Lord Huan huddled alongside Lu Bān as the doctor knelt next to Yun. His eyebrows shot up when he put his ear on her chest to assess her condition. "Too fast," he muttered. The doctor brought a shaky hand to his forehead. "How long has she been like this?"

"The last half-an-hour candle." Lu Bān's words tumbled from his mouth. "Yun said she possessed no chi and wanted to sleep. When I touched her face, she was boiling. She mumbled something about trees and fell asleep. When I could not wake her, I called you. What is wrong with my wife?"

"I will need a basin of water. Your wife's condition is acute. I only experienced one case like this in my life. I could never figure out the exact cause of *zhong Feng*." He opened his bag of herbs and potions.

A servant delivered the water. The doctor poured several

drops of lemon juice and vinegar into the basin.

"I cannot give her my normal *nepetas* remedy because she is with child," the doctor said, putting a pungent wet cloth on Yun's forehead and chest. He grimaced. "I am afraid I will lose them both."

"No!" Lu Bān screamed. "You must save her and our son!"

Yun mumbled again. She slipped in and out of consciousness, muttering words he did not understand. Lord Huan stood by Lu Bān as the doctor failed to treat her with mild herbs dissolved in the water because she could not swallow. The doctor burned sandalwood incense to drive out the evil spirit infiltrating her body.

Lady Huan's nostrils flared. She shook her fist at Lu Bān. "This is your fault," she screamed. "We have no heirs. She cannot leave this world."

魯班

Lady Huan dashed to their family altar. She fell to her knees, calling to her ancestors to communicate with the many gods and spirits.

Lord Huan followed her to the hall. He knelt, picking up their ancestral tablets, holding them to his chest. "Oh, my father's spirit, hear my plea for my daughter. Your granddaughter needs your intercession," he begged. "She is an obedient child. She does many proper deeds. Expel the evil spirit possessing her body." Lord Huan rocked back and forth as he prayed. He replaced the tablets on the altar, reaching for Lady Huan's hand. She jerked it away from his grasp. Without comment, Lord Huan returned to Yun's bedside.

Lady Huan lit candles, weeping. "I should not have been so hard on her. Please spare my child and our grandson," she wailed.

She stared at the flames. Yun's angry words replayed in her mind: "May your ancestors be ashamed and turn their backs on you."

"They may have turned their backs on both of us," Lady Huan whispered.

魯班

Lady Huan returned to where Doctor Tro worked to save Yun. The room reeked of incense and fear.

Lu Bān knelt beside Yun. "Do not leave me," Lu Bān pleaded, holding her hand and rubbing her arm. "You cannot go. I need you. Our destiny is to have a long life together and many sons."

She murmured again. Her words sounded strange. "The light. There are the beautiful trees."

"What trees?"

"I will wait for you in the magnificent trees," she said, drifting away for the last time.

"Do something," Lu Bān pleaded. Shouting, he grabbed the doctor's shoulders. "Do something!"

Despite the doctor's efforts, Yun's life left her.

Lu Bān struggled to breathe. A wave of profound grief swept over him. Sobbing, he collapsed over her body. "The Love of My Life, gone. The son I hoped for, taken away with her."

"You must mourn in silence," Lady Huan hissed. "Yun's loss of life is a matter of destiny and out of my control. This is your fault."

Lu Bān stood by as Lady Huan left in a huff, refusing to acknowledge his grief. In that instant, he vowed to leave Lord Huan's household and move as far away from Lady Huan as possible—as soon as he buried Yun.

Grief-stricken over the loss of his daughter, Lord Huan remained rooted in place. "I am sure you cared for Yun," Lord Huan said, choking back tears of his own. "She loved you so. You did everything you could to save her." He straightened his back. "Though losing our daughter is unbearable, we must mourn in silence. A child's departure is against nature and may bring misfortune to our family. Yun departed this life unfilial, unable to fulfill her filial obligations to produce a son."

Lu Bān leapt to his feet and stared at Lord Huan, not believing his ears. "Yun was my wife, my other half. She carried our son. I will not be silent! I will honor her by observing the customary three years of mourning. However, I will grieve for my beloved Yun forever," Lu Bān said through clenched teeth. "A white cloth will hang over the door. I will dress in white, place a phoenix banner outside the house as a signal to our neighbors of Yun's departure, with or without your permission."

Lord Huan said nothing further. He did an about-face and walked away.

Lu Bān knelt beside Yun's motionless body. "We made plans for a long life together and children." His tears burned like acid streaming down his cheeks. "Oh, my love, it is my fault. I lacked the strength to refuse to design war machines." Lu Bān took her lifeless hand, still warm. He held it, trying to absorb her last remaining essence.

"Yuuu . . ." he tried to whisper her name, "please forgive me."

Linda Brown Carlson

鲁班

Slanted sun's rays filtered through a canopy of the ancient trees, their fresh damp fragrances filling every part of the verdant mystical forest. The sweet scent of the majestic trees wrapped their essence around the recent arrival. An angelic girl, dressed in yellow silk, with dark eyes and hair the color of midnight, floated among the trees. A familiar spirit voice spoke from the bright light: "These magnificent guardians symbolizing the world's center, where heaven and earth touch, where all times and places converge, welcome you home."

Chapter 18

Master Sima arrived, out of breath. "I came as soon as I heard the news." He put his hand on Lu Bān's shoulder to console him. "I am sorry. I mourn with you," he said. Recognizing Lu Bān's unfocused gaze, Master Sima offered additional words of encouragement. "Lu Bān, you must not let this loss cause you to abandon your goals. You have much more to accomplish. Yun would want you to continue to improve people's lives."

"I saved many villagers' lives when I built the bridge," Lu Bān wailed. "You and I made it possible to produce more food when we learned to irrigate fields. However, I enabled General Yáng Jūn to kill multitudes of people with my inventions. I fear I am now suffering retributions in this life for my evil deeds. Taking Yun away is *my* punishment. She did not deserve this fate. She was selfless, always an obedient wife. I should be the one lying here without life."

"I understand your agony. When my wife left this world, I did not believe I could face life without her. I wanted to join her. However, in time, my ache grew bearable. I knew I had not yet fulfilled my destiny. Your life will continue, although it may be hard to accept that now."

Lu Bān heard his master's and friend's words. They gave him no consolation.

"Have you thought about what you will do next?"

"I am going as far away from Lady Huan as possible," Lu Bān said.

"Why not come back to my house while you make your plans? Your room is still there."

"Lady Huan hates me. I cannot live with someone who would not mourn for her child or grandchild."

"Although Lord Huan and Lady Huan will not grieve for Yun, I will be sorrowful with you," Master Sima said. "I will take care of the arrangements and prepare the earth to receive her body. Together, we will take her to the hill overlooking the lake."

Master Sima departed.

Now alone, Lu Bān prepared to honor his wife. He dressed in a simple, long, white hemp-cloth robe he purchased in preparation when Master Sima had fallen gravely ill the previous year. When his mentor recovered, Lu Bān never expected Yun's passing would cause him to wear it for the first time. He gathered damp cloths to wash her body, dusted it with talcum powder, dressed her in her favorite yellow robe, and covered her face with a lemon-colored cloth. He knelt beside his wife's lifeless body. "Although you are no longer in this world, I am positive you will be my other half forever. I will meet you in our next life, my love. I will come to the meadow and find the big trees, as you ask."

Lu Bān removed the jade ring from her finger, just as he had after his mother left this world. He held the now-cold jade ring in his hand. He put it on his smallest finger, rolled it around, and sobbed.

The ring warmed. Startled, Lu Bān opened his eyes. A vision of a woman with sun-tanned skin and kind eyes appeared. "My son, do not weep. Yun waits for you among our ancient shui-sa trees. She will reunite with you when it is time to leave this life. Until your time comes, continue to do magnificent works. We love you."

魯班

Master Sima returned with a cart and two servants, and together they took Yun's body to the prepared grave. Lu Bān held her jade ring in his palm.

"Remember," Master Sima said, "Jade holds magical properties and can communicate between this world and the next."

"Yes, my mother appeared to reassure me. Yun waits for me in the magnificent trees. I am eager to join her."

Master Sima read from his ancient sacred text, expressing the value of family ties beyond the grave:

We have not learned to know life. How can we know the departure from this life? Society's foundation is the unity of the family. A superior man begins with respect as the basis of love. To omit respect is to leave no structure for affection. Without love, there can be no union; without respect, love will be ignoble. To evoke love, you must love. To call forth respect, you must show respect.

He bowed three times before they placed Yun's body in the ground, along with jars of food, and covered her body with earth. They burned her remaining clothes and joss-spirit paper. The smoke ascended to the crystal blue sky to accompany her on her journey to the great trees in the world's center, where heaven and earth touch.

魯班

Lu Bān returned to Lord Huan's home in the early afternoon after the burial. Bitter, he packed his belongings, drawings, kite, tools, and worktable, eager to leave the last five years of his life behind, grateful for Master Sima's offer.

Master Sima's two servants loaded Lu Bān's things into their cart.

Neither Lord nor Lady Huan had any further conversation with Lu Bān. He left the house, closed the door, thankful to be away from Lady Huan. *I am sure you are as glad to be rid of me as I am of you.*

魯班

Lu soldiers stormed into Lord Huan's house, swords drawn, sending servants fleeing for their lives and Lady Huan taking refuge inside a blanket chest. She closed the lid but left it cracked to listen to the commotion.

"Lu Shi Huan," they called, searching room to room. Lord Huan tried to hide, but it was too late to escape. Two of the armed men grabbed his arms, jerking him to his feet.

"What is the meaning of this?" he said, drawing himself to his full height.

"By order of Duke Ai, you are under arrest."

"On what charge?" Lord Huan asked, feeling weak-kneed, but he continued to struggle against the men. The appearance of three other men, along with Ji Kanazi, the chief minister, persuaded him he had no way to escape.

"Treason, conspiring with the Qi State," Ji Kanazi said, a sneer on his face. "We have intercepted slips from your wife to her older brother in Qi, promising you would pass sensitive information to them for the right price."

"Impossible," Lord Huan sputtered, the color draining from his face. "I am unaware of any correspondence."

"It matters not whether you know. The Lianzuo System dictates you are responsible for your family's actions. Where is your wife? She is under arrest, too."

"I do not know."

"Search the grounds," the chief minister ordered.

"I am loyal to Duke Ai. He knows I would never betray him. This summons is some mistake. You have my word."

The minister chuckled. "He said you would try to give us your word."

The search party returned. "Minister, the woman is not here," the soldier reported.

Minister Ji's face reddened; his voice raised loud enough for the next five houses to hear. "Well, find her! We will take this prisoner on to the palace."

Lord Huan struggled against the men holding him until one of the other soldiers poked Lord Huan in his expensive robe with a sword to make his point. "If you are lucky, Duke Ai will allow you to take your own life," he said. "If not, you will lose your head."

The soldiers dragged their captive out of the door and into the street before tossing him, without ceremony, into a cart with bars, causing several neighbors to stop and stare, whispers passing among them. The cart bumped and jostled its passenger, his pleas still begging for mercy.

魯班

Lady Huan waited until she heard no more sounds. She opened the blanket chest lid, listened for movement, and stepped into an eerie silence. She surveyed the smashed flowers, broken furniture, and the door ajar.

It is a matter of time before they will be back. The courier betrayed me. His loyalty extended only to the highest bidder. My daughter was right; the kitchen god reported our quarrels. My ancestors have turned their back on me. I have lost everything and am doomed, for I have killed us all.

She closed the door, went to her husband's workroom, withdrew his sword, and with her final deep breath, plunged the weapon into her abdomen. She fell forward, pushing the sword farther through her body.

The soldier returned moments later to find Lady Huan's motionless body in a pool of blood, matching her crimson silk robe and ruby ring.

魯班

Lu Bān walked with Master Sima to the house that had sheltered him twenty years before, when he had no place to go. The three-bay house felt like an old, welcoming friend.

Rain pelted the shuttered windows the following morning. Lu Bān awoke, still numb, without focus. He reached for Yun, but realized he had only her memory and her jade ring. "How will I go on without you? I no longer want to be here. I want to go to the trees with you."

The ring vibrated, summoning a smiling vision of Yun. "It is beautiful among the giant old trees, but you must continue to invent things until it is your time to come. I will welcome you. Remember, I love you."

Tears washed over Lu Bān's cheeks. "You *are* my other half."

鲁班

"How did you cope when you lost your wife?" Lu Bān inquired after breakfast. "I feel empty, as if half of me is missing."

"I felt the same way, at first." Master Sima held his teacup. "I considered ending my life, but my wife visited me in a dream to tell me I had not finished my work here. In my heart, I knew the truth of her words."

"Yun appeared to tell me the same thing," Lu Bān said, his eyes wide. "She said the trees are beautiful."

"It is more important to keep the love in your heart than to care where she is now. Do not focus on the afterlife, for we understand so little about it. Instead, concentrate on your everyday life."

"My life without Lady Huan is a blessing. She hates me, and I hate her," Lu Bān confessed.

"It is easy to hate and hard to love. This is how the entire scheme of things works. All things worthwhile are difficult to achieve, and bad things come without effort. If you allow hate to enter, you allow the person to defeat you. Remember, you have the power to change your attitudes," Master Sima said, taking a sip of tea. "You are welcome to stay here as long as you like. I always enjoy your company."

"Thank you, Master. I imagine Lord Huan will make it impossible to find work here."

"Word will travel about your availability."

"I hope General Yáng Jūn does not find out," Lu Bān said.

"The general may have troubles of his own. It seems the Yue State is about to conquer the State of Wu. If this comes about, they will force him to commit suicide."

"The man whose chariot I rode home in told me he expected Yue to overtake Wu. He also said he thought the State of Chu would be the ultimate winner."

"It would not surprise me. We will all be citizens of Chu one day."

魯班

Six months later, Lu Bān gathered his belongings to journey to Ying, the State of Chu's capital, to begin his job as the palace carpenter.

He packed the last basket of his possessions in a cart before returning to the workshop to retrieve his kite and say his last farewell. He paused at the outside door, face to face with his mentor.

"My memories, standing here as a scared, trembling little boy with the village elder, wash over me," began Lu Bān. "I thought this beautiful door, carved with peach blossoms and pairs of swimming fish, had to be the door to the ruler's palace or the door to heaven. You took a poor orphaned child into your home, taught me with the patience and the kindness of a father, and mourned with me the departure of my mother and now losing my dear Yun." Lu Bān scanned the courtyard where they had spent many hours.

He continued: "Your wisdom always amazed me. No matter my dilemma, you had the right words to help me weigh my choices."

"Any knowledge I possess came from my teacher, Master Kong," Master Sima said, his voice reverent.

Lu Bān fixed his eyes, filled with tears and smiles, upon his mentor. "It is with a heavy heart I leave. I can never repay you or thank you enough."

"Master Kong took no money from his students. However, he expected us to pass our knowledge on to others. You are, without a doubt, my best student of all time. I expect you to remember all your lessons and do the same to make our world a better place. We live in turbulent times."

Master Sima reached out to touch Lu Bān's shoulder. "Last year, when illness came to me, I had a glimpse of my next life. It did not frighten me. I am old, and my eyesight is failing. My life will soon leave me. Do not worry. My servants will be with me until the end. Perhaps we will meet again in our next life."

"I give all honors to you, Master," Lu Bān said, bowing. "I hope your long life continues." He swallowed hard, trying to find his voice. "I will never forget your kindness and your lessons. Goodbye, my master and friend."

Chapter 19

Familiar with Duke Ai's expansive Lu palace complex, occupying several square miles, a sense of awe struck Lu Bān when he glimpsed the massive walls of King Hui's Chu palace stretching across the horizon as far as his eyes could see. Four-story watchtowers dotted the length and breadth of the enclosure. Yellow-bear banners flew from the tile rooftops with upturned corners, while Phoenix-like bird sculptures lined the ridges of the roofs.

The rumors are true, he realized. *A great stone wall surrounds the palace.*

The dusty road leading to the massive bronze gates bustled with chariots and riders on horseback coming and going across a wooden bridge over a moat. Two sentinels in lamellar leather armor, holding Chinese halberds on long poles, stood to protect the doors.

Presenting his slips of instructions, Lu Bān gained entrance.

Symmetrical gateways protected a central edifice, with elaborate decorations on the overhanging eaves, the roof corners upturned. Smaller structures with doors flanked the palace, guarded by golden-bear statues.

Lu Bān proceeded to a building identified as the palace's workshop. He bowed and introduced himself to the supervisor.

"Lu Bān, the great stone-bridge builder. I am Chu Bao, in

charge of all the tradesmen. We are fortunate to have a man of your talents."

"Thank you, sir. I am eager to work."

"These wooden buildings require continual maintenance. Is it true you have something to cut and smooth wood instead of using an ax?"

"Yes," Lu Bān said, withdrawing his saw and plane from his cart.

"Your first task is producing more of these tools for our workers and teaching them how to use them."

Lu Bān surveyed his surroundings. "Does this stone wall encompass the entire city?"

"Not only the city, but the whole State of Chu. Close to four-hundred miles of walls, twenty to thirty feet in most places, but they are up to forty-six feet in height in strategic spots. Chu is the first state to have a barrier."

"Impressive."

魯班

Lu Bān settled in as the palace's official carpenter, reproducing his saw, plane, and chalk line for straight marking. The following years, he added a square, an ink-marking tool, a lifting implement for burial, and a wooden, horse carriage to his list of inventions.

When King Hui learned Lu Bān invented the cloud ladder, he promoted the carpenter to chief military strategist. The promotion allowed Lu Bān to atone for his invention and naval vessels he delivered to the yellow dragon State of Wu by thinking of ways to avoid war.

Lu Bān also helped the king gain massive tracts of land from its other neighbor, Yue, with minimal bloodshed.

Chu's appetite for adding territory to their state focused their attention on the State of Song to their north.

鲁班

Mozi, a resident of Song, philosopher, and a direct opponent of Confucius's teaching, traveled ten days on foot to recruit Lu Bān to thwart the Chu king's plan to attack Song.

They met in a room filled with maps and tables piled high with records of battles, lists of soldiers, and enemy information on rolls of stitched bamboo slips. A bronze incense burner in the shape of a tulip infused the air with a sweet scent of sandalwood.

After a series of philosophical discussions, Lu Bān said, "I promised the king I would serve on this campaign. I cannot quit now."

"Perhaps you would introduce me to the king," Mozi suggested. "He regards you with favor. I want to plead my case with him. I believe he is a fair man."

鲁班

The interior of the throne room, embellished with painted rafters, elegant columns on marble bases supported bracketing carved beams, and delicate, luminous wall screens welcomed them.

King Hui sat on his rosewood seat, with a ten-foot, carved, circular translucent jade disk and multiple entwined dragons for a backrest, perched on a three-step raised platform. Two eight-foot-tall stands with three branching arms supporting fat round candles flanked the throne.

The two men bowed. Mozi started the conversation with a parable and a question.

"I saw, oh king, a man rich with chariots, silk, rice, vegetables, and meat. Yet, instead of enjoying what he had, he coveted his neighbor's shabby wheelbarrow and blanket, then stole his sack of rice. What do you think of this man?"

"He seems to be a man with a demented mind," the king offered.

Mozi listed all that is good about the land of Chu and compared it to the lack of food, fish, usable wood, and diverse species in Song. But the king cared little about Mozi's moralizing and said, "But I have new war plans."

Mozi appealed to Lu Bān to play "siege" with him, using wood chips as soldiers and siege weapons and a silk belt as Song's castle wall.

Lu Bān devised nine original tactics and different armaments, all defeated by Mozi's inventions. At the end of the game, Lu Bān exhausted all his options.

"I am frustrated, but I will still win if we siege Song," Lu Bān said. "My last strategy is excellent, but I cannot bear to say it."

Mozi agreed. "You have one last option, but I would not reveal it either."

King Hui became curious. Before he could force Lu Bān to disclose his plan, Mozi spoke.

"The last tactic is simple. Lu Bān can ask you to execute me, and we have lost all for Song. But Lu Bān is a kind man and could not bear to do so."

Before the king could react, Mozi added, "But for that too, I have countermeasures. I have three-hundred disciples in Song to defend the city. If you murder me, Song's defenses will run just as if I were there. I apologize for having put the two of you through my ruses, and I hope you do not taint your hands by killing me out of spite."

Lu Bān breathed a deep breath of relief. Mozi's last revelation resolved Lu Bān's conflict between righteousness and loyalty, helping him keep his career and reputation.

King Hui sighed. "You have made your point. I will spare your land of Song."

魯班

Lu Bān's encounter with Mozi gripped his thoughts. Impressed with Mozi's belief that people can change the circumstances of their lives, Lu Bān left his position as a military strategist. He traveled to Song to seek Mozi, to study his philosophy, turning from inventing weapons of destruction to adopting a pacifist mindset.

With Mozi's encouragement, in time, he set out for the highest mountain in the land to find the Divine Being, to cleanse his soul of his evil deeds. With the jade ring's assistance, he gained worldly wisdom, understanding, and spiritual enlightenment. He stayed there until he left his life to journey through the jade ring portal to the world's center, where heaven and earth meet.

He passed into the misty, verdant forest. A beautiful girl, dressed in yellow, with hair the color of midnight, welcomed him home to wait for their rebirth.

The End

Author's Notes

The exciting thing about writing historical fiction is the fascinating things you uncover along the way.

Ancient China is a land of varied resources and over four million square miles in area, where civilization arose perhaps as early as one million years ago and developed for centuries, almost completely isolated from outsiders by deserts, oceans, and mountains. This isolation helps explain how China's unique culture remained untouched and unknown by the outside world until the nineteenth century.

Scholars have dated the origin of China's first civilization to about 1500 to 1100 BC. We know little about these people other than their family life was matriarchal. They lived an agrarian life; raised silkworms for raw silk, developed writing, and created splendid bronze vessels and art objects. Warfare was frequent, adopting the two-wheeled chariot as a military tool.

The Zhou Dynasty overthrew the Shang ruling house in the eleventh century BC, a new warlike power. Their powerful rulers, who depended on feudal lords to supply auxiliary forces for maintaining order against nomadic tribes in the north, lasted nearly eight centuries until 256 BC.

When putting yourself in a bygone era, one must remember we come with modern assumptions and mores, and connotations of words.

My story begins in the year 500 BC. Paper had yet to be invented. It wasn't until the Chinese invented crude paper around 100 BC. Before that time, long strips of bamboo called slips served as a medium for writing with characters representing words, written with an ink brush, in vertical lines. They stitched the slips together with hemp, silk thread, or leather to form rows of text. The complete manuscript rolled up like a jelly roll, secured with a ribbon, cord, or sometimes folded accordion-style.

Common word definitions we use were not applicable in this era either. For instance, the word, Lady before a surname did not mean royalty. The ancient Chinese used it like our title, Mrs.

Words for medical conditions, familiar to us, were unheard of in this time frame, supposing evil spirits and wicked deeds were responsible for illness and death. They also did not use our words, death or dying.

Many people have asked me, "How did you come up with the idea for this story?"

The concept of two souls bound together since the beginning of time launched my idea for The Journey of the Jade Ring. Where might souls go while waiting to be reborn into their next life? Speculation abounds.

Accounts of near-death experiences appear to have similar threads. A bright light. A spirit guide. A place where a tree in the world's center connects heaven and earth, converging all times and places. A meeting place for souls waiting for their next existence.

What if two souls were to meet, find they are each other's half, and vow to meet again in subsequent lives?

When an expert in Asian jade explained the jade stone had

a magical quality to span many generations, I wondered, could this be the portal to follow the two lovers through time?

What were some things soulmates might enjoy doing together? Flying a kite came to mind. Researching the origins of the kite led me to the inventor, Lu Bān, who lived in China in the fourth century BC. This query propelled me into the secluded and fascinating legacy of Chinese ingenuity.

The Journey of the Jade Ring tells the story of Lu Bān, now remembered as the father of carpentry, who lived in ancient China during the end of the Spring and Autumn years and the beginning of the Warring States period when the Zhou Dynasty weakened. The story follows the historical timeline as the power of the nobles in each state grew, eventually rendering the dynasty ruler powerless. This political decline opened the door for the dukes in the states to vie for power, warring with each other, grabbing territory, consolidating their strength, paving the way for the ultimate destruction of the Zhou Dynasty and the consolidation of the states creating the Han dynasty, lasting over four hundred years.

It has been my earnest endeavor to use verifiable historical facts when these facts are known—considering the story's time frame, 500 BC, China, and its vast secluded territory—the western world knew little of its advanced knowledge or innovations.

Accounts of Lu Bān's life vary from source to source. Some accounts place him as the son of a carpenter or a minor lord; others have him a lowly peasant, perhaps an orphan. Written accounts of his life occurred many years after his death and varied from writer to writer, with legends and stories embellished through many centuries. Still, Chinese oral history credits Lu Bān with inventing many familiar implements, such as the frame saw, plane, chalk line, and shovel, among various other tools. Legend holds he invented a mechanical bird to carry him home to visit his wife when his work separated them. I have used these tales to give life to this talented inventor.

Lu Bān's *cloud ladder* was the forerunner to the siege ladders familiar to medieval enthusiasts. His idea for irrigation troughs with gates to divert water is still in use today. Again, folklore has credited Lu Bān with using a wedge-shaped stone, the key to the masonry arch, enabling him to construct an arched bridge over a mighty river two centuries before Romans in the first century BC.

The record of Lu Bān's wife, Yun, credited with inventing the umbrella, failed to record her surname. Thus, she and her family's names and the other supporting characters in the story are works of fiction.

I have borrowed these legends and stories to create my historical fantasy, The Journey of the Jade Ring.

The Journey of the Jade Ring

Book Two

The jade ring finds its way over centuries to a remote village in China's Shan-Si province, as a tribute to the Great Kublai Khan after two families take part in a Spirit Wedding ceremony for their deceased children, uniting them in the Netherworld until their rebirth.

Kublai Khan tucks the jade ring into a secret compartment of a jewel box he gives to his *favorite*, Sarangerel, a Manzi princess he is sending to help Princess Cocachin prepare for her marriage to the Kahn's nephew in Persia. He also promises Sarangerel to his nephew as his second wife.

On the two-year voyage with Marco Polo from China to Hormoz, Sarangerel meets Kashan, one of the Kahn's ambassadors, and his parrot, Majak, who tells fortunes.

Through Oracle cards, with Majak's help, the jade ring reveals the truth that Kashan and Sarangerel are the two souls from the Spirit Wedding.

Faced with pirates, sickness, disease, the perils of the sea, and the certainty Sarangerel will belong to the nephew when they arrive in Hormuz, the two lovers seek a way of escape.

https://lindabrowncarlson.com/

CPSIA information can be obtained
at www.ICGtesting.com
Printed in the USA
BVHW080954280722
643232BV00004B/359